PRAISE FOR
HIS UNFORGETTABLE BRIDE

"I loved every minute of reading it. So much so that I couldn't put it down. I'm a goner for royalty love stories. And second chances. Yep, loved this one with those tropes that were well done. And the ending. *Happy Sigh* It was perfection!!!"

—JULIE, GOODREADS

"His Unforgettable Bride is an engaging, satisfying conclusion to the wonderful Bride Ships: New Voyages series. The well-paced plot, with Cinderella vibes, drew me in immediately and kept me reading attentively to the end."

—CAROLYN, GOODREADS

"His Unforgettable Bride is a wonderfully worthy addition to Jody Hedlund's Bride Ships universe. Patti Stockdale shines in creating unforgettable characters and memorable storylines! I just loved the message in this story that our identity is not in our history or circumstances but in our character, and where we place our faith. I finished the last page with the happiest sigh because it was well worth the wait."

—ALYSSA, GOODREADS

"Entertaining. A page turner. A great way to spend a few hours."

—JEANETTE, GOODREADS

His
Unforgettable
Bride

BRIDE SHIPS ⚓ NEW VOYAGES

His UNFORGETTABLE BRIDE

BRIDE SHIPS ⚓ NEW VOYAGES

JODY HEDLUND

PRESENTS

PATTI STOCKDALE

sunrise PUBLISHING

His Unforgettable Bride
Bride Ships: New Voyages, Book 4

Published by Sunrise Media Group LLC
Copyright © 2025 Sunrise Publishing

Print ISBN: 978-1-963372-46-5
EBook ISBN: 978-1-963372-47-2

Scripture quotations are taken from the King James Version of the Bible.

This is a work of historical reconstruction; the appearances of certain historical figures are accordingly inevitable. All other characters are products of the author's imagination. Any resemblance to actual events or locales or persons, living or dead, is entirely coincidental.

For more information about the authors, please access their websites at www.jodyhedlund.com and www.pattistockdale.com.

Published in the United States of America.
Cover Design by Hannah Linder
Cover images from Shutterstock

Bride Ships: New Voyages

FINALLY HIS BRIDE

HIS TREASURED BRIDE

HIS PERFECT BRIDE

HIS UNFORGETTABLE BRIDE

To Kelli, Blake, and our two bonus kids,
Brian and Shannon.
Forever and Always, I love you.

"The rich and poor meet together:
the Lord is the maker of them all."

Proverbs 22:2

One

Victoria, Vancouver Island
Monday, November 1863

J ULIET DASH KNEW HOW TO SPOT A THIEF.
Once upon a time, she'd been one.

Standing in the doorway of her attic bedroom and staring at her roommate, Juliet's heart thumped in a wild clip. "You stole from the Firths?"

The cold November wind rattled the rafters as Ruby O'Reilly crouched to scoop up what sparkled like an emerald ring from the chilly floor. Juliet's roommate stood, hiding the gem inside the folds of her dingy navy cape. "I don't know what you're yammering about."

And yet Juliet had spied the ring with her own two eyes—the ring that Mrs. Firth hadn't been able to find today. "I disagree."

"Says you."

Wasn't that obvious?

A flickering tallow candle cast shadows on the unpainted walls and meager furnishings—a wooden bed, a two-drawer bureau, and a wash basin. She'd grown accustomed to the musty scent and had no quarrel with her living arrangement for the last ten months.

Other than the person who shared the space.

She and Ruby had little in common except for their employment and perhaps a thievery tie. But Juliet hadn't swiped as much as an apple since she was ten.

They certainly looked nothing alike. She was average height and had fair hair, pale skin, and blue eyes. Ruby, small-boned and red-headed, had dark, knowing eyes that appeared older than the mighty ocean on the edge of Victoria. The purplish-green bruising around her left eye had nearly faded.

Juliet undid the cuff buttons on her black chambermaid dress and glared at Ruby, who stared back. The missing emerald wasn't the first disappearing jewel in the house. A pearl-trimmed hatpin and an expensive brooch that had once belonged to the Queen's daughter and awarded to the Firth family had also gone missing over recent weeks.

There had been unannounced inspections of the servants' rooms ever since. Would another happen before bed tonight? "If you took the ring, give it back."

"Don't tell me what to do, Miss High and Mighty. You walk around with your nose tipped toward the sky day after day."

"Huh?" The opposite was true, and for good reason. The only thing Juliet had done with her nose was shove it against the grindstone. Never had she deemed herself better than anyone else because she knew deep in her heart she wasn't.

"If you must know, I dropped a trinket from my beau. That's what you seen on the floor." Ruby tossed her cape's hood over her head and stomped out of the room. A moment later, the servants' back staircase creaked as she descended.

Juliet raised her eyes to the ceiling. The slanted walls peaked like the letter A. Where was Ruby sneaking off to on the brink of bedtime? To meet her man or for another reason? A troubling reason?

What could Juliet do about it? The easiest option was to crawl into bed and pray for a better day tomorrow. This wasn't her business. She didn't need to get involved. She wasn't at fault.

After all, what if she'd been mistaken about what she'd seen Ruby drop? What if it was just a trinket? Yet Juliet's experience and gut told her no. The stone on the bedroom floor had glinted like a priceless emerald, something she'd held and seen firsthand long ago.

The truth was that thievery was wrong. Juliet had learned that lesson the hard way. If Ruby had stolen the jewels from the Firths, especially the priceless heirloom from the Queen, she needed to return them. Now.

Besides, Juliet couldn't sit back and do nothing, not when the Firths had been so kind to her over the past months of working for them. The least she could do was investigate where Ruby had wandered.

Juliet grabbed her black shawl from her drawer, tossed it over her shoulders, and tied her headscarf under her chin. Then she quietly crept down two narrow staircases to reach the bottom level and cracked open the door to a small back entrance hall without making a sound. Good or bad, she had a knack for sneaking around and doubted anyone would see her tonight.

Light shone underneath Mrs. Quinborow's office door down the hallway, and Juliet hesitated. What if the strict housekeeper was about to do one of her surprise searches? There would be countless questions if she found Juliet and Ruby missing.

One more reason to return to the attic and not get involved.

Yet, if she didn't do something now, Ruby might keep stealing. And Juliet would be just as guilty for allowing the crimes to continue.

Straightening her shoulders with resolve, she slipped from the servants' entrance and into the starry night. The moon offered a heavenly glow—perfect for catching a thief. An owl hooted a greeting. Or perhaps a warning.

With no time to lose, she dashed across the loose-stone lane used for deliveries, then hid behind an evergreen tree in case anyone else stepped outside.

If she were Ruby, what would she do next? Hide the ring to get it out of the house, but conceal it where?

Juliet narrowed her eyes to study her surroundings. The sprawling manicured gardens spread out in a maze behind the mansion. She'd seen Ruby disappear into the gardens on other occasions and had assumed the maid met her man there. But what if she'd gone out to hide the jewels instead?

Juliet crept along the pathway. At times, she had to feel her way forward in the darkness of the tall shrubs. Ahead in the moonlight, she glimpsed the fancy wrought iron fence separating the Firths' property from the neighbors'—the Lennox family—which meant she neared the back gate.

She halted at the clink of metal against rock and strained to listen. Was someone digging?

Was Ruby hiding the jewels? What if Juliet caught her in the act? Then she couldn't deny the stealing any longer, and Juliet would have the upper hand. Maybe she'd threaten to report her to the police if Ruby refused to return the jewels to the Firths.

She stepped out into the open without giving herself a chance to second-guess her plan.

Ruby was kneeling, gripping a garden trowel, and stabbing the earth.

"What are you doing?" Juliet asked, even though it was apparent.

Ruby gasped and raised her head, her face hidden in the folds of her hood. "Why did you follow me?"

"To see if you would bury the goods. Looks like you are."

"It's not your business."

Well, that wasn't true. "If you put Mrs. Firth's jewelry back where it belongs tonight and promise not to steal again, this ends here and now. No one needs to know anything more."

Ruby leaned back on her haunches. "You can't prove nothing. Where's your evidence?"

In her roommate's pocket, or maybe already in the ground?

After shooting Juliet a glare, Ruby continued to spear the earth with the garden tool. "Go ahead and tell them what I'm doing. I'll be long gone before you get back."

Juliet had seldom snitched in all her nineteen years, but if Ruby refused to cooperate, what choice did she have? None, other than to tell Mrs. Quinborow before Ruby got away.

What if someone linked her to the thievery? Shivers streaked over her skin at the mere thought.

Juliet turned and began returning to the house, winding through the shrubs, past raised beds and elegant fountains. It was impossible to know how the next few minutes would unfold. But one thing was certain. She had no intention of losing her position because of an upstart named Ruby O'Reilly. Or anyone else. No, ma'am.

Besides, she couldn't allow Ruby to hurt the Firths any longer.

Juliet loved the stability of working for the family and the routine of domestic service—the schedule of rising at dawn and cleaning the same rooms day after day. She ate every meal in the same chair and table in the servants' common room. After supper, she often completed mending or polishing and chatted with some of the other staff.

The rhythm had grown familiar and close to perfect, and Juliet wanted life to stay the same. Every day, she silently thanked Mrs. Morseby from the Immigration Committee for finding her this position when the bride ship arrived at Vancouver Island last January. Such an opportunity wouldn't have been available to a nobody orphan like her back in Manchester. Now she lived in a house with lacy white curtains, embossed velvet wallpaper, and lush carpets.

"No!" Ruby's distressed cry in the distance broke through the night. Had Ruby changed her mind? Was she telling Juliet to stop?

Juliet slowed her pace and waited once she reached the servants' entrance.

Ruby caught up with her a moment later, panting and carrying a small cigar box. "Tell the truth, did you follow me out to the back fence once before?"

"No, why would I have done that?" And why was Ruby back at the house? Hadn't she been planning to run away with the jewels?

The contents rattled as Ruby reached for the door latch. "You did so tonight, so it's not much of a stretch."

"Well, I didn't."

Ruby huffed and stepped inside, with Juliet trailing behind her. Instead of moving toward the staircase, Ruby veered down the hallway toward the housekeeper's office. Was she seeking out Mrs. Quinborow? If so, why?

They passed by the kitchen, and the dark, empty room cast shadows. Beyond the kitchen, they reached Mrs. Quinborow's door, which was tightly shut, with the light still glowing from the gap underneath.

Ruby lowered her hood and knocked.

"Enter," Mrs. Quinborow called. The woman disliked drama, particularly with her staff, but tonight she'd receive a handful, whether she wanted it or not.

Ruby opened the squeaky door, and they both stepped inside the cramped little room and were greeted by the scent of honey. Only a framed needlepoint of the Lord's Prayer adorned the walls, and a small table held a silver tea service and the honey pot. Two empty, straight-backed chairs rounded out the furniture.

Even on a good day, the housekeeper's lined face appeared strained. Now it had scrunched like a leftover winter apple. She'd piled her gray hair in a tight bun atop her head, and not a single wisp had escaped.

"Whyever are you two out of your room?" She rose behind her wooden desk, wearing her everyday blue uniform with white cuffs and collar. A thick collection of keys dangled from her generous waist.

Ruby lifted her chin. "I have something to say." A wall hook held a lit lantern, the flame matching Ruby's locks—a blend of red, yellow, and orange. Even though her roommate looked like an innocent angel, she wasn't.

"I need to tell you something too," Juliet said. "Something important."

The housekeeper crossed her arms. "Can't this wait until morning?"

"No, ma'am," Juliet said simultaneously with Ruby.

"Then proceed, and don't dawdle."

Ruby glanced at Juliet before releasing a rapid-fire spew of words. "She dropped a fancy ring on the floor in our room. I wager it's the missing jewel that belongs to the mistress."

Juliet's breath caught in her chest. "That's a dad-blamed lie."

Mrs. Quinborow's brow wrinkled. "What's this?"

"What Ruby described is what she did, ma'am. Afterward, she went outside. I followed and found her digging in the yard, but I didn't stay to learn if she was collecting something or hiding the ring."

"Juliet unburied a box, then I grabbed it to show you." Ruby opened the front of her cape and withdrew the cigar box, which she set on the desk next to a stack of papers. Then she raised the lid to display a handful of stones. "Don't know the reason for the rocks, but thinking Juliet planned to hide the ring inside here." She tapped the container. "She probably snatched the mistress's other jewels too."

Juliet thumped a hand on her waist as anger shot through her. "Another lie. I followed you outside, and . . . you retrieved the box, not me. When I said I was leaving to tell Mrs. Quinborow, you charged after me, cooking up this . . . twisted version of what happened."

Ruby burst into tears.

What? Not only was Ruby a good thief but also a top-notch actress.

The housekeeper withdrew a neatly folded white handkerchief from her desk drawer and passed the cloth to the weeping woman. "Do either of you have physical proof that the other stole the jewels?"

"Ruby has the ring on her person, I believe."

Mrs. Quinborow's expression grew more severe—if that were possible. "Remove your cape and empty your pockets, Miss O'Reilly. You do the same, Miss Dash."

Juliet followed the instructions, and Ruby also heeded the order. Mrs. Quinborow thoroughly examined them from head to foot and found nothing suspicious.

Where had Ruby stashed the ring?

Juliet's mind raced, trying to piece together a solution to her predicament. All she'd hoped to do was the right thing and protect the Firths. But nothing was going according to her plans.

"I've been employed here for ten months and have a clean record." What else could she say to convince the housekeeper she'd done nothing wrong? "The stealing didn't start until after Ruby arrived months back."

"Maybe you was waiting to get comfortable." Ruby sniffled. "Then you figured you could pin the blame on me since I'm newer."

When Mrs. Quinborow pursed her thin lips, they nearly disappeared. "If clear-cut evidence existed, I'd immediately send for the constable. Instead, I only have a box of rocks and two differing tales."

The housekeeper sighed deeply as if she'd stored the breath in her chest all day. "These insinuations now cast doubts on your characters. Therefore, pack your things, both of you. You're fired, and I shall not give you letters of recommendation."

Juliet huffed out a breath of exasperation. How was this happening? "But I'm innocent."

"I can't take the chance." Mrs. Quinborow stepped around her and Ruby before opening the door. "I'll escort you upstairs to gather your personal things. Naturally, I'll report this incident to Mrs. Firth in the morning."

The world was tipping out of control, and Juliet placed her hand against the wall to steady herself. Where would she go? Her two friends from the bride ship, Willow and Daisy, had married and lived a boat ride away. Willow's sister Sage lived next door but had left town with her employers, the Lennox family. And Juliet didn't know why.

Would Mrs. Moresby help her find a new job despite the accusation? All the other women who had arrived on the bride ship from Manchester had either wed or resided with their employers. Nobody lived at the marine barracks, their first home on the island, anymore.

The housekeeper left the room as her charges filed behind her, silently parading to the attic. In the bedroom, Juliet quickly crossed to the dresser, opened one drawer, and retrieved her empty flour sack before stuffing her belongings inside—tattered shoes, scant clothing, Grandfather's precious journal, and other small items. The uniform on her back belonged to her, the cost removed from her wages.

Ruby packed as well, grumbling as she did.

Afterward, they retraced their steps to the back service door before the housekeeper dismissed the women outside. The wind cried in the trees, and Juliet swallowed her tears of frustration. The stars shone dimmer than before. Or did she only imagine the lack of luster?

Ruby slung her bag over her shoulder and glared at Juliet.

Emotions whirled inside her, with anger and desperation near the top of the heap. "This isn't my fault. You stole the jewelry."

Ruby's shoulders sank. "You can't imagine how much trouble I'll be in for this."

"Losing your job?"

"Losing everything."

"Trouble with who?"

When Ruby failed to reply, Juliet turned and strode down the service lane, her feet as heavy as her heart. She had better things to do than worry about Ruby, starting with where she might lay her head tonight. The wind gusted, and she tightened her shawl over her shoulders. Several paces later, she rounded the brick house and a rosebush hedge, moving toward the main road and cutting through the grass.

Losing her job wasn't fair. But dwelling on what was just and what wasn't had never done her a speck of good.

Ruby caught up with her in a few steps, and they walked side by side in the house's shadows. "My man, that's who. He wanted the Queen's brooch."

The rare heirloom was probably worth thousands of pounds, if not more. Losing it was undoubtedly a giant failure.

Would Ruby pay the price? Another black eye? Or worse?

Juliet's chest tightened. As mad as she was at her former roommate, Ruby didn't deserve someone hurting her or pressuring her to commit crimes.

"You still shouldn't have stolen it or any of the jewelry, Ruby." Undoubtedly, she sounded self-righteous, but maybe she had earned the right tonight.

"And you shouldn't have interfered."

"I didn't."

"Then how did the rocks get in the box?" Ruby's voice turned threatening.

Juliet sidled sideways a pace, her heart clamoring. "I have no idea."

"I think you know more than you're letting on." Ruby started to lunge at Juliet's neck, her empty hand like a claw. "Maybe you've stowed the brooch somewhere and plan to keep it yourself."

Juliet blocked Ruby's arm and quickly unsheathed the small knife tied to her calf. She'd carried it with her since her orphan days of living on Manchester's streets. "You keep to yourself." She pointed the knife at Ruby and let menace fill her voice. "And I'll do the same."

Ruby backed up several steps. "Tell anybody about what happened tonight, and you'll regret it."

A bluff? Probably not.

She watched as Ruby disappeared into the night's shadows. With the weapon still in her fist, Juliet moved west toward downtown. A woman never knew what to expect on the streets alone at night, but Juliet was accustomed to caring for herself. She'd had lots of practice.

It was too late to bother Mrs. Moresby. She'd have to wait until morning to explain tonight's disaster and ask for help finding a new position.

Fortunately, Mrs. Moresby was a good woman, and Juliet could use one of those now. She hadn't known many in her lifetime. There was Willow, Daisy, and Sage. And Molly, her friend from the orphanage.

She shifted her gaze toward the starry night sky and pictured God somewhat like her grandfather who'd raised her for a while—trustworthy, wise, kind, and loving. But after his death, God had disappeared too. Still, she paused and squeezed her eyes shut.

"Dear God. . ." A minute passed, then two. "I'm still sorry for all the mistakes I've made."

Quick as a pickpocket, a heaviness pressed against her chest, almost stealing her breath. "What will become of me?" she whispered to the night.

Although Juliet no longer believed in fairy tales, she wished she did.

Instead, a hard reality stared back at her. She was homeless again.

Two

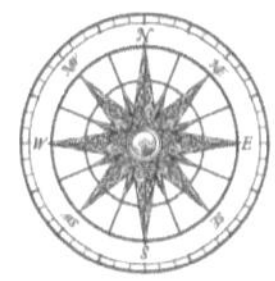

Saturday

YOUR BROTHER IS DEAD.

Henry Graighton drew a trembling breath, dropping his mother's epistle into his lap after reading the first sentence. "Dead." Such an empty, hollow word.

"Who?" Henry's valet and lifelong friend, Dobbin, closed the wooden wardrobe's door inside the Victoria Hotel.

"Sutton." It was easy for Henry to picture his older brother, almost like gazing in a mirror. Blessed with sturdy frames, they both had to duck through doorways. Their brown, wavy hair often misbehaved. Sutton's dark brown eyes duplicated their father's, and Henry's matched their mother's light brown hue.

"I am incredibly sorry." The window behind Dobbin revealed a gray, early evening sky. The faint light also highlighted the young man's posture, straight as a steeple. His blond hair was neatly combed, and his suit was impeccable as always.

"He was too young to die." At twenty-three, Sutton was only a year older than him. "He was not supposed to perish, especially before. . ." Henry could not finish the sentence aloud. But the ending echoed in his heart—they forgave each other.

But honestly, how long would that have taken?

Henry's heart swelled and pressed against his rib cage. From where he sat in a wing chair, mere feet from the hissing fire in his elegant room, he focused on his breaths, striving to keep them steady.

A couple of hours ago, the royal ship had arrived in Esquimalt Bay, where patchy hints of fog had settled over the water. There, his entourage transferred onto a smaller vessel to reach Victoria. Most everyone had already settled into their rooms in the establishment.

Mother's waiting letter was not the greeting to the island he had anticipated. According to the hotel proprietor, the correspondence had arrived several weeks ago, which meant the news was old.

He could admit that he had fallen behind on the itinerary his parents had meticulously honed for his one-year worldwide sojourn. Because of the interesting people he had met, he had extended their stay in San Francisco an extra week. But had he not done the same in Portugal, Morocco, and Chile?

His parents' goal, and the purpose of the trip, was for Henry to grow up and settle down. Or, in his father's words, "Stop your irresponsible pursuits."

But obviously, he hadn't done that yet.

"Do you mind if I sit?" Dobbin asked.

"No, do as you wish. However, I beg you to play the role of friend tonight and nothing more."

"Certainly." Dobbin sank into the plush matching chair on the other side of the fireplace. "What happened to Sutton, if you don't mind my asking?"

"Of course not. I was about to learn that myself." Henry retrieved the letter from his lap and read aloud.

> *"Your brother left this earth during the night after suffering from pneumonia. He disregarded the seriousness of his ailment until it grew too dire to ignore. How unlike him not to heed the royal physician's advice."*

The stationery crinkled as Henry's fist tightened. "Sutton displayed his stubborn side every day of the week, but how dare he jeopardize his health? Risk our country's welfare?" Henry shook his head. "More than once, I heard him claim he led a charmed life."

"Perhaps an accurate statement until recently."

Henry smoothed the crease with his finger. "Mother also writes . . .

> *"You shall soon receive an official notification from the palace, but I wanted you to learn the news from me first. The King is beside himself. Naturally, we are all devastated. It is a loss, but we understand God numbers our days according to His plans.*
>
> *"Son, I am confident this letter cuts deeply even though you have worked hard to carve the distance between you and your brother."*

Had he? His mind wandered back to a day when he was eight.

"Do you recall when we raced ponies with Faith as children?" She was not only a family friend but also Sutton's eventual fiancée.

"I do, and if I remember correctly, we were beyond weary of her boasts about her superior equestrienne skills. Then you challenged her in an open meadow."

"How better to discover if she told the truth?"

Dobbin nodded.

Sutton, a well-known tattler, attempted to dissuade the match, threatening to tell the King. Henry called his bluff, and the contest began in earnest. "I led the entire distance from oak tree to oak tree—just as we expected."

"Indeed, you did."

Then Henry had twisted back around after crossing the finish line, probably grinning like a joker. He had spotted Faith lying in the grass with Sutton at her side. Later, they discovered she had broken her leg. "That was the first time Sutton yelled he would never forgive me for what I had done."

"Even back then, he'd loved the girl."

Henry nodded. He and his brother shared the blame for their frequent feuds over the years. The more spirited of the two, Henry knew how to provoke his sibling and purposefully needled him. Eventually, their thorny relationship grew even pricklier.

And now, no more opportunities to make amends.

He raised the letter again but read silently.

> *If you are reading between the lines, and I assume you are—the wisest of my wonderful children—it is time to accept your duties and reorder your plans. I am sorry to clip your wings, though I bid you to return home post-haste. My dear heart, you are now the next in line to the Bascandy throne.*

Henry's stomach muscles clenched as if primed to receive a punch. Of course, he had reached that conclusion himself, but seeing the written words stirred something soul-shaking inside him. He had always wished for an ordinary existence—no pressing appointments regarding the monarchy, no expectations to lead a life of duty, and no pressure to be anyone but himself.

Such a wish was selfish, unkinglike, and nothing but a fairy tale.

He pictured his homeland—a small sovereign country off the coast of France, with English as the official language. The monarchy held weight in Bascandy, but a prime minister led a parliamentary government. Long ago, larger nations attempted to conquer their small island. Yet Bascandy had persevered, held firm, and earned respect worldwide.

"Do you wager peace will continue to govern once I rule, or shall I ruin the streak?"

"When it's your turn, you will be as strong of a leader as your father."

Henry scoffed. "You, my friend, are incredibly biased. According to him, I am too carefree. Too playful. Too irresponsible. All true, I suppose."

"I disagree, though you are far different than Sutton."

Sutton had always been disagreeable toward Henry, but over the years, they had learned to cope with one another. But then, on Henry's tenth birthday, the King brashly suggested that he strive to be more like his older and more responsible brother.

Father's harsh comment had built resentment inside Henry, festering over the years so that all Henry desired was to be the opposite of his brother. If Sutton announced he loved peas, Henry proclaimed he hated them. Sutton adored fencing, so Henry convinced himself he loathed the sport. Almost since birth, his brother only had eyes for one female, which convinced Henry not to rush finding a marriage partner.

"You have the makings of a wonderful king," Dobbin spoke quietly and with assurance. "You're admittedly headstrong, yet decisive, brave, and willing to learn. Once you return home, your father will teach you everything you need to know."

Henry sighed and picked up where he left off with his mother's letter.

It is time to face the facts. You must now wed Faith since Sutton cannot. I have no doubt you shall both accept the new plan in time. Your father believes the match is for the best.

Although an advantageous pairing based on wealth and connections, the King did not need to increase his riches or standing. He primarily desired to join families with his oldest and most loyal friend, Faith's father. "I cannot."

Dobbin leaned forward, his hands on his knees. "Can't what?"

"Marry Faith, who will undoubtedly love Sutton forever. I shall never measure up to my brother in her eyes either."

Besides, Henry had always hoped to wed for love. Among all the things he would have to give up, he did not wish to abandon that dream.

He read the letter's closing and lowered the stationery embossed with the royal seal to his lap before pinching the bridge of his nose. A stack of additional correspondence sat unopened on the pedestal table beside him. But reading through them would have to wait. He needed time to absorb the news of Sutton's death before doing anything else.

The room's heat suddenly stifled him, and he longed for cool air.

He stood, folded the letter, and tucked it inside his trouser pocket.

Dobbin's brow rose as he stood. "Are you fine, Henry?"

Of course not. How could he be? "I desire to step outside. Perhaps it shall clear my head."

"I'll join you." Dobbin moved to the door, his hand on the latch.

As much as Henry wanted—needed—to be alone, it would be a royal sin, or at least dangerous, for him to wander by himself. At home, a bodyguard or a soldier always accompanied him. But during the trip, he had grown somewhat sloppy about the protection because most people he met did not know his identity as a prince, which was precisely what Henry wanted. The royal ship was unmarked for a reason.

His security would intensify with the announcement of his new royal status. A dreadful thought.

Dobbin's kind eyes radiated with sympathy. "We both know my mother would box my ears if I failed to care for you properly."

Henry forced a smile, picturing the cook, a small yet formidable woman with a penchant for correcting her son. Despite her firm hand, Henry held a soft spot for the cook who had given birth to Dobbin on the same day as Henry was born on the same property. Except one birth had occurred in the palace and the other in the head gardener's cottage.

While Henry studied history at Oxford, Dobbin learned at the knee of Sutton's valet. Balancing the dual roles of servant and closest confidant had sometimes proven difficult for Dobbin. But they had made strides since leaving Bascandy in May, followed by Henry's best six months of life.

He donned his evening coat and top hat, pulling the brim low as Dobbin opened the dark-paneled door. They entered the empty, dimly lit hallway and closed the door in their wake. Soon, they descended the staircase. Wall sconces lit the thick banister and the rich, dark mahogany woodwork prevalent in the hotel.

A few guests milled in the lavish lobby, which boasted decorative pillars, groupings of plush chairs, and a shiny wooden floor. Avoiding eye contact with anyone, Henry quietly moved toward the exit and strode outside.

On the cusp of dusk, Henry led the way toward the shoreline to reach a sandy path, leading away from Victoria. Dobbin dutifully followed behind in silence. Patches of heavy, misty clouds shrouded the water, waves rolling in the wind. Nearby but hidden, a seagull cried into the night.

A stand of fir trees and the ocean lined their walkway with waves crashing against the shore. The fresh air and intermittent raindrops soothed his still-warm face as he stepped over a dead fish in their path. The sharp scent of seaweed was unmissable as they wandered farther from the city.

A sense of loneliness stirred inside him for the first time in a long while. Yet, the scattered fog held a soothing quality. "I desire a couple of minutes alone. Perhaps I shall sit on that flat stone overcropping the water and reread Mother's letter."

Dobbin bowed. "I'll wait here until you're ready to depart."

Henry tugged Mother's letter from his pocket and advanced toward his destination. Had he missed anything in the first pass? He climbed onto the hip-high stone and sat before unfolding the stationery and squinting at the words.

The wind gusted, slapping the waves against the shore, the spray inching closer. He read the message twice, then ran his thumb over the scar on his wrist. Minutes seeped away, and his thoughts jumbled until his fingers slowly curled around the letter, crumpling it into a ball. He squeezed with all his strength, then hurled the clump into the ocean. Almost immediately, the paper disappeared, and regret stabbed his chest.

The epistle connected him to home and his family, and he had carelessly tossed the link aside, much like his relationship with Sutton. With his chin raised, he asked, "Why, God? Why did You take my brother?"

"He ain't going to answer if that's what you think."

The scratchy voice wasn't Dobbin's. Henry glanced over his shoulder to find two strangers cloaked in the fog and the fading evening.

Henry slid off the rock to the sandy beach. "May I help you?"

"You certainly can." The man garbed in darker clothing lifted one notable accessory—a long-barreled weapon—and pointed it at Henry's head.

Dobbin, a keen shot, always kept a revolver with him. Henry

glanced toward his friend and winced. Dobbin was lying face down in the grass amongst the weeds.

Had the two men attacked his valet? Possibly killed him? Please, no.

His pulse spurted forward with dread, and he started toward his friend.

He made it only two steps before the man with the weapon thrust the barrel of the gun into Henry's side. "Stop!"

Drawing a steadying breath, Henry turned slowly back around. "What do you want with me?"

The one without the gun, missing his front teeth, held a deadly glint in his eyes. "Our sister works at the Royal Hotel and says mail had piled up for Prince Henry Graighton. We believe he is you."

Unbelievable, or at least unacceptable, behavior for a hotel employee. But then the welcoming committee before him—two men and at least one gun—were also highly objectionable.

"You see," the toothless man continued, "a few of us been waiting on you for days, hatching a plan. You were to arrive before now. Then we heard your ship docked and tracked you to the fancy hotel. It was our lucky day when you slipped outside."

Henry scanned the shoreline for an escape route. Could he outrun the duo? Could he hide in the fog or jump into the ocean and swim to safety?

The stranger waved the barrel of his weapon back and forth and stepped closer. "If you're smart, you won't try to escape. I never miss what I aim for."

Perhaps the pair only intended to rob him. All Henry had on his person was his clothing. "Is it money you seek?"

Laughter rumbled from the toothless man's chest. "Why else kidnap a prince for ransom?"

Kidnap? Not today, at least not without a fight.

He was a strong swimmer and could perhaps escape if he dove into the ocean and disappeared under the waves. It would be cold but not any more frigid than the North Sea, where he had learned to swim.

He took a step back. But before he broke away, the man with the long-barreled weapon swung it hard and slammed the butt against the side of Henry's head.

Instantaneous, gut-wrenching pain swallowed Henry whole. He crumpled, then thudded into the sand, hitting his head.

Three

"Y OU KNOW, A DEAD PRINCE IS WORTH far less than a live one," a gruff voice said.

Henry was not dead yet, but he had no intention of correcting the man's assumption that his last breaths were not imminent. Lying on the cold floor, perhaps of a steamboat, if the steady rumble of an engine was any indication. He kept his eyes shut and his body still. His head throbbed. The scent of blood, most likely his own, mixed with hay and the ripe stench of manure. He fought the urge to shiver from the cold.

On cue, a cow mooed. Was he stuck down with the animals on the lower deck of the steamer going . . . where?

When he strained to recall his attack, his head threatened to explode. He'd been struck. In the side of the head hard with the gun, but that did not account for the throbbing at the back of his skull. Had he smacked against a rock when he fell unconscious?

He drew in a steadying breath. How was Dobbin? Was he on the ship somewhere?

Henry prayed his friend had not been captured too. Even worse, he hoped Dobbin had not been left dead on the beach.

Dead. Like Sutton.

Henry flinched, hoping his captors failed to notice. The anguish of losing his brother washed over him anew. If only he had done more to amend their differences. But now it was too late . . .

If only he had done more to fix the problems with his father too. But they had parted ways on unfavorable terms, especially after Henry's last escapade before leaving on his voyage.

He had donned a disguise and entered a horserace, betting a large sum on himself as the winner. But his horse drew up lame, Henry lost, and the King learned about the stunt. During his reprimand, his father threatened to cancel Henry's trip. But Mother intervened, believing time apart was best. She hoped Henry would soon realize his actions impacted the entire family.

Guilt pressed against him again. What would it take to turn his life around? Indeed, Sutton's death and the kidnapping were strong contenders.

Of course, he disliked upsetting his parents, who must have been consumed with grief over losing their firstborn. His four younger sisters—Amanda, Charlotte, Nora, and Maureen—were undoubtedly mourning Sutton's loss too. The girls adored their older brothers, and the feelings were mutual. If Henry failed to survive his unfolding ordeal, he would shatter their tender hearts even more.

He had to fix his predicament, but how?

"I tell you what, the prince should have awoken by now, you'd think," came a slurred voice—probably the toothless one. "There's a doctor in Everly. Suppose we get off there, have him give the prince a once-over, and then we catch a later boat."

How long had he been unconscious? Was it still the same night as his attack? The next day? Or longer yet?

"Don't be an idiot," replied the gruff voice, belonging to the man who had carried the gun. "The last thing we want, you see, is someone to catch us with royalty. Use your head. We're going straight to Hope, like the boss said. That's final."

Was Hope a city, a secret hideaway where criminals plotted underhanded deeds? Or did his imagination run wild? Perchance, both possibilities rang true.

"What do you suppose is the going rate for a prince these days?" the toothless man asked.

"Hard telling, but I wager it'll be hefty."

Moments later, one of them released an obnoxiously loud yawn. "Must be past midday. Gonna go stretch my legs."

"While at it," said the gruff voice, "check how long until we dock."

The toothless man mumbled as hay rustled and the floor creaked. Soon, footsteps sounded and faded.

With only one foe guarding him, should he attempt to escape?

Henry slit his eyes to examine his surroundings. It was broad daylight, and cloudy blue skies floated past above the deck railing. If it was past midday, then he had been unconscious since at least last evening.

His elbow itched, and he glanced at his arm. Dried blood stained his sleeve. Why did he only wear ripped undergarments? No wonder he was cold. Was his clothing removed to deter him from fleeing? If so, his captors had judged him incorrectly, for nothing would stop him other than a bullet.

A body length away, the assailant with the gun resting in his lap casually leaned against a plank that perhaps shielded the animals from the chilly water's spray. His legs stretched before him with ankles crossed. The brim of his hat rode low, covering much of his shadowy face. Regardless, Henry had no trouble identifying him— the assailant who had rendered him unconscious with his rifle.

Every muscle in Henry's body tensed. He would sooner take a

chance on fleeing than remain complacent. But what advantage did he have over a man with a weapon?

But then his guard released a snore, a deep-chested rattle—a positive development.

Any minute, the man's partner might return. Therefore, Henry had to be clever, inconspicuous, and on his way. Silently, he rose, then paused to regain his bearings and combat his dizziness before tiptoeing around the cows, sheep, pigs, and a horse tethered to posts. Once he moved away from the livestock, he halted again to catch his bearings.

The rumble of an engine nearby and the steady slap of a paddle-wheel told him that he was indeed on a steamboat. Ahead of the steamer to the east, the rocky shoreline and harbor surrounded by a small town seemed to beckon him. It could not be more than a quarter of a mile away. Was this the Everly his captors had mentioned?

Voices and footfalls drew near, and he ducked behind a mound of crates. Two deckhands passed by, perhaps getting ready to dock soon.

Should he search for the captain and report his kidnapping? His heartbeat thumped in his head, tapping a message to find a doctor. He touched the laceration at the back of his head from where he had hit something. It was still slick with blood. He winced, though he doubted the wound required stitches, and wiped his hand on his underclothing.

A steam whistle split the air with a long, slow bellow as if an-nouncing the steamer's ever-nearing proximity to the shore. At the noise, the pain in his temple sharpened. He braced his head until the throbbing subsided before rising and moving along the rail. Should he jump into the water and try to swim to shore? When in Bascandy, he swam the pond length at the palace daily, sometimes twice.

More than anything, he wished he was there now.

Was jumping over the side his best option? Or, in his weakened and injured condition, should he wait until the gangplank was lowered? It wouldn't be long.

He kept to the shadows as the steamboat chugged into the harbor. With another whistle, this one with three shorter blasts, the vessel drew alongside a wharf. The deckhands began to secure the boat, and a few minutes later, Henry sidled toward the gangplank, now being lowered with chains and large iron hinges. He paused to watch, willing the escape route procedure to move along faster.

A few workers glanced sideways at him, and why not? Barefooted, filthy, and in his undergarments, who would not raise their eyebrows at his appearance?

"Hey!" The slurred voice belonged to his toothless captor. "Stop that man!"

Undoubtedly, *that man* was Henry.

Without glancing behind him, he hopped onto the gangplank, which had just barely touched the shore. His head and feet were pounding with each step. Charging forward, he perused the scene before him. A line of passengers was starting to board a steamboat pointed west—presumably toward Victoria.

Of course, its destination could be anywhere. But anywhere appealed more than his current position.

An idea formed around the edges of his mind. What if he raced on board, fooling his pursuers into thinking he intended to hide on the ship? Instead, he would leap into the strait. But only after he reached the front, putting distance between himself and everyone else, ensuring his pursuers failed to notice his escape.

Except he was a spectacle in his unmentionables. In theory, his plan could succeed. But then again, based on his injury, he may drown. Still, he had to take the risk, mainly because shouts from his kidnappers trailed behind him.

Henry charged down the wooden wharf, dodging passengers, livestock, and carts headed toward the departing steamer. He spun onto the crowded gangplank and jostled travelers as he maneuvered forward. "Apologies, apologies," he repeated countless times.

A giant of a man in a coonskin cap elbowed Henry. "Watch where you're going."

"Please forgive me." He hurried forward, aware he exhibited deplorable manners, yet plowed toward his goal. Otherwise, he may lose more than a footrace.

When Henry's feet hit the slippery deck, he bolted forward yet maintained his balance. He veered to starboard, needing to disappear.

Ideally, his pursuers would search high and low for him. With any luck, the steamer would pull away with the kidnappers still aboard, offering Henry ample time to swim to safety. If he survived the next twenty-four hours, he may even book a passage back to Victoria as early as tomorrow morning.

What a tale to relay to Dobbin upon his return . . . if Dobbin had survived. Hopefully, his friend was safe, sound, and at the hotel, though he would undoubtedly suffer physically from his assault and mentally with worry over Henry's disappearance. Dobbin would blame himself for neglecting his duties and allowing his charge to vanish mysteriously. But the kidnapping was not his friend's fault.

Henry reached the deck's railing and glanced behind him. Finding nobody nearby, he climbed over and dropped into the icy water, praying he did not splash.

Or freeze to death.

The shock to his system nearly made him gasp, but he clamped his lips shut. The cold pierced his skin, and he struggled to focus as the blasted misery consumed his thoughts. With hard, swift strokes, he swam, forcing himself to remain underwater until his lungs threatened to burst.

If he surfaced, would he be seen? Had his captors fallen for his ruse? Did they now search for him on the second steamboat?

He raised his head enough from the clear water to gasp a deep breath and gauge his location. Thankfully, the afternoon tide barely hampered his progress. He slipped back under the surface, his feet numbing from the cold, and continued to swim underwater parallel to the shoreline, hoping to put a safe distance between himself and his captors.

When the town's shoreline was no longer in sight, he fully rose to his feet, slipped out of the strait, and onto an empty, pebbly beach. Water dripped from his hair, chin, arms, and undergarments. Shaking and exhausted, Henry stumbled forward over twigs and rocks that poked at his tender skin until he reached a pine tree on the beach's fringe.

He briefly paused behind it to catch his breath. Between the cold and his aching head, the swim had nearly ended his life, yet he had persevered. Rarely, if ever, had he given up on a challenge—not a horse race, chess match, or fistfight with his brother.

His current life-and-death nightmare was not the time to change his habits.

He peered around the prickly edge and tried to see down the shore toward the steamboat he had abandoned minutes ago. As far as he could tell, nobody was following him. But Henry needed another blessing—a safe, friendly place to warm up and stay out of sight. Who would help him in his current state? If not mistaken, he smelled like a dead fish and probably looked worse. And he had no money.

Should he venture back toward town and search for the help he needed? Or should he wait in the woods along the community's edge until more confident his kidnappers no longer searched for him in the area?

A distant whistle blared a quick, powerful blast. Was the steamboat he had temporarily boarded preparing to leave the harbor? And were his kidnappers on board?

Merciful heavens, he hoped so.

Just in case they had decided to scout the town, Henry would be safest if he stayed hidden in the woodland for a while longer, preferably away from the shore.

Every muscle was stiff from the cold as he swerved around the impediments in his path—trees, stumps, a thorny hedge, and a canoe in the weeds. He crossed a muddy road and soon sneaked past the rear of a livery with penned horses.

Moving north, he climbed a hill and entered a more residential area to one side of him with dense timber on the other. When the hill crested, he paused to lean his hand against the trunk of a birch tree, winded.

Ahead, a sprawling lawn separated him from a stately house and outer buildings. Perhaps someone would step outside and, after a bit of coaxing, offer him dry clothing or a warm blanket. Or should he search for a church? Surely, he would find assistance there.

A gunshot echoed in the distance. His kidnappers or a hunter, perhaps?

Unsure and shaky, Henry spun and staggered into the woods. He listened for voices or footsteps but only heard a whooshing inside his head.

Another gunshot cracked the air, closer this time.

Was someone coming after him? Probably not. Why would his kidnappers be shooting? Even so, he could not take a chance and had to move farther from the town.

He wove deeper into the thick woods, pinecones and twigs stabbing his feet. With each step, the throbbing in his head roared louder until nausea rose inside him, and lights flashed at the backs of his eyes.

A wave of dizziness hit him while he stumbled over a root. He was falling but could not find the energy to brace for the impact. In the next instant, his body collided with the ground.

Four

HOW LONG UNTIL EVERLY RESEMBLED home? Perhaps never.

After Juliet lost her job with the Firths a week ago, she spent one night in a quiet, empty church and left before dawn. Then, when a reasonable hour arrived, she visited Mrs. Moresby, who invited her into her home. Juliet explained the situation at the Firths', telling her every detail about her firing.

Not only did Mrs. Morseby believe her, but she also agreed to help her find a new job and allowed her to stay in her home for nearly a week. Juliet would never forget her kindness.

Friends Mrs. Moresby had met while traveling from England to Victoria had recently written, asking for help locating a servant to assist in their home and future tearoom. Their current part-time employee had taken ill and didn't intend to return. Mrs. Moresby had immediately written to the sisters about Juliet. They'd sent word back, agreeing to hire Juliet for some unbeknownst reason, even after learning about her firing for possible theft and lack of an endorsement.

Why? Juliet was stumped, for certain. Could she picture pouring tea to society folks? Not even for a whisper of a second. But nobody else was lining up to give her a job, either.

After leaving the wharf minutes ago, she paused her ascent up a hill and ripped off her drenched headscarf, hoping her hair would dry faster in the afternoon breeze. It couldn't get much wetter. Even her flour sack stuffed with belongings was dripping. What a miserable way to meet her new employers—soaked to the bone. "Ugh," Juliet said to nobody but herself.

When a whistle screeched from a steamboat in the harbor, she peered over her shoulder. The town was nestled on a cleared hill that sloped gently toward the water at the Fraser River Delta's fork. Whitewashed houses mixed with shops on Everly's Main Street at the foot of the hill. A fishmonger along the shore hawked his wares, his voice echoing.

Against the backdrop of mountains to the north, the town sat on the mainland of British Columbia across the Strait of Georgia from Vancouver Island, a seven-hour steamboat ride. The northern range, with its rocky peaks and massive forests, was a magnificent sight, especially from the hilltop where she now stood.

She spun around and continued toward her destination, taking her merry time. The town had not yet built wooden walkways in the neighborhood. The higher she climbed, the fancier the houses. A hefty breeze rippled the puddles. A vast grassy park stood to her left, and evergreens hemmed the town on three sides and the mighty Fraser River behind her.

Her sodden shoes squeaked with each step. Her stockings stuck to her legs, and her cold skin had shriveled and sprouted gooseflesh. She stopped walking and yanked up her skirts to wring out all the moisture she could summon as she tried to recall Mrs. Morseby's specific instructions.

Didn't she say the respectable sisters resided across from Queen's Park in a pink-and-green two-story house with a copper roof on Birch Street? Also, the dwelling had a lattice and a turret, whatever that was.

Her gaze swept across the road and over the surrounding houses, halting abruptly at two women staring at her from the front steps of a property that matched Mrs. Morseby's description.

Snakes alive. She dropped her skirts. Had they watched her hike her garment above her knees? Well, of course, they had.

Juliet's stomach sank.

Both appeared to be middle-aged based on the lack of youthfulness on their faces. The shorter sister wore more white ruffles than should be allowed and an enormous flouncy hat. Long of limb, the other one held a closed umbrella. Her oatmeal-beige dress was fancy yet simple at the same time.

Although Juliet had learned to stand up to a gang of no-good hoodlums in England, high-class ladies made her quake. Now she risked losing her job before stepping foot in their house, and she couldn't let that happen. No, ma'am.

Focused on the house, she strode forward. Buildings offered no judgment. Two chimneys stuck up on each end. The remainder of the home included four upstairs windows, three down, an imposing door left of center, and wrought iron railings beside the steps. Shrubs trimmed the front and large side lawns, probably keeping the neighbors from snooping too much.

Juliet, her resolve firm, didn't stop until she stood near the bottom of the stairs, below the two women. She straightened her shoulders and offered a tight smile. "I'm Juliet Dash. Mrs. Moresby sent me. I'm here for a one-month trial or something along those lines."

The lady in beige had sharp, bright eyes, more green than blue.

Although willowy in build, she had a staunchness about her, perhaps due to her arrow-straight posture and raised chin. Her hair, the color of weak tea, was gathered and trapped in a crocheted netting at her nape. "Allow me to introduce my younger sister and myself. This is Livy Sherwood, and I'm Tabitha Pierce. It's lovely to make your acquaintance."

"I apologize for looking like a wet cat, but I got caught in the rain."

Livy offered a genuine, welcoming grin, descended the steps, and closed the gap between them. Everything about her appeared as soft as a pillow—fleshy chin, plump rosy cheeks, and whatever hid beneath her shapeless dress. Her red nose signaled a cold. Pearls trimmed her monstrous hat, covering all evidence of hair, and her greenish eyes were as inviting as her smile.

"We were going to the park since the rain stopped." Standing before Juliet, Livy tilted her head as she examined her. "Let me get a good look at you instead. You have beautifully high cheekbones, a fine figure, and the starkest blue eyes I've ever seen."

"Umm . . . thank you." Over the years, boys and men had praised her looks, but she didn't put much stock in compliments. Sometimes, hearing flowery words was nice, but all too often, the compliments came with a motive or a price.

With her lips pursed, Tabitha clasped her hands behind her back. "I'm afraid I must mention the inappropriateness of you wringing out your skirts in the street moments ago, Miss Dash."

Juliet had no excuse for her careless actions and would never conjure up such a thing. But now the ladies likely deemed her a wild hoyden. She truly wasn't, not anymore. "My behavior wasn't ladylike. I know that, and I'm probably not what you expected."

Sure as shooting, they'd fire her. Now that they'd met her, they'd see she didn't belong in a tearoom. "Do you want me to leave?"

Livy reached for Juliet's wrist, her fingers warm. "Of course not. Isn't that correct, Tabitha?"

"It is." Her tone and facial expression were frank and unconvincing.

Livy's oversized hat bounced as she nodded. Any minute, the breeze might pitch it across the lawn. "When Mrs. Moresby wrote, she explained your unique circumstances."

Unique? That was one word for it. "Yes, ma'am."

Tabitha's face somehow grew even tighter than before. "A young lady in our care does not chase wherever her impulses lead her. Is that understood?"

"Yes, and I'll do my best to stop doing that, starting now." Except Juliet's whims sprinted every which way far too often.

A raindrop plopped onto Juliet, quickly followed by more, cooling her suddenly warm face.

"Let's assemble inside, shall we?" Livy turned and led the way, hurrying up the broad steps and opening the door wide.

Tabitha entered the house ahead of her sister, but Juliet remained rooted where she stood.

"Hippity hop, Miss Dash," Livy called from the doorway. "Otherwise, my lovely hat may slump in this weather. I was convinced the sun wanted to shine, but alas, I was mistaken."

By all accounts, it appeared they expected their new servant to waltz through the front door. Juliet had never heard of such a thing. Not once had she crossed the front entrance at the Firths'.

Then the rainfall strengthened, prodding her forward up the stairs and through the door. Inside, she stood rigid on the doormat, dripping wet again and not wanting to dampen the floor more than necessary. But her eyes wandered everywhere as she carefully wiped her shoes.

Two gold-rimmed mirrors stood on either side of the door, and narrow wood planks covered the floor. The large entrance hall led to a staircase that curved midway. Although less grand than the Firth residence, the house still impressed.

Juliet stretched her neck to view the impossibly high ceiling. She caught a whiff of something delicious wafting from the other end of a narrow hallway. Was it a warm, hearty soup? Oh, she hoped so.

Tabitha lowered her umbrella to the stand and sat on a nearby spindly-legged chair before unfastening her side-lacing boots. "We don't stand on ceremony, Miss Dash. Our staff is small—you and our part-time cook. His wife previously filled the role you're assuming and recently quit due to her health. They reside elsewhere alongside other natives on the outskirts of town."

"I see." Mrs. Moresby had explained Juliet's role as a maid in the household and a server in the tearoom, which had a grand opening scheduled days before Christmas, weeks away. Furthermore, Mrs. Moresby had informed her that Tabitha's husband had died during their first year of marriage, leaving her childless but wealthy. Livy had never wed after being jilted at the altar long ago.

Such a thing could break a person's heart.

Livy removed the long pin from her hat and hung the giant headpiece on the brass wall hook behind her. Sandy-blond, curly hair capped her head. "Why don't we show you to your room? After you put on something dry, we'll give you a tour of our home, followed by the carriage house, which we're converting into the tearoom. May we call you Juliet?"

"Of course, though"—she raised her soggy bag—"all my garments are drenched, including my maid's uniform."

Tabitha rose, now wearing mule-brown slippers with a rounded toe. She straightened Livy's hat on the hook to perfectly center it before facing Juliet. "A uniform isn't required inside the house. We'll provide what you need for the tearoom."

No uniform? That was odd. But Juliet wouldn't complain. "How generous. Thank you."

Tabitha perused Juliet from head to foot. "My castoffs will likely fit you. I keep them at the back of the wardrobe in the bedroom where you'll sleep. You may wear what you please."

The sisters' kind behavior didn't make sense, no matter how she twisted their angle. Why treat her like a cherished guest instead of a possible thief?

"This way, Juliet." Tabitha moved toward the staircase.

"Yes, ma'am." At least her bag wasn't dripping anymore as she followed on the stairs' carpet that matched red wine. Pretty carved rosettes decorated the rails, and she longed to run her finger over the ridges, yet stopped herself.

At the top, she paused to count six closed doors, three on each side of a wide hallway. Then she hurried after Tabitha and entered the last room on the right, next to a rear staircase. One pace inside the room, she paused again. The Firths' four attic bedrooms equaled this one in size.

She gazed at two large windows facing the back of the house, each framed with tied-back pale-yellow drapes. Undoubtedly, the view captured the impressive mountains. Her stomach fluttered at the thought of waking to the beautiful picture every morning.

The room was furnished with a half-tester bed, a wooden wardrobe, a washstand, a writing desk, a chair, and a flat sandstone hearth. Framed floral pictures and a long, narrow mirror hung on the same wall. No reason to give her water-logged appearance a once-over.

Surely this fine chamber wasn't meant for her, and if it was, not just for her. "There must be some mistake. This room can't be for me."

"It is for you." Tabitha gazed around the chamber with critical eyes.

First, the sisters had her strolling through the front door. Now, she was to sleep on the same floor as all the other bedrooms. "But I'm the servant. Why not put me in a dormer room in your attic?"

"Our attic isn't suited for a bedroom. Besides, we have several unused rooms on this level. Class distinctions are not something Livy and I put much stock in, although we value good manners and proper behavior from everyone, regardless of their station in life. It also makes sense for you to eat your meals with us as well."

Huh? Juliet had never heard of such a thing. A bedroom to herself was more than she could imagine. But eating in front of the sisters sounded like a nightmare. Undoubtedly, she'd tangle herself in a fit of worries, thinking she'd break her bread wrong, spill too many crumbs, or use the incorrect utensil. "If it's all the same to you, I'll just eat in the kitchen. Alone."

Tabitha nodded. "If that's your preference." Then the prim woman launched into a discourse about the newly developed town—a hodgepodge of military personnel, business folks, lumber mill workers, natives, and people drawn to British Columbia to seek gold. The thriving village served as the primary port of entry to the Fraser River. More and more imports, including livestock, firearms, food, and clothing, occurred daily. Plenty of gold, lumber, fish, and cranberries exited Everly via steamers. Or was it blueberries?

Juliet wondered if she should take notes and if the woman intended to quiz her later about all the facts.

Livy popped through the doorway, dabbing her nose with a wadded handkerchief. "Are your sleeping quarters satisfactory?"

"It's a dad-blamed palace. And I'm far from a princess." Even though her grandfather had called her the sweet fairy tale name. She twirled in a full circle to admire the loveliness. "It's perfect. That's what it is."

Tabitha opened the squeaky wardrobe's doors. "We're pleased you like it, though the term dad-blamed is considered slang, and proper young ladies never utter slang."

Mrs. Quinborow had corrected Juliet's speech a time or two and specifically instructed her not to say *dad-blamed*. But the word still slipped out now and again anyway.

"And Juliet?" Livy asked, fluffing her hair with her hand.

"Yes, ma'am."

"One of our goals in opening the tearoom is to bring culture to the community. We expect you to help us in that effort. Therefore, you'll need to mind your p's and q's."

Her what? That was all well and good, except Juliet was the last person to convert folks into well-mannered, classy citizens.

Why had Mrs. Morseby sent her here?

Oh, right, because there were no other options.

Juliet held back an exasperated sigh.

Grandfather had tried to raise her right, but the years had faded some of his teachings. Others she'd shoved to the side because circumstances had forced her to do things she wasn't proud of. However, she'd learned additional niceties at the Firths' house.

Yet she didn't know proper conversation with well-to-do folks or when to curtsy, if ever. Nobody had taught her to pour tea or greet a gentleman caller. She had other know-how, but her street smarts couldn't help her now. "I'll try my best."

Tabitha smoothed the bedspread with her flat hand before straightening. "That is all we ask for, Juliet. If you'll excuse me, I must speak to Icala briefly."

Who was he? Juliet nodded as Tabitha left the room.

Livy moved to the bed and sat, creaking the springs and disturbing the spread Tabitha had straightened seconds ago. "Now that I've mentioned our goals for the tearoom, I'm wondering about yours, Juliet. What are they?"

"Mine?" She tightened her grip on the flour bag.

"Yes."

"Goals?"

"Yes, indeedy."

Never had anyone asked her that question, not even herself. Her friend Daisy had opened a sewing shop, and Willow farmed—both worthy ambitions. Sage favored her position as a lady's maid. "I guess I want a roof over my head and to feel safe."

"What else?" Livy persisted. "Have you ever considered what you want out of life?"

What did she desire more than anything else? "I don't mean to speak poorly of myself, but I'm not trained for much more than what I'm doing now. You'll soon teach me about tearoom duties, according to Mrs. Morseby." Juliet shrugged and continued to ponder her answer. "I'm a good maid and like doing honest work."

Livy's sharp stare had Juliet running her moist hands over her skirt. "I understand your grandfather raised you until his death. May I ask what happened to your parents?"

"They drowned when we crossed the River Irwell to visit my grandfather. I was but two. I don't recall our boat tipping over, nor the stranger who fished me from the water and hauled me to a church. Grandfather fetched me from there."

"I'm sorry for your loss." Livy stood and stepped closer, her eyes kind. "Have you ever had an older woman's influence?"

"Only a smidge. Mrs. Moresby treated me nice, and the housekeeper where I worked in Victoria taught me a few polite particulars."

"Long ago, someone bestowed kindness upon Tabitha and me, though I won't get into the details." Livy patted Juliet's forearm. "Feel free to refuse, but would you enjoy learning how to be more genteel overall, training that would extend beyond the tearoom?"

What exactly was this kind lady proposing? Juliet cranked up her eyebrow. "Why do that for me?"

"Because we can." Livy chuckled. "Truthfully, the notion just popped into my head, and Tabitha must agree to the plan before we set anything in motion. It's simply an idea. Some days, I'm full to the brim with them."

"It's good you have all that room in your head for such things." Livy's eyes widened.

Juliet clamped her hand over her mouth. Had she just insulted

the woman by insinuating that her head was empty? "I'm sorry . . .
I misspoke . . . I was only trying to compliment you."

Livy waved a dismissive hand. "Mrs. Moresby said you'd be perfect for us, and I believe she was right."

Juliet wanted to be perfect for herself, but still . . . holy Moses.

An unexpected glimmer of hope buzzed inside her, but she told
herself to calm down. If the sisters taught her the ins and outs of ladylike behavior, she'd become more respectable, and that sounded
awful nice for a change. "I believe it's to my liking."

"Very well. After you change, please join us downstairs, and
we'll start the tour."

"Yes, ma'am." Livy excused herself, and Juliet quickly dried off
with a plush towel. Then she grabbed a plain brown dress with
buttons from the waist to the collar from the wardrobe. She tugged
it on, draped her wet garments near the fire, and spread her few
other meager belongings on the gold-carpeted floor to dry. Even
her grandfather's journal had damp, but not ruined, pages. She
bent to kiss the cover, grabbed her hairbrush, and pulled the bris-
tles through her locks.

Already, she adored everything about the room. What if she
fell madly in love with the place and then had to leave? How long
could she stretch her stay in paradise?

Based on her employment record, not long enough.

Juliet abandoned the hairbrush on the bureau and rushed downstairs. At the front of the house, she entered the empty drawing
room, decorated in greens and blues. A noisy grandfather clock
interrupted the quiet. Next to a square piano, an empty birdcage
dangled from a hook attached to the ceiling.

Juliet stepped closer. Scattered seeds covered the bottom. Someone had carved the words *Dearest Peaches* onto an attached brass
plate above the open door. Though she knew nothing about bird-
cages, the latch appeared busted. Had the cherished pet escaped?

Later, she'd investigate the home and the bird mystery more

thoroughly, but now she needed to meet with the sisters. She briefly poked her head into a library, then a dining room, and finally a sitting room with a bed shoved in the corner. Each one charmed her as much as the next. Yet she failed to locate the sisters.

A glorious aroma led her down the remaining hallway to an expansive, welcoming kitchen with a black-and-white checked floor. Iron hooks held a mix of pots, kettles, and a griddle. A blackened vessel with a burping lid perched on a massive stove built into the wall. The remnants of a squash, a knife, and a wooden spoon claimed space on the sideboard.

She closed her eyes and savored the rich, nutty scent only briefly. The last thing she wanted was for the sisters to think she plodded along. Were they in the carriage house? There was only one way to find out, and she moved toward the rear door and opened it.

The second she did so, a green bird with a yellow head and bright orange beak swooped past her head, whistling as she escaped.

What in tarnation?

But then again, if Juliet lived in a cage, she'd probably try to flee too.

Juliet charged outside in pursuit of Dearest Peaches.

Five

NOBODY HAD EVER CALLED JULIET silly. But chasing after a dad-blamed bird was nothing less than downright foolish.

For pity's sake, the sisters would fire her for losing Dearest Peaches, hoisting her skirt in the street, and uttering common words. One mistake they might overlook. But three?

She kept her eye on the beloved critter. "Get back here, now."

A damp breeze brushed her cheeks as she tore down a cobblestone path, pursuing the fowl. Desperation and mist swirled as she sped past a lattice fence, gardens, fruit trees, and three outer buildings of various shapes and sizes.

She pinpointed the two-story structure as the carriage house. A tall, wide-centered doorway large enough for a buggy stood on one end. The building featured a steep roof, dormer windows, and two smaller, closed doors.

She ought to peek in and see if Tabitha and Livy were waiting for her inside. But if she paused to speak to them, she'd lose track of Peaches.

Oh, blame it all.

The pathway ended, and a pine and cedar tree grove stood yonder. Or was it a vast forest big enough to lose a person, let alone the nuisance of a bird? Her sensible shoes slapped against the soggy grass as the bright yellow-headed critter, not much bigger than a sugar bowl, swooped high and low over bushes and through trees but never landed.

Please, don't enter the woods.

Peaches soared straight into the forest. Because, of course, she would.

"Snakes alive." Juliet followed, weaving around trees as fast as she could. The temperature dropped inside the thicket, and her borrowed dress offered little protection. Pine needles, long as a shark's tooth but hopefully not as sharp, scattered underneath her shoes. A woodsy tang swirled around her.

After a few more steps, she stopped. Her odds of catching the creature with bare hands were higher than the treetops. Although she didn't believe in curses, sometimes she wondered about her long streak of misfortune.

Today was one of those days.

She should swallow her pride, admit defeat, and accept the facts—she'd never catch the bird singlehandedly, especially without a butterfly net like the one the Firth daughters had used for play on the lawn.

Peaches darted past, almost close enough to snare. Like a ninny, Juliet lunged for the creature, only to stumble and fall, landing hard on her chest with an *oomph*. She winced. Pine needles poked at her face, and she slowly rose onto her elbows. Grime clung to her sleeves and skin as she peered over her shoulder to determine what had caused her stumble.

A pair of legs poked out of a pile of brush. Real human legs. With bare, pale feet.

Her pulse jumped in her veins. What in the world?

She pushed up until she was kneeling and could see more clearly. It was a man, based on the size of his feet. Was he dead? Of course, since he was lying on his belly motionless and halfway buried in the woods.

The whistling bird dove past. Only this time, Juliet ignored the critter's teasing, stood, and focused on the body. Who was he? Had someone killed him? If so, how long ago?

Unfortunately, she'd seen dead bodies in Manchester, and not just her grandfather's. People died on the streets for an assortment of reasons—fights, starvation, diseases, and who knew what else.

But what if this fella hadn't taken his last breath? What if he was merely unconscious?

Juliet crouched and brushed debris off his back and head. Dried blood matted his dark, wavy hair. His shoulders were broad, his middle whittled, and his legs extra-long. Even though his face pointed away from her, she noted the start of a beard on his cheeks and chin. An angry, long, red scratch on his forearm. Her best guess had him stepping into his twenties not too long ago.

Tentatively, she reached for his wrist. Was he dead or alive? There was only one way to find out. Her pulse quickened even more as she pressed her fingers against his cold skin.

Life pumped through his body.

Juliet surged back to her feet and glanced in the direction she'd come from. The man required shelter and medical know-how. But could she drag him to the house by herself? If she left to fetch help, would she be able to find him again? Somewhere, a dog howled, or perhaps a wolf. Uneager to learn the answer, she hitched her skirt to unsheathe her knife laced with a leather cord to her calf.

She squatted and sliced off a dingy white portion of his drawers below his knee. Why did he wear nothing but filthy underclothing? It was odd, but the entire day was strange. She trimmed the cloth into a dozen smaller pieces.

Determined to save his life, she quickly returned her knife to where it belonged and retraced her steps, dropping makeshift breadcrumbs along the path. She broke through the dense trees and raced toward the carriage house as heaven began to dump more rain on her chilly frame. She flung open a side door and crossed the threshold in a flurry.

The sisters stopped rummaging through a crate stuffed with straw in the room's heart to stare at her. Tabitha's brows rose toward the ceiling, and Livy clutched her cameo.

The room lacked furnishings but had plenty of parcels, boxes, and hampers. Plus, it reeked of horses. She knew little about tearooms, but the dirt floor, partially constructed walls, and a high loft-like ceiling with open beams fell far short of what she pictured.

Then her attention snagged on a lean native gripping a dainty teacup and standing beside a row of barrels toward the back end. The yellow-orange light from a nearby lantern brightened his carved jaw and sleek black hair that reached his shoulders. He wore gray trousers, a white shirt, and a black eye patch. Maybe he had reached the age of thirty.

The fellow nodded at her. "I'm Icala, part-time cook and jack-of-all-trades. Hello."

"Hello." Winded, Juliet placed her hands on her knees before straightening. "A man in the woods isn't moving, but he's alive."

"Oh my." Livy rushed forward, wringing her hands.

Tabitha strode slowly, her nose scrunched, and her eyes narrowed to examine Juliet's dirty apparel. "You're wet again, muddy from top to bottom." She reached for her tan coat strewn over a nearby barrel. "Did you say he's in the woods?"

"Yes, ma'am."

"Why were you there?" Tabitha shoved her arms through the sleeves, her brow creased.

A knot formed in Juliet's belly. She had to confess that Dearest Peaches escaped. Even if she lost her new job, it was the right thing to do. "When I left your house, so did your bird. I chased her until I tripped over the body. I'm truly sorry."

Tabitha finished donning her coat. "Don't despair over the parakeet. She belonged to Father, and I'm afraid she's an afterthought these days."

Juliet swallowed hard, and a sense of kinship to the creature stirred inside her.

"The cage's latch must have broken again," Livy said.

With her thumb, Juliet pointed toward the woods. "I need to fetch the fellow before he dies. Who will help me?"

"I will." Icala returned the teacup to the crate, collected a folded tarp from the ground, and moved toward her with long, graceful strides. "Plenty of folks have helped me. Seems it's my turn now."

Why did he wear the patch over his eye? An injury? Why was his English perfect? The closer he drew, the lighter his skin appeared. Perhaps he had one non-native parent.

Livy's eyes widened. "Oh, Tabby. What if it's Alex? We must bring him home posthaste."

"Who's Alex?" Juliet asked. Their brother? A neighbor or a friend? She shook her head. Why the onslaught of questions? Holy Moses, she just asked herself another one.

Tabitha buttoned her coat up to her chin. "Alex is our nephew, whom we expect any day now." She dropped her hand onto her sister's shoulder. "Since you're still recovering from your cold, why don't you prepare the bed in the sitting room for our guest? Retrieve one of Father's old nightshirts and any leftover medical supplies. Start the fire, as well."

"And you'll assist Juliet and Icala?"

"Exactly. Many helpers make a task easier."

Rain pelted the carriage house roof in a rapid rhythm. But they couldn't allow the weather conditions to hinder their rescue. A life may depend on their efforts.

Tabitha withdrew a pair of black gloves from her pockets. "Please lead the way, Juliet."

She wasted no time darting outside, crossing the yard, and hoping her little trail markers hadn't blown off the path. Soon she entered the thicket and wove around trees and brush, following her white trail. When they reached the injured man, Juliet crouched to double-check his breaths, placing her finger under his nose.

"Is he . . . still with us?" Tabitha leaned over Juliet's shoulder.

"Yes, does he look like Alex?"

"We've not seen our nephew in twenty years, making me a poor judge of his identity."

"Oh." Juliet twisted to gaze up at the sister. "Why haven't you seen him?"

Tabitha frowned. "It's impolite to ask, and this is not the time for questions."

Juliet had a bad habit of saying too much and speaking too freely. Although she'd been trying to limit her chattiness since working for the Firth family, it was a genuine struggle half the time.

Or, more accurately, most of the time. "I apologize for my nosiness."

Icala was spreading the tarp on the ground as best he could, but the sparse open space prevented him from extending the edges. "Whoever he is, let's pray he recovers."

"Amen," Tabitha whispered.

Juliet crawled over a mossy log alongside the body. With Icala near the man's feet and Tabitha next to his head, they spun him onto the canvas, laying him on his back. He made no sounds or movements, even though she wished he would. Scratches covered his ashen, swollen face. A large bump on his forehead was red or perhaps bruised. His temple sported an ugly, blood-crusted marring. And then there was the bloody spot on the back of his head. No doubt his mix of injuries had caused his unconscious state.

Together, with Icala in the lead and she and Tabitha bringing up the rear, they slowly hauled him through the woods. The chilly rain had sputtered out by the time they reached the clearing. Juliet's handhold grew slippery, and she tightened her grip on the tarp. Tabitha grunted now and again. Little by little, they made progress, weaving around the stumps in the yard.

Finally, they dragged him through the kitchen, down the hallway, and into the sitting room. In their wake, a mud trail streaked the floor, and Juliet promised to mop it later. They fully lowered and released their load onto the sitting room's navy carpet to clean him up a smidgen before transferring him onto the bed.

Lanterns and a budding blaze combined to offer adequate lighting on a dreary day. A metal-framed bed and an unusual chair made from a sugar barrel, the cushion covered with plaid fabric, sat on either side of a stone hearth. A *Harper's New Monthly* magazine draped over one arm of a deep burgundy settee.

Clucking, Livy rushed forward, dropped to her knees beside the patient on the tarp, and gazed at him with love in her eyes. She covered him with a thick, deep green afghan. "It's him. Our dear nephew. Thank you, Juliet, for finding our precious Alex."

"What makes you confident it's him?" Tabitha removed her gloves, and her voice labored as she strode to a small corner table brimming with medical bottles, ointments, and bandages. "He could be anybody."

"Intuition, I suppose." Livy expertly tucked the blanket around the long form on the floor.

With a huff, Icala placed his hands on his hips. "Should I collect Doctor Pooley?"

A small sigh slipped past Livy's lips. "I'm afraid he's working beyond town this week and possibly the next. Therefore, it's up to us to care for our patient."

Everyone broke into motion. Livy ran a wet cloth over the man's bruised face. Tabitha applied an ointment to his cuts, and Icala bandaged his pale feet. Did he suspect frostbite?

Unsure how to best assist, Juliet padded toward the hearth to boost the small fire. She added another log and jostled the wood into place with the wrought iron poker before turning back around but remaining next to the warmth. She'd caught a chill outside, but her measly woe fell far short compared to the patient's list of concerns.

Although tempted to slip outside to wring the moisture from her heavy, dripping skirts, she would never do that again.

Mrs. Quinborow had taught her not to stare openly at her betters, yet Juliet studied the injured man. How could she not? His wounds failed to hide his rugged handsomeness in the better lighting. A chiseled jaw, full lips, and shoulders built like a Viking. However, his skin had a sickly pallor, and his stillness was alarming. Although his straight nose held a noble perfectness, his wavy, untamed hair was imperfect and utterly appealing.

A notion struck her to crouch beside him and remove a twig from his locks, but she refused to act on her whim for a change. She moved the poker from one hand to the other, ready to ensure the room remained well-heated for the patient.

Tabitha rose, shed her coat, and draped it over the back of a chair before sitting on a corner chair beside the table. Her weary face slumped, but her hair twisted like ivy climbing a wall. "You should be on your way, Icala. I know your wife is unwell today, and we've kept you far longer than planned. Thank you for helping."

The cook stood and returned the roll of bandages to the table. "I hate to leave you in a lurch."

"You're not," Livy added. "We'll be fine."

Icala hesitated, his eyes roaming to the patient one last time before saying farewell and leaving the room. If the part-time cook hadn't helped cart the wounded man into the house, they'd still be struggling in the woods.

But now they had another task. "Shouldn't we ask Icala to help lift the patient into bed?" Juliet asked.

"We'll manage." Livy was cleaning the fellow's dirty hands, delicately and lovingly wiping between each finger with her cloth. "We often assisted our father in and out of bed during his illness, didn't we, Tabby?"

"Yes, but he was never unconscious." Tabitha mopped her brow with the back of her hand. "Before we move him, I must rest a stint longer. I'm exhausted. Then Juliet and I shall change into dry garments."

The fire crackled, and Juliet turned to reposition the logs with the poker, recalling how she'd once played a nursemaid. "When my grandfather suffered after a fall, I fed him soup, gave him his medicine, read him Bible stories, and changed his garments."

She added another log to the flames, set the poker in the brass holder, and turned around.

Livy was smiling at her, sympathy in her eyes. "How old were you?"

"Eight."

"What a blessing you must have been to him." Tabitha tidied the table, grouping the similar medical items. "However, you'll not assist with our patient's personal care. We dare not shock your sensibilities."

Truth be told, Juliet's sensibilities had received a robust jolt long ago. Just as she'd seen dead bodies back in England, she'd also witnessed naked ones on the streets. If the sisters learned the truth, they'd probably suffer from heart tremors.

Juliet decided a change in subject was in order. "So what about your family? If this is your nephew, what brought him here?"

Livy sat back on her haunches. "Our brother served in the Royal Navy and raised his family beyond England. It's the reason we haven't laid eyes on Alex in years. According to one of his letters, he's in a dire financial bind, partly why he's coming to reside with us."

Tabitha bent to unlace her mud-caked shoes. "By the time Livy and I arrived at the colony fourteen months ago, he'd already moved north to Barkerville to mine gold."

"I see." Taking Tabitha's lead, Juliet removed her grimy shoes and placed them near the hearth to dry. Then she straightened to glance at the unconscious man again. Was he the sisters' relative, or merely a poor soul left in the woods to die?

Livy picked a leaf from his shoulder, which she discarded on the tarp. "Our father built this house to reunite his family under one roof. Unfortunately, he passed on a few weeks after we arrived."

"I'm sorry." Even though Juliet's grandfather had died eleven years ago, the sting remained sharp as a claw. She hadn't wanted to eat, drink, or live after he perished. In time, the loneliness seeped away little by little, but it never ran empty. "Do your brother and his wife also live here?"

A moment passed before Livy added, "Nolan and Katherine returned to our manor between Bristol and London after our father's death. And we're not offended by the slight if their departure had anything to do with our arrival. Tabby and I are too busy planning our tea shop to fret over such things."

It was clever how the sisters pointed toward the future, not the past. If Juliet paid attention, she might learn more than manners and how to pour tea. Would they genuinely help her become more ladylike? If so, could she possibly wed an upstanding fellow one day?

Tabitha stood and held her dirty shoes away from her body. "Perhaps one of us should collect the constable."

Constable? Juliet shuddered. Her one encounter with the law had ended in disaster. A lawman had hauled her to an orphanage, which still starred in her nightmares. Even though being on the streets homeless had been bad, the orphanage had felt like a prison.

She'd been alone, bullied, and hungry. Quickly she'd adopted a motto: offer the legal authorities a wide berth.

Livy rose and wiped her hands with the wet rag before depositing the cloth on the table. "Involving the constable may cause more problems than help."

Tabitha leveled a stern look at her sister. "What if this young man's family searches for him and has contacted the local authorities? It certainly is a possibility."

"But if he is our nephew, and I fully believe he is, he'd prefer to avoid all lawmen."

Why? Was Juliet not the only person in the house with a criminal past?

Frizzy hairs now framed Tabitha's serious face. "In my opinion, it's a mistake to assume he's our relation based on nothing but intuition."

Livy waved her hands as she spoke. "In my opinion, it's better to be optimistic than pessimistic."

Based on Tabitha's tight expression, she probably wanted to roll her eyes but was too much of a lady. Instead, she spoke calmly. "I'm not a pessimist. I'm cautious."

Tension hummed in the sitting room as a small sigh passed over Livy's lips. "We're both frazzled. I'm sorry if I offended you, sister."

"You haven't, though we're not setting a good example for Juliet. It's time she and I left to change our garments."

Livy offered Juliet an apologetic smile. "Please forgive us."

"Of course. Don't fret about your tiff." Juliet collected her shoes. "Compared to some of the knock-down brawls I've viewed, your spat is next to nothing."

Tabitha blinked her wide eyes. "Oh, my stars. I must say, Juliet, you have much to learn before you're ready to serve guests in the tearoom, especially regarding proper conversation."

Her stomach knotted as she lowered her eyes to the floor. Was she teachable? With her whole heart, she wanted to be. But maybe she didn't have it in her. "Yes, ma'am."

Six

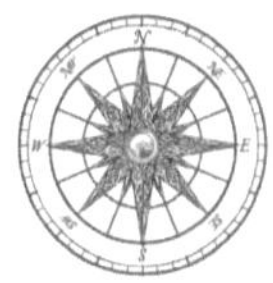

SOMEWHERE, A GRANDFATHER CLOCK chimed three times.

Had someone kicked him in the head? The constant pounding rivaled a dozen horses racing around a never-ending track. Slowly, he opened his eyes, his vision blurry.

A thick quilt covered him, and he untucked his arms. His fingers explored his face—a scrape on his chin, dry lips, and swollen eyes. A swath of thick cloth encircled his head, starting above his eyebrows. No wonder his head throbbed, especially his left temple.

One by one, he wiggled each limb. A sudden wave of darkness threatened to plunge him into unconsciousness, and he closed his eyes and counted his breaths, hoping to ward off the dreamlike state that beckoned.

Was he at home? The bed possessed a tolerable softness, and

the room radiated a pleasant warmth. But the scent of something pungent and medicinal watered his eyes. His mouth had the opposite problem and was drier than a desert. He would pay a king's ransom for something cool to quench his thirst.

Slowly, his dizziness receded, and the pain slightly lessened. He cracked his eyes open to concentrate on the plain, plastered ceiling. Then he broadened his view to the heavy burgundy drapes near the bed. No daylight seeped inside around the edges.

One lantern lit the room, better resembling a parlor than a bed chamber. As he turned his head toward the crackling fire in the hearth, his gaze met a silent woman kneeling before the flames. Was she praying? Her light blond hair cascaded in waves down her back, hiding her profile. A flowy nightgown concealed her form, though he deemed her build slender.

How odd that he could not recall her name. Perhaps she was a new servant. "Who are you?"

She rose and twirled toward him, shoving her hair behind her ears as her crystal blue eyes widened. "Holy Moses. You're alive and awake. I thought you were a goner for certain."

Despite the rapid words that flew out of her mouth, she had a warm, soothing voice. Her simple nightgown landed at her ankles, and her feet were bare. A vibrancy radiated from her beautiful eyes, set off by her ivory skin. Her face held multiple angles, hollowed-out cheekbones, a straight-carved nose, and a delicate but sharp chin. She had a long, almost regal neck that he instantly appreciated.

An unforgettable face, yet he had no recollection of her. What was wrong with him?

She approached the bed and stopped beside him. "Are you Alex?"

The name held no familiarity. "Who?"

"Alex Sherwood. Livy and Tabitha's nephew."

A second pain knifed his temple as a soul-shaking question

dawned—who was he? He floated between mindfulness and oblivion. A wave of nausea surfaced, the room spun, and he clutched the bed's blanket as darkness rose to choke him.

Remaining perfectly still, he waited until the rotating subsided, grateful he had not emptied his stomach on the floor or himself. How long had it been since his last meal? Unfortunately, he could not recall.

Nor could he remember anything beyond two minutes ago. How had he come to be in this bed? How had he gained his injuries? What was his name? His age? Who was his family?

Why could he not remember the answers to any of those questions?

A strange sense of panic swelled inside, and again, he gripped the bedsheets, his nerves growing taut. How long would it be before he swirled back to nothingness?

Gradually, he reopened his eyes, squinting in the dim light. An overwhelming sense of loneliness settled into his bones. Where had his memory fled, and how long until it returned? A moan from deep inside him grumbled in his chest, then burst to the surface.

"Sir, may I fetch you anything?" The strange woman was still present and hovered above him with worried eyes.

"Why do I not know the essential facts of my life?" The desire to ask more questions battled against the quake of his body. He clenched his jaw to stop the shaking and failed. The room would tilt again any minute now, sliding him back to oblivion.

But miraculously, he stayed present.

"Don't know, but you're trembling." She tucked his covering on the side closest to her, sliding her hands under his legs, hip, and torso. "I slipped down to stoke the fire moments ago, and it should soon remove the chill. Or can I fetch you another comforter?" She leaned dangerously close over the bed to administer the same procedure with the covering on his other side.

Merciful heavens. Her flowing hair, gorgeous eyes, and elegant face made her the most beautiful woman he had ever seen. Or maybe not. She also carried the scent of lemons and heaven. Had he died? He swallowed hard. "I am utterly confused."

She straightened, compassion creasing her brow. A lock of hair draped across her cheekbone, and she corralled the strand behind her ear. "Tabitha thinks you suffered a coma and a concussion."

Tabitha. Coma. Concussion. He shut his eyes and drew a deep breath into his lungs, failing to distress his ribs. They must be intact, a fragment of positive news. Was he supposed to know someone named Tabitha? "Do you know how I sustained my injury?"

"Hard to say. But it looks like someone beat you. Robbed you, as well."

Who would wish to harm him? Besides his memory, what else had his attacker stolen? Or had multiple people caused his wounds? Or nobody at all? When he finally opened his eyes, he latched on to hers—a beacon in the darkness. "How did I come to be here, in this room?"

"I tripped over you in the woods behind the house yesterday, and then Tabitha, Icala, and me hauled you here."

None of the names resonated. "Where is *here*? What city?"

"Everly in British Columbia."

That resonated even less. What was wrong with him?

She touched the bandage on his head. "How are you feeling?"

Empty. Groundless. Lonely. As if he had fallen off a cliff and landed on his head. Perhaps he had. "I shall survive, I believe."

"I agree, now that you've awakened."

"Whose home is this?"

"Two sisters. Livy thinks she's your aunt, and Tabitha sounds doubtful. Do you suspect you're their nephew?"

Instead of finding clarity, he grew more bewildered. Was he not asking the right questions? Or was he stuck in a dream, a nightmare? "They are in this house?"

"Upstairs. I couldn't sleep and crept down to check on you and the fire. But the sisters don't know I'm here. However, I didn't want you cold and alone like I. . ." Her words trailed off, and her eyes dropped to the quilt. "Do you care for a dipper of water before I fetch them? They'll want to know you've awakened."

"Yes, I desire water." At least he knew that.

She swirled and began to cross the room, her nightgown rising inches to expose her shapely ankles. Even in his hampered state, he appreciated the view and watched until she disappeared through the open door into a dark hallway.

His temple continued to throb, and he touched the precise spot. Did he suffer from amnesia? He knew little about the subject other than it explained his affliction.

And how did he understand complex medical conditions and not his name? And why did one possible aunt recognize him and the other not? Maddening. Would he be more lucid in the morning? If only he had identifying papers or a monographed handkerchief to spark a memory.

Perhaps he did.

After several long minutes, the young woman returned and slowly approached the bed. She held a dipper with one hand and her other cupped beneath it. "I apologize for being garbed like this, but I wasn't expecting you to awaken."

"You do not offend me in your nighttime garments. Far from it."

Her chin cocked, and her eyes narrowed as if she measured him. Based on her frown, she disliked what she assessed.

His comment had absentmindedly tumbled from his mouth. What type of man was he? He would need to ponder the possibilities later. "When you discovered me, did I possess belongings besides my clothing?"

"Just soggy underdrawers and a shirt. Livy says they were cut from a fine quality fabric."

How peculiar. "Nothing else?"

"Nothing else, at least according to the sisters. They swapped your wet clothes for dry ones while I waited in the hallway. Afterward, the three of us hefted you into the bed, and Livy put more balm on your wounds."

A new tightness gripped his chest, and it had nothing to do with his injuries. Three strangers . . . or perhaps one stranger and his aunts had gone to great lengths to rescue him and save his life.

The woman—the maid, or whoever she was—glanced at the doorway. "They wouldn't find it proper, me here alone with a gentleman at this hour. But let's give you that water before I go."

"I could drink the ocean dry."

She softly chuckled, and he liked the pleasant sound. "I'll raise your head a notch, and you tell me if anything ails you."

Ever so slightly, he shook his head. "I have neglected to inquire after your name."

"Juliet Dash."

"Since I cannot tell you mine, I shall remain a man of mystery for now."

"Fine, unless you're a low-down murderer or someone of that ilk."

He was tempted to laugh yet lacked the strength. But then again, perhaps he did possess a dubious character. He could not deny the possibility. "As far as I can determine, I am an innocent man."

"Good." Without spilling, she snaked her free hand underneath his head, lifting him a measure. At the same time, she drew the dipper to his lips.

For a reason he could not explain, her tender touch anchored him. The cool metal touched his mouth, and the liquid soothed his lips. Heaven blessed heaven. He swallowed twice before she returned his head to the pillow.

"Enough for now. Otherwise, you'll spit it back up, and neither of us wants that. I nursed my grandfather and had to be mindful of such things."

Clearly, Juliet was not a gentle lady who used perfect diction and followed every protocol of polite society. He was unsure how he knew such a thing, yet somehow, he did. Her evident goodwill and charitable compassion, two admirable traits, shone a bright light in the middle of his dire situation.

She took a step away from the bed. "Will you manage if I leave you alone for a minute or two?"

"Yes." Honestly, he wanted her to stay. All too soon, he might spin back into the emptiness that had enveloped him earlier. "May I call you Juliet?"

"Only when we're alone. I'm just a servant who started working here yesterday. That sure seems like a dozen lifetimes ago."

What a bizarre first day of employment for her. Although he had no idea what had transpired to lead him where he now lay, he assumed his immediate past had not been stellar either. The pain in his head intensified, and his stomach muscles pinched. He closed his eyes, hoping to ward off another round of intense discomfort. "You are dismissed."

"Well, then, goodbye to you too, fella."

Had he offended her? Was he too curt? "I shall try not to forget you."

"That's a good plan." Her voice held sarcasm as her footsteps padded from the room.

"Can you open your eyes again?" A sweet voice, not Juliet's, awoke him.

Strangely, he had dreamed about the beautiful maid. They had shared a picnic by the water, she in her nightgown and he in day clothing. They laughed and launched paper boats on a lake that matched her eyes. The instant he tried to draw her close for an embrace, she disappeared in the same fashion as his memory.

His heavy eyelids refused to lift, almost as if someone had nailed each one shut. Why was his body and mind failing to cooperate? One more mystery to add to the growing list.

"His face is less gray, and his pulse beats stronger than last night." Another new female voice held authority as she clasped his wrist with cold fingers. Did the comment belong to one of his possible aunts?

When he tried to force his eyes open, dizziness came rushing in, and the bed seemed to rotate. The same as the last time he had awoken.

"During the night, he said he doesn't recall his name or past." Juliet's voice. How much time had lapsed since she left him?

"Based on a few books I've read, medical forgetfulness is rare," said the firm voice above him, "though not unheard of."

"You read doctoring books?" Juliet again.

"Yes, and a multitude of other subjects. I've always had a keen interest in the sciences, and our dear father helped secure whatever reading material I sought."

"How long does it take for someone's memory to return?" The sweet voice entered the conversation.

"It's impossible to know," replied the firm woman. "A few days, weeks, months. . ."

Months? His heartbeat accelerated. Although not well-versed in amnesia facts, he assumed his state was a temporary inconvenience. Not a life-altering, forever type of problem. He breathed in steadily, hoping to counter his anxiety. If he gazed at his possible aunts, would they look familiar, even vaguely?

"But surely it will return in time." Unmistakable hope wound through Juliet's words, and he longed to share her sentiment.

He suddenly wanted to open his eyes and gaze upon her again. She offered something to hold on to, a connection he desperately needed. Maybe because she had been the first person he had viewed after regaining consciousness?

"I wonder if anyone is looking for him," Juliet said. "Is your nephew married?"

"Not according to his last letter," the sister with medical knowledge said. "The good news is the young man appears strong, and his body will heal, I assume. Perhaps faster than his brain. We'll need to watch for seizures and avoid additional bumps to his head."

Not married—the answer to one question. Although it was impossible to know for certain, he sensed he was not wed. And the last thing he intended to do was injure his head again.

"We'll ensure that doesn't happen," the sweet-voiced sister remarked earnestly. "Alex is coming to us for a fresh start, and I believe nobody in town should know about his past crimes." The lady heaved a breath. "Poor, poor Alex."

A wave of dread and a sense of guilt struck his core. Was he *poor, poor Alex*? A felon? He fastened his hands onto the sheets. He had to resist the sleepiness that beckoned. Otherwise, he would not learn more about the offenses.

A soft hand touched his brow, and he opened his blurry eyes, straining to focus.

Three women gazed back at him. One garbed in lace, another in brown, and Juliet, smiling as radiantly as the sunshine streaming through the windowpane behind her.

"Good morning," said the shortest of three—the one with the sweet voice—as she withdrew her hand from his forehead. "How is our patient this fine day?"

His throat scratched, and he covered his mouth and coughed. "Excuse me. Recovering, I believe, and grateful to see sunshine again."

"Indeed." A tall woman with a tight face and gold watch pinned to her bodice stood behind the other two. "I'm Tabitha, and this is my sister Livy." She nodded to her sibling. "I believe you met Juliet a few hours prior."

He forced a weak smile, letting his gaze linger on Juliet as he admired her shiny locks, bright eyes, and the simple dress that showed off her enticing figure. "Yes, she met my immediate needs."

Juliet's chin cocked to a discerning angle again. "Are you thanking me?"

Apparently, he should have. "Yes. Was that not clear?"

"More muddy than clear. Any chance your memories returned?"

He searched his brain, hoping to awaken the slumbering part, and studied his long fingers and hands. Not a callus anywhere. Did he not labor for a wage? Where was he from? What was his lot in life?

He waited for the answers to arrive as he had the last time. But nothing came to him, not even the barest of specifics. Disappointment rushed through him. "I continue to lack details about my life."

Livy gently fluffed his pillow. "We're expecting our nephew Alex any day now. He's coming to help convert our carriage house into a tearoom since he has carpentry skills. I, for one, believe you're him."

A carpenter. Like Jesus. Livy had given him a name and a profession. Was the information a starting point to rebuild his life or aiming him in the wrong direction?

"They've not seen their brother's son, for many years." Juliet had pulled her hair back into a long tail and played with the end. "It's why they're uncertain about your genuine identity. We may have to wait until you can tell us the truth yourself one day."

His eyes roamed between the sisters, who appeared nothing alike. One was tall and the other short. One was thinner than a single portion of bread, and the other resembled the whole loaf. One stood stiff, and the other fluttered nonstop. "Although I do not recognize either of you, perhaps I resemble your brother or his wife."

Livy said, "Yes," as Tabitha uttered, "No."

"What if you examined yourself in a mirror?" Juliet nodded as if to urge him to agree to her suggestion. "Seeing your reflection could poke at a memory or two."

"A wonderful idea, Juliet." Livy beamed. "There's one on the top of my bureau in the room to the left at the front of the house. Will you please collect it?"

"Yes, ma'am." She twirled and hurried from the room as she did last night when she delivered his water. But today, she wore shoes, stockings, and a long skirt.

Livy leaned closer to his bed, almost too close, as she examined his face, the scent of rosewater perfume clinging heavily to the air around her. "In my opinion, you're the identical image of your father, Nolan, especially along the jawline." She straightened.

The name failed to register. But the pain in his head certainly did, perhaps made worse since he was unable to stop wondering what crime he may have committed. His eyelids tugged to drift shut, and he drew in one breath. Two breaths. Three . . .

Clamoring footsteps grew in volume until Juliet burst into the room, the tail of her blond hair swinging to and fro. Her blue eyes held a shiny brightness as if excited on his behalf, hoping he would indeed recognize himself in the mirror. "Here it is."

Tabitha clucked her tongue. "Proper young ladies never run. Particularly indoors."

Juliet slowed her approach to the bed. "Yes, ma'am."

He reached for the heavy silver hand mirror with a floral design etched onto the back. Their fingers brushed, and he nearly grasped her hand so she would not leave him again. What an unexpected response, yet she somehow soothed him. Already, he considered her an ally in his battle to regain his memory.

Slowly, he raised the mirror to view his image.

A swath of white bandages capped his head. A few brown tufts of hair stuck up beyond the tight binding. How long ago had he sustained his injury? He could inquire about today's date, but what difference did it make?

Time in the past held no meaning.

His gaze dropped lower, and he studied his swollen face. A bruise's bluish-green discoloration flawed the skin below his left temple. His eyes were more red than white, and the irises had a golden-brown hue. He ran the back of his hand over a layer of scruffiness on his jawline.

"So?" Juliet's voice pierced through his confusion. "Do you recognize yourself?"

"No." He set aside the mirror, turned his gaze to the ceiling, and heaved a frustrated breath. "I am even a stranger to myself."

Seven

"Y OU AND I NEED TO HOLD A FRANK conversation," Tabitha said from where she stood with her back to the sideboard in the kitchen, a stone's throw from Juliet seated at the table bathed in a streak of late afternoon sunshine. The sister had tugged her brown hair into a severe bun on the top of her head, and her thin face was drawn equally tight. Even her tone carried a distinct sternness.

Juliet stopped polishing a brass candlestick. Uh-oh. What had she done? Clearly, something terrible. She set aside the candlestick and rag on the table and gave the sister her full attention. "Yes, ma'am."

"I apologize for not addressing this before, but I've been busy with the patient."

Was she talking about the parakeet's escape? But hadn't Tabitha said not to fret over the bird? "It's all right."

"Most definitely, it is not all right. Attending to the patient alone, barefooted, and"—Tabitha lowered her voice—"in your nightgown is unacceptable. What would people think if they knew you were in such a state around a man?"

"I won't tell nobody if you don't."

After Tabitha closed her gaping mouth, she folded her hands. "Please tell me you understand what I'm saying."

"My behavior was . . . wrong."

"In so many words, yes."

Juliet wiped her sweaty palms on her skirt. Starting a new position twenty-four hours ago and falling short in her employer's eyes was dismal. She'd do almost anything not to lose another job. "I'm sorry."

"I accept your apology." Tabitha turned around, collected two floral teacups and saucers from an open shelf, and set them on the counter. She continued speaking over her shoulder. "There are certain rules a young woman in our household must heed, such as this one."

"I understand." Holy Moses, she had tried to do a good deed last night. Instead, she'd blundered and committed an indecent one. But she hadn't expected the patient to rouse. Wasn't the fact he'd awoken the more critical matter?

Tabitha opened a canister of tea. "I expect you to follow the rules precisely."

"I'll surely try." Juliet resumed her polishing chore. She doused the rag in sweet oil and rubbed the cloth against the next tarnished candlestick, starting at the top.

She sighed. "I still have memories of waking up scared shortly after my grandfather's death. Sometimes, they torment me. I was cold, alone, starving, and filthy. Back then, I'd have given anything to know someone cared. I aimed to spare the patient from feeling likewise."

"Thank you for telling me." Tabitha finished scooping tea into a silver infuser, closed it, and lowered it into the teapot. "And I'm sorry for your hardships, Juliet. You've had a heavy cross to bear, especially for a child. Nonetheless, modesty is a moral virtue."

Although unsure what a virtue was, she nodded. "I'm not complaining, only trying to explain myself."

"I understand."

Life and Grandfather had taught her to offer a helping hand whenever possible. He often assisted the widows at church and even a bird with a hurt wing once upon a time. Deep inside, Juliet longed to be more like him.

Was that why she'd been so quick to help when she'd stumbled upon their patient unconscious in the woods? Maybe she was more like her grandfather than she'd realized.

It surprised her the patient had joked about drinking the ocean dry and calling himself a man of mystery. Not everyone in his situation would have jested in such a manner. Still, he had an arrogant bent, though she shouldn't judge him too harshly since she barely knew him.

After he'd gazed into the mirror earlier today, he'd rolled onto his side, away from the women, and had grown silent. What was it like to peer into a looking glass and see a stranger? Crushing, most likely.

She hadn't talked to him since. But her thoughts had wandered to him frequently as she'd completed her chores. The sisters had kept her busy opening shutters, starting fires, hauling soiled clothing to the washroom, cleaning mirrors, removing sparse cobwebs, wiping down the woodwork, running a feather duster over everything . . . and now polishing the silver.

Had she ever seen a less dusty, musty house? No. A suspicious person might think the sisters were plotting to keep her busy with chores and away from the patient. If so, their plan was working without a hitch.

Tabitha finished arranging the items on the tray and then carried them to the table. "I hope you like peppermint tea."

Her employer was bringing her tea—Juliet, a servant—and after a scolding. What could that possibly mean?

She rested the cloth and candlestick on the table again. "It's my favorite."

"Mine too." Tabitha placed the tray on the table. "I've ordered a variety of teas from India and expect the shipment to arrive any day now."

"To serve in your tearoom?"

"Correct." Tabitha lowered herself to the chair across from Juliet. "Do you have something more to say? Based on your quizzical expression, I believe you may."

Juliet relaxed her facial muscles the best she could, not realizing she looked puzzled, even though she was. "I'm stewing because I thought you were angry with me. Instead, you did something kind. Thank you."

"I'm not mad. However, if you haven't noticed, I am persnickety, particularly regarding manners."

Juliet had noticed, all right.

After the tea was steeped, Tabitha poured the liquid into each cup.

Juliet lifted her cup and blew on the steamy beverage.

"A lady never blows on her beverage to cool it."

"Why not?"

"It's impolite. She must wait to sip until it's not too hot to burn her lips or tongue."

"Well, I'll be." Juliet lowered her cup, clattering the saucer. Thankfully, not a drop spilled.

Tabitha's gaze turned intent as she raised her cup, then peered over the rim. "Livy told me about the conversation you shared upstairs yesterday regarding us teaching you manners and more. Is that what you want?"

Did she? "Are you offering to assist me?"

"I'm asking you a question."

"What I like is learning, always have. What I don't is being disrespected or thought less of because I'm . . . improper sometimes. So yes, I'd be grateful for the opportunity, I suppose."

A long moment passed before Tabitha spoke. "It will be a challenging undertaking, most likely."

"For all of us, I wager."

"Indeed. If you fully cooperate, Livy and I will instruct you. I'm not sure what that fully entails yet. However, long ago, someone helped us improve our lives. Now, we're called to extend a helping hand similarly."

Juliet's heart hammered with a new intensity. "Like how you're aiding the patient in the sitting room, whether he's your relative or not."

"Somewhat like that, yes."

No matter what, she'd always be a woman with a thieving past. But maybe she could hide the truth better if the sisters prettified her manners. "I'd be much obliged."

"If all goes according to plan, we'll proceed with the first class in a day or two."

Since arriving in the household, all Juliet had done was make one error after another. Other than her grandfather, who had ever helped her without expecting something in return?

There had been her friend Molly, whom she'd first met at an orphanage. After the mill closed back home, everyone lost their jobs. Juliet had moved into the tiny apartment Molly shared with her husband. About the time her friend learned a baby was coming, her husband collected two bad habits—drinking too much and calling Juliet beautiful daily. It hadn't taken long for Molly to ask

Juliet to leave. The request hadn't been unreasonable and had likely been for the best, but it still stung.

Juliet sighed. Of course, the women from the bride ship—Willow and Daisy—only wanted friendship from her. Sage too. Mrs. Moresby had kindly assisted her twice.

Perhaps there were others, but she couldn't think of anyone. Now she could add Tabitha and Livy to the tally. But the offer was almost too good to be true. Wasn't it?

Juliet reached for her cup and sampled the hot but not unbearable tea. It boggled her mind that blowing on something scorching was impolite. What else had she been doing wrong all these years? The list was likely long.

The back door's latch rattled, and she turned toward the noise. A fanlight, with small stones and white marble, was built into the wall above the door. How fancy for a kitchen. The door opened, and Icala entered, whistling after running an errand for the sisters. "Doctor Pooley's wife says he's still out of town."

After he shed his dark overcoat and hung it on a metal hook near the door, he turned toward the table. His black shirt and trousers matched his hair, pulled back from his face, revealing his broad forehead. Even his eye patch matched his appearance.

At least Juliet had the good sense not to ask why he wore it. But she'd sure love to know.

He moved toward the stove with long strides. "The good news is that Peaches circles the yard."

Relief flooded Juliet. The bird's return would hopefully erase one of her errors. "Maybe he'll swoop back inside if we open the door."

"We will do no such thing." Tabitha rose from her spot and picked up the tea tray. "There's a chill in the air. If Peaches chooses to reenter, she'll have to dive in the same method she snuck out."

As if that would happen. Juliet almost snorted. Was Tabitha trying to teach the bird a lesson? Were parakeets that smart?

After putting away the tea supplies, Tabitha excused herself to check on the patient. Icala gathered and chopped vegetables on the sideboard as Juliet continued her polishing.

The rhythm of the native's knife *tap, tap, tapped.* Then he lifted the lid from a black pot and sniffed. The scent of last night's squash soup wafted through the kitchen. It smelled delicious and had accompanied moose steak, carrots with turnips, baked apples, and mince pie for supper—the best food Juliet had ever tasted. The competition wasn't even close for second place.

Juliet pressed a hand against her growling stomach. "How'd you learn to cook so good?"

"My father, a white man, owned a restaurant in Montreal. He taught me everything I know."

"Your soup was delicious."

He glanced over his shoulder and grinned. "I know and thank you."

"How'd you come to work here?"

"My father knew the sisters' father, and I worked for him first. Mr. Sherwood was a first-rate man, much like his daughters. Well, except they're females."

Juliet chuckled. His approval of the sisters confirmed what she pondered in her heart—she'd been given a fresh start with a good family, and she must not ruin things. At the Firths' she never forgot her station. Here, she slept alone in a room fit for a queen and drank tea with her employer.

Juliet helped herself to another sip.

Holding the spoon, Icala turned around, dripping soup. The man was as messy as Tabitha was tidy. Good thing Juliet hadn't cleaned the floor yet today. "I wonder if the patient is ready to eat something?"

Before Juliet could reply, Tabitha bustled into the kitchen, her skirts rustling. "I believe he is indeed. Juliet, please carry whatever

Icala has prepared for the young man. Thankfully, he's awake and alert."

Finally, she could check on the fella's welfare for herself.

With a tray of food, Juliet followed Tabitha, mindful not to spill. They entered the patient's room and found him upright in the bed. Livy was sitting in the sugar-barrel chair shoved close beside him. Tabitha positioned herself in front of the fireplace, and Juliet delivered the tray to the table in the corner, shoving bandages aside.

Then she turned to assess the patient. Dark shadows bloomed under his eyes, but a dab of color flushed his cheeks. His thick dark hair matched worn leather.

His handsome face could easily tongue-tie a young woman, even in its bruised and swollen state. And his soulful eyes carried a sadness that made her stride closer to the bed. How could she best help him?

Livy leaned forward, her plump face creased with concern. "Alex. Does your name trigger a memory?"

"Not in the least."

"Sher-wood." Livy drew out the two-syllable word as if the man's brain needed extra time to operate. Maybe it did. "Do you recognize your last name?"

"It means nothing to me." He rested his head against the headboard, a slump to his shoulders.

Was there a better method to spur his memories? For a moment, Juliet closed her eyes to scour her brain. Grandfather's friends had called him Cobbie because he toiled as a cobbler. Her eyes popped open. "By any chance, has your nephew gone by anything other than Alex? A nickname, perhaps?"

"Now that you mention it, he did," Tabitha said. "Our brother's hair turned gray by the time he reached the age of thirty. Back home, it's common to call such a man's eldest son Grayson. Alex went by the name for years, though I'm unsure if he still does."

The patient straightened, his eyes growing vast and almost wild.

"Gray resonates with me." He placed his chin in his palm as silence gathered until he continued. "I may be mistaken, but I sense Gray is my name. Even the word Grayson carries a vague familiarity."

"Oh my. Oh my." Livy rose and gently embraced him before standing beside her chair. "I knew you were family, and we're elated your memory is returning. Aren't we, Tabby?"

"Indeed." Tabitha spoke the word dryly.

A skeptical thread wound tight inside Juliet. Hadn't Livy leaped to a three-story conclusion? Yes, ma'am, she had. Couldn't the name Gray belong to a horse or a family dog? Or maybe the street from where the man once hailed?

On the other hand, perhaps he'd discovered a link to his past. Who was she to cast doubt? "It's a good, strong name."

Clearing his throat, Icala slipped into the room. "Peaches flew inside."

Livy clapped her hands. "Thank the Lord."

Juliet drew in a breath of relief. "Yes, praise be."

Icala's expression, however, looked anything but pleased. "Another shipment has arrived for the tearoom, and I'm afraid everything fragile is shattered."

"Oh my goodness." Livy's face turned pale, and she fanned herself. "That's terrible, terrible, terrible."

Tabitha hurried from the sitting room without a word but with her lips pressed tightly, followed by Livy and Icala.

Juliet stared at the door. Should she stay with the patient while he ate? Someone had remained with him constantly since he'd awakened, but was she the best person for the task?

At least she was wearing something other than her nightgown.

Society folks tended to assume a young man and woman couldn't resist each other romantically while unchaperoned. What a crock full of nonsense, especially regarding her and him. Whyever would they need a chaperone? Not when he was battered and bruised and bedridden.

"I brought you soup. Would you care for a taste?"

"It smells wonderful."

"I won't argue with you on that score." She retrieved the tray from the table and carried it to the bed. Carefully she set the offering on his lap. "Would you like me to feed you?"

"Feed me?" One of his dark brows quirked, and brown eyes homed in on her with a strangely arresting playfulness. "Tempting, very tempting. Though I shall manage unassisted, you may accompany me while I eat."

"Hmm…" She wrinkled her nose. Bossy, wasn't he? "I've known men like you."

"Amnesiacs?"

"Men who make offhanded comments that women prefer not to hear, especially when they barely know the fellow."

He lowered his spoon to the tray, the playfulness fading away. "I did not mean to offend."

Was he being genuine and respectable, or the opposite? Not once had a slick-talking man ever caught her eye. They usually proved to be insincere and self-important.

She narrowed her gaze to him. Was he a womanizer? She'd give up two pence to know the truth.

He helped himself to a spoonful of soup, then another. "This nourishment is delicious, and I am feeling somewhat better."

"I was going to ask but figured you might be weary of the question."

"The sisters indeed fuss over me, although they mean well." He took another taste of the soup. "My head still aches, though less intensely, and my memory continues to elude me, unfortunately."

"I wish I knew how to prod your recollections, but sadly, I don't."

His brow arched. "Are you telling me you are not an expert on amnesia?"

"I've never heard the word until you arrived." She tilted her head a notch. "With such a condition, how will you determine who you truly are?"

He wiped his mouth with the linen napkin. "I cannot stop thinking about that very question. For one thing, I shall confer with the constable at my earliest opportunity. Perhaps someone has reported a missing person."

Why involve the law? Was there another way to learn the answers he sought? Maybe not. "You'll go to him instead of him coming here, right?"

"Does it matter?"

Probably not. After all, she hadn't done anything wrong at the Firths'. But Ruby had been so intent on regaining the stolen jewels, especially the Queen's brooch. What if Ruby had alerted the law and persisted in accusing her? Would the crime eventually catch up to her here in Everly?

She could only pray it wouldn't. After all, Ruby didn't know where she'd moved.

Regardless, Juliet didn't want a run-in with the local constable. Could she convince their patient to put it off? "The sisters said their nephew committed a crime. Are you sure you're ready to meet with a lawman? Why not give it some time? Your memory might return before you know it."

"What if it does not? I demand answers and must investigate the matter posthaste. Or whenever I am free of this bed."

Juliet swallowed her additional protest and nodded. "Of course."

How could she deny this poor man any leads that might help him discover his identity? She couldn't. Doing so would be selfish. In fact, she understood better than most people what it was like to lose a family and be alone. He deserved her sympathy more than anything. And she intended to deliver it.

Eight

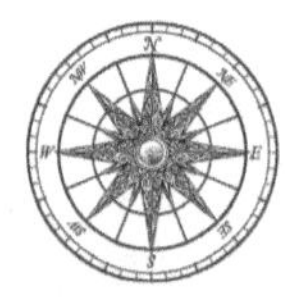

"I SENSE YOU HAVE AN AVERSION TO CON-
stables." An easy deduction as he sipped his soup.

Juliet gazed out the window at the sun starting to set. The view of her profile emphasized her sharp features—the point of her chin, the straightness of her nose, and the arch of her cheekbones. As she stretched, her black dress molded around her curves. Did she realize how beautiful she was?

"It's a long, tedious story."

He finished the last bite of the savory meal and placed the spoon back on the tray. "Believe it or not, I have a clear agenda to hear your tale."

The hint of a smile reached her lips, yet she said nothing. She had intrigued him from the beginning, standing barefoot in her nightgown. She had warmed his room, tucked his covering into place, and brought him a drink to quench his thirst.

Most importantly, she had diminished his loneliness.

Was he a man who genuinely valued others, no matter their station? Was he fair? Considerate? Had he adequately thanked Juliet for her assistance, even once? Most likely not. "If I neglected to mention the fact earlier, I have appreciated your aid."

When she turned and fully smiled, his breath hitched. Why such a strong reaction to a woman he barely knew? Of course, Juliet had shown him nothing but goodness, but his physical response to her was extreme. Was it not?

Had beautiful women always turned his head? What kind of man had he been, particularly regarding how he treated women? *Why did You choose this path for me, God?* His hand roamed to his bandages, and he tentatively touched the most tender spot at his temple. Had his faith been strong or lazy in the past? Perhaps the latter since he failed to sense the answer?

Over recent hours, the hammer in his head had finally dulled, though the pesky beat refused to stop completely. Tabitha had insisted he swallow laudanum twice, even though he first refused. The medicine had turned him drowsy. As eager as he was to uncover his past, he had to temper his expectations and timetable. He had only regained consciousness thirteen hours earlier.

Juliet moved to the sugar-barrel chair and plopped onto the cushioned seat. "A lawman once hauled me to an orphanage, and that's hard to forgive or forget."

Merciful heavens. What had she endured?

Since realizing he suffered from amnesia, he had mainly dwelled on himself. Granted, he had a valid excuse for self-absorption, but it was time to think about something different. Perhaps something better. "Why? Were you in need of a home?"

She slumped and held the blue and maroon checkered pillow in her lap. "In time, I found a home of sorts after my grandfather died when I was eight. There, I had good food, a safe place to sleep, and friends."

"Did relatives take you in?"

"No. I got none. The place wasn't perfect, but I was off the streets." She squeezed her eyes shut briefly. "Looking back, I suppose going to the orphanage was for the best. Eventually, it changed my life for the better. But back then, I hated the Wunderlin House for Children with a passion."

"Was it like *Oliver Twist*?" He had read the book by Charles Dickens, although he did not recall where or when. All he remembered was that the story had painted a bleak picture of life in an orphanage—little food, little comfort, and little hope.

Her brow wrinkled. "I am not familiar with that orphanage. It must be in London."

Obviously, he knew how to read and was educated. What about her? Perhaps she could only read a little, if at all.

Her gaze probed him. "Do you have memories of London?"

What did he remember about the place? Anything? He had a fleeting thought of the city, that he had been there, had crossed the London Bridge, visited St. Paul's Cathedral, and had perhaps stopped at Buckingham Palace.

To the palace? That could not be right. Perhaps he had walked past it.

"Speaking of memories," she persisted. "You've recalled something from your past. Your name—Gray Sherwood. I think that is grand. It truly is."

"I fear I need more than one or two familiar words to believe I am a Sherwood thoroughly."

"You know what? I was thinking that, too, even though Livy seems convinced you're her relation."

If he was indeed Alex "Gray" Sherwood, then he was likely from a good family of some means since the sisters were wealthy gentlewomen. But enough about him. He wanted to learn more about this charming young maid. "What brought you to British Columbia?"

"A bride ship."

A bride ship? He had a vague recollection that occasionally ships were sent to colonies to provide wives. Had she joined such an endeavor? "If you arrived on a bride ship, is it safe to assume you are married?" The personal question fell out of his mouth before he had the good sense to stop it. But he truly wanted to know.

"Not yet. On board, someone said there are ten times more men than women around here. It's why I like my chances to wed one day."

She could change her marital status in a heartbeat based solely on her gorgeous eyes, which resembled brilliant cut sapphires twinkling throughout their many facets. He gripped the bedsheet. Was he a romantic? Merciful heavens. He rather hoped not, though he was unsure why.

"Then you must already have a serious suitor?" As soon as the question escaped, he shook his head. "I apologize for my forwardness, and obviously, you need not answer me."

She shrugged. "I courted two men back in England. One couldn't stop looking at other women, and the second had a temper like a tiger. Good riddance to them both. I climbed on a bride ship for a good reason—to find a decent man, someone kind and stable. However, in the ten months I've been in the colony, I haven't located him yet, but I will."

Surely she had men interested in her since arriving, especially if there were ten times more men than women in the area. How many of them had she turned down? The question pressed for release, but he had already prodded more than was proper on the personal topic. "Was it a good ocean crossing for you?"

Her head tilted to the side, her blond tail dangling. "Aren't you the curious one?"

He softly laughed. Minute by minute, he was learning something new about himself.

"The voyage was a mix of good and bad, I suppose. In the beginning, I fought seasickness. There were too many rules on board, such as where we could roam. Lots of boredom, but I had friends, which helped."

Too many rules. Was he inclined to dislike them, as well? Although he sensed the answer was yes, he had no reason to hold the belief. And how long had he carried the opinion? Based on his accent, he was most likely from England or thereabout. What had brought him abroad? A ship, of course. But why and when?

She glanced at the doorway. "Want to place a wager with me?"

Why not? She reminded him of a chess game. What direction would she move next? "Precisely what are we wagering on?"

"How long until Livy or Tabitha fly back to the sitting room, realizing we're unchaperoned."

Since Juliet had entered the room, he had barely thought about the two women. "I hope not for a while."

Her brow quirked. "Don't you care for the sisters?"

"Of course I do. It is just that"—he paused to weigh his next words—"I rather enjoy conversing with you . . . someone closer to my age. And having nobody censure our conversations." One or both sisters had accompanied him since dawn, and he had peppered them with questions while awake. But there had been no sign of Juliet since he glimpsed his image in the mirror in the forenoon.

"Do you think they're your relations?"

"Who can say? Until I recall my identity, all I have is an intuition that my name is Gray."

"What if we call you that for now?"

Everybody had a name, and he needed one too. "Very well. Though I reserve the right to change it again one day."

"By all means. There are worse names, like Poindexter."

"Or Amadeus." He liked her humor without question. Had he

always gravitated toward a woman with wit? "I hope it is not too forward to say so, but I am fond of your name."

"Thank you. It was also my grandmother's, as I understand it." She stood and removed his tray of food from the bed.

Was she leaving?

He hoped not and scrambled to find a way to continue their conversation. "How did you occupy your day?" Apparently, if the dull question was any indication, he was neither suave nor charming.

"Cleaning mostly, though I kept wanting to check on you." She placed the tray on a nearby table, then resumed her place in the chair at his bedside. "However, I stayed too busy."

His brow arched. "You did?"

"Have multiple chores, yes."

"No, want to check on me?"

"Of course. It's ridiculous, but I feel responsible for your welfare, being the one who found you. I don't suppose you remember how you ended up in the woods."

"Not even an inkling." It was as if his life started when he first awoke in this bed. Was he the sisters' gold-mining nephew with carpentry skills? Or how else had he earned a wage? No answer surfaced, but had he truly expected one?

"It'll take time, I suppose. Don't lose heart. I used to tell myself those same three words."

Had he ever known anyone as forthright as Juliet? More than a little, he liked that she played no coy games and freely spoke her thoughts and opinions. He held her gaze and admired her symmetrical face, thin and angular. More oval than round. Her faint brows barely registered, perhaps because the stark blueness of her eyes garnered his attention more.

His heart rate accelerated. What was she thinking as she stared intently at him?

"I should go." She dropped her gaze and fidgeted with the edge of his cover. "At first glance, I'd say the sisters have more doilies than dust, but I'm not done with the polishing. Also, the kitchen floor still needs mopping."

Chores. She had been thinking about household cleaning. Regardless of her daily tasks, he selfishly wished her to remain with him longer.

The sisters, especially Livy, fawned over him. Tabitha studied him as if he were a medical anomaly. Perhaps he was. Juliet appeared to accept him as he was, a man trapped in a peculiar circumstance. "Surely you can stay with me a little longer. Tell me about your grandfather."

She pressed her hand against her chest. If not mistaken, love filled her eyes as she recalled the man who raised her. "Once upon a time, I rode everywhere on his shoulders, and we competed to sing the loudest. Shouted, really. He prided himself as a storyteller and often spun tales about princesses. I still recall the scent of leather as I watched him cobble shoes."

"He sounds like a man I would have enjoyed meeting."

She nodded. "He was wonderful."

"Do you remember your grandmother?"

"Gone before my birth. My grandfather cried whenever he talked about her, and the same with my mother. As a child, I hated to see him in pain, so I stopped asking questions about the dead people we loved." She hugged the pillow again. "Looking back, though, I wish he'd told me more, particularly about those two women."

"He sounds like someone who felt loss deeply, which means he probably also loved deeply."

"He reared me the best he could. He broke his back after he fell from a roof, helping a friend patch a hole. Then he caught the consumption." Her voice dropped to a whisper. "He didn't last long after that."

Undoubtedly, her past had shaped her in multiple ways, and

likewise, so had his. Yet Juliet had rallied the strength and courage to start a new life in a new country. "It is a pity you lost him so young, but it sounds like he set you on a good course."

"Mostly, though, I've had a few wrong turns." Her blue eyes latched on to his. "However, I never discuss my darker days."

A firm knot tightened in his stomach. If he was Gray, he apparently faced darker days too—darker days he would rather not remember. "Tell me more about your brighter ones. I like learning about you, perhaps because I know nothing about myself."

Her sweet face scrunched with emotion before she detailed how her grandfather taught her to play checkers, marbles, and card games. And how they had a kitten named Bing. Throughout her recitation, her voice carried a happy lilt.

She barely grabbed a breath before sharing a little about her time working at a textile mill, bypassing the period between her grandfather's death and the orphanage. "For a few years, I labored as a weaver in a spinning room. It was hot, dusty, and horribly loud, but the payment satisfied me."

What was fair compensation for such a position? He had not the foggiest notion. "I see."

"After the mill closed, I briefly lived with my friend Molly, then boarded the bride ship where I made two life-long friendships. No matter what, I can always count on Willow and Daisy."

Did friends miss him? Search for his whereabouts? Or was he more apt to seek solitude? Moreover, how long until he remembered these and all the other confounding questions darting through his brain? "Good friends are a blessing."

How did he know such a theory was true?

Juliet leaned forward, her hands on her knees and her brow furrowed. "One day soon, you'll tell me about your past."

"Let us pray it is so."

She studied him intently. "If you don't mind my saying so, you don't talk like anybody else I know, not even Tabitha and Livy. Your speech is . . . fancier."

Was it? "I assume it is based on where and how I was raised."

In a flurry, Livy rushed into the room with wide eyes and flushed cheeks.

Juliet jumped to her feet, bumping the bed with her knee.

"Oh dear, oh dear. I completely forgot about the two of you." Livy was wringing her hands as if she had just caught them in an improper embrace.

Juliet stepped away from the bed toward the window. "I didn't want to leave the patient alone since he was eating. I'm sorry if that was a mistake."

"I asked her to stay." He refused to let Juliet take all the blame.

Livy halted behind the chair Juliet had vacated. "Tabitha and I have never had a young man and woman under our roof together, and we want to keep Juliet's reputation intact and spotless."

"Yes, ma'am." Juliet took another step away from him.

"Both of your reputations, actually," Livy continued. "One day, you'll thank us, especially when it's time to find a marriage partner."

Marriage? Matrimony was the last thing on his mind.

Livy stepped closer, slipped a hand behind him, and began to plump his pillow for the dozenth time. "I keep forgetting to ask why you're wearing Tabitha's black mourning dress, Juliet. Could you find no other options in the wardrobe?"

Juliet glanced down at her dress. "All my clothing needs laundering. When I picked this from the collection, I knew people mourned in black but didn't realize it wasn't worn otherwise. My uniform at the Firth residence was black."

"Have no fear." Livy's round face dimpled in a cheerful smile. "During your upcoming etiquette lessons, we'll cover topics such as what to wear when and much more. Soon, you'll be a brand-new Juliet."

Etiquette lessons? Was something wrong with current-day Juliet? In his opinion, following high-class standards and protocols mattered far too much to some people. "While everyone may benefit from polishing in one form or fashion, let us not forget that Juliet has value as she is. If she had not stumbled over me in the woods, I may have died."

Juliet nodded at him appreciatively.

Tears formed in Livy's eyes. "Heavens to Betsy, Juliet. I didn't mean to imply you were inferior. Please forgive me."

Juliet shifted her focus to Livy. "There's nothing to forgive. I'm much obliged for all your kind help."

"It will be our pleasure, dearie. We'll take the instructions one day at a time." Livy untucked a lacy handkerchief and dabbed delicately at the edges of her eyes. "I've always suspected I'd make a superior teacher."

"No doubt you will," he said. A moment passed before he added, "Was anything in your shipment salvageable?"

Livy shook her head, her curls bouncing. "All of it shattered. It will be a shame, but we may need to postpone the open house due to the broken china and the slow pace of the renovations."

Undoubtedly, he could hammer a nail, but converting a stable into a workable tearoom stirred up doubts. Perhaps after he viewed the building's interior and learned what work remained on the project, he could gauge how to proceed. "If possible, I shall look at your future tearoom tomorrow."

"Let's assess how you feel in the morning and go from there, young man."

"Juliet suggested I begin going by the name Gray. I concur with the plan."

Livy nodded. "Well, it is your name."

Truthfully, he could be a Sherwood or a servant like Juliet. But based on his speech alone, he doubted the second possibility. He had a whole life waiting for him somewhere. Now he just had to find it.

Nine

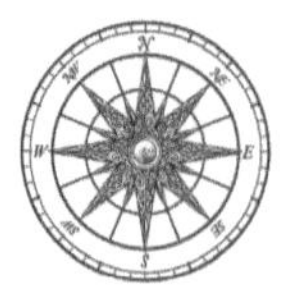

"NEVER MUTTER, DRONE, OR STUTTER," Juliet whispered as she entered the empty dining room. She liked muttering and saw no reason to stop, provided she did it privately. Livy's other specific instructions were tastier to swallow.

Juliet glanced at the shiny brass clock on the dining room mantel she'd polished two days before. Her first formal etiquette lesson was to have begun forty-five minutes ago. Where was Livy, the one leading the instructions tonight?

Juliet carefully lowered a heavy pitcher of water to the sideboard. An oil painting of a distinguished gentleman and his black hunting dog hung on the wall and stared back at her. Most likely, he was the sisters' esteemed father, though he barely resembled his daughters, other than the grimace he shared with Tabitha.

Livy poked her head into the room. A crocheted shawl covered her shoulders, and she'd fastened a small doily adornment with a pink ribbon into her curly hair. Evidently, she dressed to please herself. "I seem to have misplaced my manners manual. Have you seen it?"

In addition to running late, Livy also tended to lose things. "I don't believe it's in here."

"Very well. After it's found, we'll start your instructions in earnest. But before I forget, a true lady must have a pure heart. All right, off I go again. Hippity hop." Livy bustled back down the hallway, heading toward the front door.

A pure heart? What did that mean? Had Juliet done something impure? Not that she could think of. Besides, did anybody on earth genuinely have a pure heart? She hadn't turned the pages of a Bible in years, but based on her recollections, the answer was no.

Juliet stepped closer to the long dining table she'd set for three upon Icala's instructions. Candlelight flickered on the white plates with silver trim and sparkled on the abundance of silverware. Who else would join the sisters for supper? Not her since she still preferred eating alone in the kitchen. Perhaps a friend. Or maybe Gray was a possibility, though he hadn't left the sitting room since his arrival.

Honestly, it could be anyone.

All day her thoughts had drifted to him as she'd cleaned fireplaces, swept floors, and listened to Livy advise her about muttering and such things. She couldn't stop wondering about his identity. What was his livelihood? Based on his gentlemanly ways, he probably held a gentlemanly job. Was he a banker? A jeweler? An attorney?

Perhaps he was the genuine Alex Sherwood. Nobody else by that name had arrived, and the open house wasn't that far in the future—approximately five weeks—if they received a new shipment of supplies in time.

Apparently, Alex had agreed in a letter to visit several weeks ago and assist with building the tearoom. Even though he was a gentleman, he'd picked up carpentry skills while living in the wilderness towns of the mountains, where such skills were necessary for survival. If Gray wasn't him, where was the real nephew, and what kind of man would leave his aunts in a lurch?

A lousy one, for certain.

Even though Gray had an uppity bent, he had surprised her by inquiring about her grandfather and childhood, then listening without interruption. Was there a better gift than someone wanting to hear what a person had to say? She thought not.

"Coming, Juliet!" Livy called from another room. "Go ahead and take a seat."

Juliet moved to the far end of the table, scooted back a chair, sat, and plopped her elbows on the table's edge.

Twenty-five random kitchen items for her lesson stared back at her, everything from sugar tongs to a nut pick.

Breathless, Livy rushed into the room, opening her book. When she reached Juliet's side, she tapped her arm with her manual. "One must never prop her elbows onto the tabletop."

It was just a minor mistake and hopefully the last one for the night. Juliet straightened her spine like the room's fire poker. With perfect timing, the blaze in the hearth crackled.

"Where was I?" Livy perused the pages of her floppy-paged manual. "Furthermore, a lady never interrupts a meal's harmony by uttering phrases such as 'this dish is too salty' or 'so-and-so burnt the beef again.'"

What an odd little book, complete with peculiar little rules. "I've not lived in your home for long, but I don't think Icala would do either of those things, ma'am."

"Of course not. He's a fabulous cook. I only offer examples." Livy resumed reading. "Also, a lady never eats too fast or too slow. And it's improper to use your napkin as a handkerchief."

"What if Icala adds too much pepper and I sneeze?"

"I suspect you tease. Nonetheless, here's a tip. When the first twitch of a sneeze arrives, do this." Livy placed her forefinger in the middle of her top lip. "It stops the itching straight away. Isn't that ingenious?" Livy's ample bosom puffed out as if she were pleased with her helpful hint.

"Yes, ma'am."

Tabitha and Gray entered the dining room, with her supporting his elbow. They paused just inside the door. Tabitha's brow spiked. "Oh, you're not finished with the lesson."

"We've barely started." Juliet stood, and her pulse elevated. She'd never seen Gray fully cleaned up and dressed in anything besides drawers or a nightshirt. Even though he now wore baggy clothes—dark trousers and a white shirt once belonging to the sisters' late father—she still noticed how his broad chest trimmed to a narrower waist.

Although Gray's head still pained him, and he suffered double vision from time to time, his facial bruising and swollenness had faded, revealing the perfect angles of his nose and cheekbones. Tonight, his eyes held a bright alertness. A bandage still covered his head, and he remained unshaven, the scruff adding to his appeal.

What a handsome, handsome man.

Juliet shook her head. Snakes alive. What in tarnation had come over her? She ran her hands down the front of her dress, another castoff from Tabitha.

Over the last couple of days, she'd helped take care of him occasionally under either Tabitha's or Livy's supervision. She'd also tidied his room now and again. But she hadn't had a chance to talk to him alone again, and she'd not mind another opportunity.

Although tall herself, Tabitha glanced up at the man at her side. "It seems we're early for supper, Gray. Would you prefer to return to your room or wait here?"

Not here, not here, not here. How embarrassing if she failed her etiquette lesson in front of him, in front of anyone. But especially him.

"I prefer a change of venue if nobody minds."

Oh, she minded with a fervor, but she couldn't say so, could she?

Tabitha accompanied him to the opposite side of where Juliet stood. His strides appeared capable and steady, and then he sat with ease while Tabitha began to light the candelabra at the center of the table.

Livy smiled at him tenderly. "Your pallor is much improved from earlier."

"I am much improved overall, thank you."

The knot in Juliet's belly tugged tighter. What if she mixed up the gravy and soup ladles or mustard and salt spoons during her etiquette lesson? If so, he'd have a front row seat as she performed like a fool. But she couldn't very well kick him from the room, now could she? "Any new flickers of memory today?"

"Not yet, though I keep hoping it is only a matter of time."

Was he as optimistic as he proclaimed? If so, his stance should serve him well. In his place, she would probably burrow in bed until her Maker called her home. On second thought, she wouldn't mind forgetting the bleaker parts of her past.

"Are you eager to learn the differences between finger bowls and preserve dishes?" His voice held a huskiness she hadn't noticed or appreciated until now. Coupled with his teasing tone, the combination appealed a little too much. In the candlelight, his light brown eyes reminded her of cider. And she sure loved cider.

"Do I have a choice?"

Tabitha's all-seeing eyes trapped Juliet. "Come now. Do you want our help to become more ladylike, or have you changed your mind? Because if you have, we'll move on to our meal sooner rather than later."

The sisters exchanged knowing glances.

Obviously, they were giving her a choice, hadn't coerced her, and were full of graciousness so far. "I'd be a numbskull to miss out on this opportunity. I need to corral my worries, that's all."

"Worries about what, child?" Livy closed her book and pressed the manual against her hefty chest.

Concentrating on anything other than the man at the table. Possibly failing miserably at the lessons. Disappointing the two women. Perhaps even showing everyone that she could never be more than a poor, mannerless orphan.

"My worries aren't important." Delicious scents rose from the kitchen, and she drew a hefty whiff. "But maybe you all should eat first? Icala's wonderful roasted beef and fixings smell heavenly."

"It will keep." Livy rattled off the names of every item on Juliet's end of the table, starting at the upper left corner. When she finished, she smiled much too cheerfully at her. "Show me the tea knife."

The temptation to roll her eyes struck hard, yet Juliet refrained. Tea knife. Was the question a trick? "A knife for tea don't make no sense."

"Any sense," the sisters' voices chimed together.

Gray caught her eye and motioned toward his right, where only one knife sat on that side of the table.

Juliet swiped up the utensil. "Here it is!"

Livy clapped daintily. "Hurrah."

Tabitha was busy surveying her place setting. "Show us the dessert spoon."

Gray reached for his water glass but, before doing so, touched a spoon that sat above the plate.

Juliet grabbed a matching utensil in front of her. "Here."

"I'm such a good teacher." Livy pracktically preened.

When Gray's lips quirked into the beginning of a smile, Juliet couldn't resist a grin of her own. Maybe learning to be ladylike would be easier than she suspected. Especially if he became an ally.

Ten

NOT FOR A MINUTE HAD GRAY EX-pected to find himself in the middle of such a pleasant evening.

The group had gathered in the drawing room. Livy delivered a thick knitted blanket of blue wool to where he sat in a comfortable, well-stuffed chair. "We can't have you catching a chill."

He raised his brow, not cold in the least. The pain in his temple mainly had subsided, and his strength had rallied. First thing tomorrow, he hoped to speak with the constable, then venture to the dock to investigate which ships had arrived in port recently. Hopefully, the name of a steamer, a city, or a person on a sailing log would trigger his memory.

Lord willing, something would register soon.

Juliet sat beside him in a rosewood chair, her ankles crossed. Had he been wicked to have helped her cheat with her dining room lesson before dinner? He wanted to think of himself as a hero who had come to her rescue, but something about the exchange told him he had once been a bit of a rogue . . . and perhaps still was.

He had recognized every item on the table, another reason to believe he was raised in a well-to-do home. Or else he had an unusually keen interest in dishware.

The sisters had invited Juliet to stay at the table for the evening meal. But she declined and insisted on eating her nourishment alone in the kitchen. Although he had enjoyed the supper with the sisters, he could admit he would have liked it more with Juliet present.

Thankfully, she'd rejoined them now in the drawing room. Tabitha had stepped out to retrieve a photograph of her brother and his wife. Livy continued to flit around, striding past another grouping of chairs at the far end, including a deacon's black settee, large enough for three or four people. She paused beside the piano near the entrance and Peaches's cage. "Where is my etiquette manual, my pretty bird? It seems I've misplaced it again."

The delicate creature whistled in reply.

Gray studied Juliet, who now pumped her toe. Was she growing restless? He did not want her to leave when the evening was still spread before them. "Do you care to play chess or perhaps checkers?" Both games were set up on small side-by-side tables near where they lounged.

Before Juliet could reply, Tabitha entered the room with her posture perfectly erect and holding a picture frame. He had not recognized himself in a mirror. Would viewing the faces of anyone else lead to a different outcome?

Tabitha handed him the silver-framed images. "This was taken the day Nolan and Katherine sailed back to England."

Slowly, Gray turned over the picture and stared at the grainy photograph, longing for an emotion, anything other than disappointment.

The lady's large hat shadowed her eyes. But most of her small, delicate face remained open to inspection. Compared to him, her chin was pointier, her nose was slimmer, and her round, puckered mouth resembled the button on his cuff. His did not.

A generous display of facial hair covered two-thirds of the man's face, and his large forehead revealed a receding hairline. Gray patted the top of his head to ensure the strands sticking out of his bandages remained. To his relief, they did. A pair of deep-set eyes bore no resemblance to his either.

He desperately wished for a familiar chord to connect him with this couple, but that chord failed to strum.

When he glanced up, all three women stared back at him. "Perhaps it would help if I heard more specifics regarding your brother and his wife."

Livy had settled into the chair next to Juliet. Between them sat an oval table and a unique lamp, designed with a cut glass chimney, a pink reservoir for the oil, and a brass base. A vague memory resurrected, and the lamp seemed familiar. Had he been in this room at least once before amnesia addled his brain, confirming he was Alex Sherwood?

Livy leaned forward. "Your father's middle name is Alfred, and your mother's is Louise."

Not beneficial.

"Oh." Livy raised her finger and stood. "I've thought of something else that may awaken your memories. Please excuse me while I collect it."

"Of course." He tried to keep his tone pleasant, though he remained doubtful.

Livy left the drawing room, humming to herself.

Tabitha moved to take Livy's vacated seat, but before she

perched on the cushion, she tapped Juliet's knee. "Young ladies never sit with their legs apart. It's grossly unbecoming."

"Thank you." Juliet slapped her legs together, the fun from the earlier lesson gone and now frustration written on her face.

His jaw tightened, and he strongly suspected he had also failed to meet someone's rigid standards once or twice before. But whose? Did he have a stern taskmaster in his life?

He knew the sisters only meant well, but a kinder way to point out someone's error would be to pull them aside and provide the instruction one-on-one, not in front of others. Was that not common courtesy, or was he mistaken? "Would you care to view the photograph, Juliet?"

She squared her shoulders before reaching for the image he handed her. "Do you recognize even the slightest kinship toward the people in the picture?"

"Not yet, I fear. Tabitha, what else have you not disclosed about your brother and his wife? Anything substantial?"

"Katherine is French."

French? Could he speak the language? *Oui.* A litany of French words rattled inside his head, not enough to fill a dictionary, but several pages, at least. Was he raised in France? No, he primarily spoke English. Perhaps he had visited his maternal relatives there. "Are Katherine Sherwood's parents still living, and what was her name before marriage?"

"Last I knew, her family still resided in France. If I correctly recall, the name was Moreau."

Gray waited for the name to stoke a memory, but none sparked inside him. Was he expecting too much progress too soon? Putting his life back together would take time. Therefore, maybe he should temper his expectations instead of losing what remained of his mind.

Still, what if he traveled north to where Alex Sherwood had served his sentence? Yet how could he leave town and simultaneously assist the sisters? He had an obligation to help them with their tearoom, did he not? They had fed, sheltered, and saved his life, for mercy's sake.

Yet he could not stop wondering if he possessed the know-how for the project.

Juliet passed him back the frame. "They're a fine-looking couple."

"Indeed. That could help explain my good looks, could it not?"

A delightful laugh burst from her lips, bringing life to her face and a light to her eyes. To see and hear her happy again removed a weight from his shoulders.

Tabitha shook her head. "A lady never guffaws. It's . . . vulgar."

Juliet squeezed her chair's doily-ridden armrests and clamped her mouth shut. Never mind that she had merely expressed joy. Never mind that calling laughter vulgar was absurd. And never mind that loud guffaws were inappropriate in certain circumstances, but not always.

Was Tabitha incapable of softening her many criticisms?

It was clear he needed to come to her rescue again. "Your charming laughter reminds me of music, Juliet. Bach, perhaps."

Smiling, she waved off his praise. "You're quite the charmer, aren't you?"

Tabitha was watching his face. Did she see his disapproval of her criticism there? He hoped so.

"Joviality has its place, I suppose." The sister seemed to be choosing her words carefully. "But I have read the etiquette manual Livy carries around from cover to cover. It clearly states that speaking loudly, talking out of turn, and laughing boisterously are ill-bred and . . . vulgar."

Juliet's brows knitted. "I mean no disrespect, but I was raised believing laughter was happy and joyful."

Gray nodded. "The Bible mentions laughter in a positive vein more than once. I trust that book more than any etiquette manual ever written."

"I do, as well." Although Tabitha agreed, her eyes and voice held a frostiness.

After a moment, he cocked his brow. "Did you and your sister attend finishing school?"

"Naturally."

"Then I presume," he continued, "you already know everything necessary to deliver etiquette lessons with good sense and a gentle hand."

Tabitha picked at a piece of lint on the arm of her chair. "Perhaps we have been overly harsh in our methods. I'll consult with Livy, and we'll determine whether to proceed with or without the manual." She shifted toward Juliet. "I apologize if I've been too exacting, but we're trying to prepare you for the open house and dance afterward. Life in general, as well."

"Dance?" Juliet's voice squeaked. "I never learned how."

"Don't worry. We'll teach you whatever you need to know beforehand."

Juliet rubbed her hands on her skirt. "I am grateful for all the lessons, even if I muck them occasionally. Well, frequently."

"You're doing fine. However, memorizing our teachings isn't enough. They need to sink into your soul and match your deeds."

Juliet's blue eyes carried a keen sincerity. "I'll work my best on that."

"I found it!" Livy waltzed into the room, carrying a rectangular gold box. When she reached his side, she handed him the item. "As a boy of two, our nephew loved this music box. It belonged to our mother."

An inlaid circle of brightly colored flowers and fruit covered the lid's middle portion. When Tabitha slid a lever, the top lifted, music played, and a feathered bird in blues, reds, greens, and purples popped up and spun.

Held captive, a memory gathered shape, and he pictured a child sitting at the knee of an older man, admiring such a contraption. Was he the youngster?

His temple pulsated as it typically did when straining to recall his past. He tried to blink aside the pain, which threatened to send him back to his bed in the sitting room. Slowly, he drew a deep, helpful breath.

A loud knock came from the front door, startling them all.

Tabitha stood, her brow furrowed. "Who is at the door at this hour?"

"I suggest we go and see." Livy withdrew a tiny gold key from her skirt pocket and handed it to Gray. "If you wish to crank the box again, go ahead. We'll return shortly."

Juliet rose, as well. "I'll wash the teacups from earlier."

Tabitha nodded before she and Livy turned to leave, whispering as they exited the drawing room, Juliet trailing behind them.

He glanced around, uneager to return to the sitting room where he had been confined the past few days. Should he read a book? Challenge himself at chess?

Why not dry a dish or two?

Yes, that was a fabulous idea. He could put himself to work.

After standing, he lowered the blanket, key, and music box to the chair and crossed the room. His stride was stable, and his legs were strong. Although headaches still nagged him daily, his physical strength had fully restored.

As he slipped out of the drawing room, the sisters stood in the doorway at the front entryway, speaking to someone outside, and did not seem to notice him as he made his way to the kitchen.

He slipped into the spacious room to find Juliet reaching for a pot dangling from a metal hook. When he realized he was staring at her pleasing form, he raised his eyes to her equally pleasing face.

Her brows were quirked as if questioning his arrival in the kitchen.

"I came to help you."

"How so, exactly?"

"After you wash a dish, I shall dry it." He glanced around the kitchen. "Where would one find a towel for such a task?"

She wrapped one hand around the kettle, and the other found her shapely hip. "I suspect you've never dried a dish in your life."

"Perhaps I have done all sorts of shocking things."

"Most likely, my past would surprise you twice as much as yours would me."

"Oh, really? Have you ever startled someone with a kiss?"

Her brows shot high as either mirth or astonishment danced in her beautiful eyes. "Are you telling me you remember kissing someone?"

"No."

"Then why mention it?"

Why indeed? "I have determined I was raised a gentleman, but maybe I am also someone who speaks his mind, laughs at least once a day, and . . . flirts with pretty ladies."

A moment passed before her eyes widened and she realized he had referenced her. A teasing smile curved her lips. "I don't know whether to applaud or slap your cheek."

He chuckled. He appreciated her straightforwardness, how she was easy to like, and how a tendril of her flaxen hair lay against her cheekbone.

Juliet's face grew suddenly somber, and she unflinchingly studied him. "Smooth, flowery talk doesn't impress me. I've heard it all before, mister."

"I am not trying to impress you. I am merely being me, I believe. However, your message is noted."

She nodded. "Thank you for coming to my aid with the etiquette lesson in the dining room and your comments with Tabitha regarding my laughing. It was nice of you."

How easily she offered gratitude. Did he, as well? If not, perhaps it was time to take a lesson from her. "I propose since you saved my life, I shall help smooth the way for you however I can."

Her brow cocked. "How exactly might you do that?"

"I may make you laugh when I think you need it. Or, again, show you what fork to use with dessert."

Her eyes sparkled with that same conspiratorial glint as earlier. "What kind of dessert?"

"What's your favorite?"

"Chocolate cake."

"Excellent. If Icala ever bakes a chocolate cake, I shall ensure you use the proper utensil to devour it. And on occasion, I might remind you that learning something new takes time."

"I'll try to remember that."

"Me too." Wholeheartedly, he approved of Juliet, ladylike or not. Together they would determine how to proceed in a world, or at least a household, foreign to them both.

The clacking of heels in the hallway drew near, and in the next instant, Livy stepped into the kitchen.

Juliet moved toward the basin, then reached for the dipper, quickly busying herself by filling the pot with water to warm it.

Livy paused beside the table, her usual cheerfulness replaced by a frown. "Our visitor was the constable, making his rounds. Apparently, we left the double door to the carriage house open earlier, and he shut it on our behalf. He didn't want an animal or trespasser slipping inside."

"Is he still here?" Gray's pulse raced. "If so, he shall save me a trip in the morning."

"No, he's already left for home. However, Tabitha asked if there were recent reports of a missing man in the area, and Mr. Blake assured us he hadn't received any. Unfortunately, or maybe fortunately, nobody has asked about you, Gray."

He could not stop his shoulders from sagging just a little.

Juliet cast him a half smile that seemed to offer encouragement, yet the news was not what he had hoped for.

Livy started to leave, then turned back around. "I did inform him that our nephew finally arrived and has moved into our home."

"The constable was aware of my . . . I mean, Alex Sherwood's pending arrival?"

"Oh, yes. Tabby and I are good friends with his wife and attend the same church. We haven't mentioned Alex's criminal record, and I believe it's still best to keep that detail to ourselves. No need for others in the community to form negative opinions of you from the onset."

"There." Juliet's smile widened. "You don't need to go to the constable after all."

Perhaps she was right. What good would it do if the constable had not heard of a missing man in the area?

Maybe it was time to consider that he was Alex Sherwood. More and more missing puzzle pieces had been coming together to create that picture.

However, he detested what he had learned about the sisters' nephew thus far. Maybe that was why, somewhere deep inside, he felt dissatisfied with himself, because he had not been living an upright life.

What if God had given him this hardship to turn things around and become a better man? If so, he must not squander the opportunity.

Eleven

J UST AS I AM," JULIET WHISPERED THE sentence printed on the front page of her grandfather's worn journal before closing the book. Why those four words? It wasn't the first time she'd asked herself the question, and it probably wouldn't be the last since she had no answer.

Sighing, she deposited the journal on top of the chest of drawers, exchanging it for the letters she'd written to Willow, Daisy, and Sage. Since leaving Vancouver Island five days ago, she'd had little time to write to her friends. They'd want to know how to reach her. One day, and hopefully soon, she'd invite them for a visit.

Eager to show off the tearoom upon its completion, a little thrill rolled around inside her as she left the bedroom, descended the back staircase, and entered the kitchen. Tabitha handed her

"

two more envelopes. "The post office is inside the workplace of Stipendiary Magistrate J.B. Elliott. Go straight down the hill until Main Street, one block from the river, and turn right. Keep going until you reach 10 Seventh Street on the corner."

"Yes, ma'am."

Icala turned from the stove, a knife and a loaf of fresh bread in one hand. The yeasty aroma smelled like heaven. "There's a rumor someone in this house adores chocolate cake, and that person might find it on the menu tonight."

"Really?" Juliet recalled her recent conversation with Gray. The man kept surprising her in the best possible ways. Maybe she'd pegged him wrong from the start. "I can barely wait, and I thank you both."

After too many lean years in England, her stomach always craved more. Maybe one day, her gut would stop grumbling.

As she stepped outside, the mid-morning sky matched a pewter goblet. A sharp northern wind from the mountains snuck inside her scarf. She tightened the knot below her chin and rounded the house to reach the street. Children frolicked in Royal Park across the road, their laughter carrying on the wind.

Juliet strolled down the hill. Perhaps she'd bump into Gray on his way back from the dock. He'd hoped to learn what ships had arrived in Everly the day before he regained consciousness. But how much time had passed between his attack and her rescue? Based on the dried leaves and brush atop his form, a couple of days, maybe.

Ideally, he'd begin laboring in the carriage house as early as this afternoon, and then they'd all discover his level of carpentry skills.

When she reached downtown, only a few folks roamed the raised wooden platform that served as a sidewalk. She paused to wait as a buggy crossed the muddy street, spitting up sludgy dirt. She strode past a watchmaker's shop, a law office, and a tannery before reaching a sky-blue hotel on her side of the road.

The fancy three-story structure featured a balcony with a decorative cast-iron rail, towering snow-white pillars, and a macadamized drive to reach the large front entrance. The place created an inviting picture, and she considered stepping inside. Hotels had always intrigued her for a good reason. Her father had labored as an innkeeper, where he'd met Juliet's mother.

But there was no time for snooping around today. Livy had lessons planned on proper posture, proper letter writing, and proper books to read to polish her mind. Truthfully, much of what Livy deemed critical teachings ranked far from necessary in Juliet's opinion.

However, she wasn't an authority figure on manners, now, was she?

Juliet soon passed a twin-spired church. Its white stone walls, steeply pitched roof, and three gorgeous stained-glass windows in a row impressed her at first glance. Was it the sisters' house of worship? Tomorrow was Sunday, and she would learn the answer firsthand.

Then she reached the intersection she sought and squinted at the address proudly carved on the two-story, brick-fronted building. 10 Seventh Street. Juliet hurried forward but paused at the sight of an older man slumped on the bottom step.

Wearing a loose sack coat, he doffed his beat-up straw hat, revealing scant white hair. His blue eyes held a piercing sharpness that was difficult to ignore. "Good morning to you, miss." When he inhaled, he faintly wheezed. "I'd stand, but I have an achy leg."

"No need, sir, but thank you." She sidled past him up the rest of the steps into the lobby with welcoming chairs of light oak and apple-green seats. Nobody would mind if she brought the man on the steps inside, would they? The blustery November day better suited the birds.

In less than two minutes, she handed the postmaster her mail, received a passel of letters for the sisters, and returned to the fresh air outside. The older gentleman still occupied the steps.

Twisting toward her, he smiled, revealing a large gap between his upper front teeth. "That was quick."

She descended the stairs until she reached his side. "I don't tend to dawdle."

"And I seem to do it endlessly these days."

Did he need assistance due to his hurting leg? "May I assist you somehow, sir? Fetch a family member?"

"Kind of you to offer, but I'm alone now. Wife died two years ago, and then my brother and I built a cabin in the mountains, which we share. The name is Cy Kelly." On closer examination, he was as thin as a scarecrow, his cheeks chapped from the wind, and his coat threadbare. "Came to see the doctor about my leg, but he's out of town."

"I see. I'm Juliet Dash, and sorry about your wife." A light sprinkling of rain was beginning to fall.

"Pleasure to make your acquaintance, Miss Dash."

"How long have you been in town?"

"Close to a week. With the weather changing up in the mountains, I'm told the passes have blown shut with snow, which means I'm probably stuck here until spring."

She wiped the raindrops off her face with the end of her headscarf. Based on appearance, Mr. Kelly partially resembled her grandfather, particularly his straight nose, slight build, and midnight blue eyes. "Can you stay at a boarding house?"

"I have been, though it's too expensive to continue. God will provide."

"Once upon a time, I had nowhere to stay either. But I'm a servant at a fine house up the hill these days."

Although she occasionally grumbled to herself about the strict and seemingly random lessons, she had few complaints. And then there was Gray, who'd compared her laugh to music. He was a little too interesting and more than a bit mysterious. It was hard to say what she liked more—his good looks or his charm. Undoubtedly, a toss-up.

Yet she had no designs on the man. For one, he was a gentleman and above her class. And two, if he was Alex Sherwood, he had a criminal past. Sure, people changed—and he seemed decent enough. But what if, after he recovered from amnesia, he decided to return to his crimes?

She'd had enough lawbreaking in her past and didn't want it in her future.

"Ideally, I'd raise an umbrella to shelter us from this rain," Cy said. "But I have nary a one. This confounded dampness troubles my gout, I'm afraid."

"Sounds like you're down on your luck."

"'Tis true, but don't fret over me. I'm what you call a survivor."

Juliet's stomach muscles tightened. "Me too."

"Years back, I labored as an architect and builder. Then my Elizabeth got sick, and I had to care for her. At about the same time, I was swindled out of a large sum of money. Yet I always land on my feet."

"My grandfather used to say the same thing until he fell off a roof." She glanced at the nearby hitching post where three horses stood tethered. Did one belong to Mr. Kelly? Surely, it must. She doubted he could amble far in his condition.

"I've been asking around town about work. Even with my bad leg, I can still manage."

An idea began to take shape. "So, you know something about building and carpentry?"

He laughed. "I don't just know something. I know everything."

"Then I might have a job for you." In Gray's weakened condition, he could use the help. Wouldn't that be a blessing? And how could the sisters object to having Mr. Kelly assist, especially if they hoped to be ready for the open house on schedule?

The idea was growing by the second. What if Tabitha and Livy didn't only hire Mr. Kelly to help with the tearoom but also allowed him to stay at their place for the winter months? After all, they had three empty bedrooms upstairs.

Juliet had no business meddling, but how could she ignore someone in need?

When she'd been homeless, how many times had she prayed for a helping hand? Did Mr. Kelly whisper the same prayer?

She tucked the sisters' mail under her cloak to shield the bundle from the rain. "I'm not promising anything, but I might return for you."

His eyes twinkled. "I'd be much obliged, and you know where to find me."

"That I do." Outside on the cold, lonely street. A place she knew all too well.

Juliet turned and trudged back up the hill, growing rain-soaked with every step and growing more convinced not to ignore Mr. Kelly's need for help. At the very least, she'd ask the sisters if he could stay in their home until he found other accommodations. She was a great judge of character, had learned to be over the years, and something about the man told her that he was good and kind but just down on his luck.

"There you be," a voice called from behind Juliet.

Lost in her thoughts, she jumped and twirled around, dropping the sisters' mail onto the street alongside the park.

There, a few feet away, stood a soggy Ruby. A new bluish-black bruise had swollen her eye, reducing the opening to a slit. "Surprised to see me?"

"What are you doing here?" Juliet's heart thundered as she gathered the envelopes, wiping the grime on her skirt. "And how did you find me?"

"I have a way of getting information."

Blame it all. Who had given away her whereabouts to Ruby?

Indeed, not Mrs. Morseby. Had Ruby paid for the information, or had someone assumed she and her foe were friends?

Juliet scoffed and stood. The pesky woman was anything but a friend.

A young woman approached, pushing a rattly pram, the child wailing as the drizzle soaked them both. Juliet turned her shoulder, not wanting anyone to catch her conversing with Ruby. Everly was supposed to be Juliet's fresh, clean start, away from all the problems chasing her from Victoria.

Neither of them spoke until the lady and child moved beyond earshot.

"I just got to town. Seems nice enough." Ruby glanced around as if truly admiring the lovely homes that bordered the park. "Who was that old man you was yapping with?"

Chitchat? Did Ruby seek chitchat? Juliet fastened her hand to her hip. "Nobody of your concern. Now tell me why you're here."

"To fetch what's mine. I need the Queen's brooch, all the jewels, actually." They both knew the valuables belonged to the Firths.

But Ruby watched her expectantly, wiping her nose with her cape.

Juliet wouldn't have recognized Ruby's lack of manners not long ago. But life had changed. She'd changed and didn't want Ruby causing problems and jeopardizing her new position with the sisters.

Juliet rubbed the tight muscles in her neck. "For the last time, I didn't take what you buried, and I don't know what happened to the jewels."

Ruby's eyes narrowed. "You sure found me in the yard quickly that night we got fired. That can only mean one thing. You followed me the other times too."

Juliet could claim her innocence twenty times a day for a year, and Ruby probably would continue to ignore her. But she had to try again. "I don't have the jewels, and I promise I have never touched them. Why don't you please let this go?"

"Can't. My life just might depend on me getting them back." Ruby glanced around warily as if she expected someone to jump out and blacken her other eye. "Either you help me find who took the jewels or give me the money they're worth, I'm thinking."

"What?" Juliet could only gape at the young woman's nerve to make such a demand. "You can't be serious. We both know servants don't make big sums, especially whatever that brooch was worth."

"Somebody has to pay for it. Why not you? Get the money from your new fancy employers."

Juliet tightened her grip on the mail. Did Ruby know where she lived and who she worked for? Was she suggesting Juliet steal from the sisters? Never. She'd walk away before harming Livy and Tabitha.

Hardening her face, Juliet dropped her hand onto Ruby's shoulder. "You need to leave and not return. Or I'll tell the local constable you swiped Mrs. Firth's jewels."

Ruby wiggled out of Juliet's clutch. "Mrs. Quinborow didn't believe you. The constable won't none neither. I'm mighty convincing when I put my mind to it."

Ruby spoke the truth for a change. Hadn't she wept genuine tears in front of the housekeeper? Of course, she'd stoop to the same shenanigans in front of Everly's constable. But who would the lawman believe? "For the last time, I didn't take what you seek."

"Prove it."

She couldn't prove anything and wouldn't let Ruby come to the sisters' house and rummage through her belongings. That would raise questions Juliet didn't want to answer. And besides, when Ruby didn't find anything among her possessions, she'd assume Juliet had hidden the jewels.

Ruby crossed her arms. "Since I'm nice, I'll give you some time to raise the money."

"That's not gonna happen, Ruby—"

"I've spoken my piece, so I'm catching the next boat out of here. If you don't give me back the jewels or come up with the money, you'll force me to take revenge one way or another." Looking mighty satisfied with a smug grin, Ruby turned on her heel and began to stroll down the hill.

The rain continued to drench her, yet Juliet remained rooted, waiting until Ruby disappeared from view. Her shoulders slumped. What was she to do? She couldn't allow Ruby to return and possibly steal from the sisters and disturb Juliet's new life.

But she had the feeling that's exactly what would happen.

Juliet raised her chin to heaven. "Please help me, God, and don't take Everly away."

As usual, no answers arrived, only the splat of a raindrop on her upturned forehead.

Twelve

*Select the kind of business that suits your
natural inclinations and temperament.*

HAD HE EVER CONSTRUCTED ANY-thing with a hammer and nails? Gray strongly suspected the answer was no—not a birdhouse, not a cradle, and certainly not a tearoom.

Similarly to how Juliet had struggled in her dining room lesson the previous evening, Gray only identified a handful of the equipment poking from a splintered toolbox near his feet. He bent and retrieved a hammer with a wooden handle and a tarnished head. "To be clear, does your nephew make a living as a carpenter or only dabble in the profession?"

"According to his letter, he picked up the trade out of necessity during his time mining for gold in Barkerville." Tabitha crossed the dusty carriage house, brushing her hands together as if dirty.

Learning a craft *out of necessity* was far different from earning a living as a carpenter. A novice could easily forget the tricks and tools of the trade, could he not?

The rolled-up blue etiquette manual poked out of Livy's overcoat pocket as she paced the length of the room waving her hands. "Here's where we would like one wall to divide the front room from a kitchen at the back."

Late-morning raindrops snaked down the windowpanes and tapped on the roof. The building was vast for an in-town property, approximately twenty-five feet wide and perhaps fifty feet deep. Apparently, the sisters' father had collected buggies and carriages and constructed the enormous building to store his vehicles.

Cleared out and primarily empty except for the building materials that the local lumber mill had delivered, the space would likely be relatively simple to finish . . . if a person knew how to accomplish such a task.

He had hoped the sight of the tools and lumber would bring back all his knowledge about using them. But it had not. "Before gold mining, how did your nephew make a living?"

"I suppose you could call him a businessman." Livy retied her bonnet's blue silk ribbon underneath her chin into a bow. "He attended university in Paris, then briefly came to Everly before moving north to find his fortune. Alas, he discovered misfortune instead."

Gray tightened the grip on the tool's handle. Would he rest easier if he knew the crime he may have committed, or never rest again? The law often ignored a gentleman's unruly behavior, but not this time it appeared. Was he a thoroughly dishonorable man?

Merciful heavens, he hoped not. "You are referring to his incarceration, I assume."

Livy sighed. "It is a dreary topic, is it not?"

Tabitha nodded. "But Gray deserves to know all the missing bits and pieces we might provide. Our father was a nobleman, inherited a sizeable estate, and generously shared his wealth with his family. Upon Father's passing, our dear brother inherited everything."

"But Tabitha bought this house from him," Livy interjected, as open as always. "She has wealth since her husband's death."

He had wondered about the sisters' ability to own a large home, fund the carriage house conversion, and operate a business. The ladies' ambition impressed him, and he was ready to ignite his determination as well.

Tabitha pursed her lips, her expression severe. "However, I fear Alex has squandered his portion and made several mistakes, especially over the last year. I wish we could tell you the specific nature of his crime, but he hasn't told us. Perhaps he's ashamed."

Ashamed of what? Murder or some other dreadful mayhem? The thought was enough to drive him mad. "One way to determine if I am a Sherwood is to travel to Barkerville and speak with a jailor and others. Either they recognize me or not."

"I suppose," Tabitha said. "But Barkerville is a long distance from here, and this time of year, the mountain roads may already be too difficult to traverse."

"Of course." He had already decided that he could not leave now anyway, that he needed to stay and help the sisters with their project.

Livy's eyes turned soft with compassion. "We realize it must be overwhelming and frustrating to lose your memories, Gray."

"Honestly, it is." He ran his hand through his hair, his head notably lighter without the bandages. His trip to the dock in the forenoon had proved a waste of time. He had hoped to discover which ships had recently arrived, perhaps view the passengers' logs and learn the steamers' origins.

A good plan, except the record keeper failed to report to work today. Therefore, Gray would have to venture to the harbor again soon and, hopefully, leave with a better result.

A noise at the door drew everyone's attention.

Juliet bustled inside, her cheeks pink, and her clothing flattened to her body. A howl of wind accompanied her. "I'm back."

"We see that, Juliet, and you're dripping wet." Tabitha's voice carried a note of irritation. "Did you bring back our mail?"

"Yes, and I placed it on the kitchen table." She removed her headscarf to reveal her hair pulled back from her damp, shiny face. Moisture from the rain had clumped her eyelashes together. Wet or dry, she was equally appealing.

Tabitha brushed flecks of sawdust from her overcoat sleeve. "We were just showing Gray around the carriage house. Any day now, we'll put him to work."

Except he could barely recall which end of a hammer pounded the nails. "Do you know anyone in town capable of instructing me, at least until more of my memory returns?"

"As a matter of fact, I do." Juliet smiled. "Cy Kelly needs a place to stay for the winter. Perhaps he could teach you in exchange for room and board."

"Cy Kelly?" Both of Livy's brows rose. "Where and when did you meet this stranger?"

"When I exited the post office, he and I struck up a conversation, and he told me he's looking for work."

Tabitha crossed her arms. "And this stranger possesses carpentry skills?"

"He was once an architect and builder and said he knows everything there is to know about such things." Was there a better available candidate in town? Not likely, or the sisters would have hired him before now.

Tabitha's eyes were lit with interest. "Tell us more about Mr. Kelly, Juliet."

"He's a widower and appears older, perhaps in his fifties. He lives in the mountains but came to town because of a hurting leg and now doesn't think he can return until spring."

The prospect of obtaining carpentry assistance certainly appealed to Gray, but who was this man? "Should we not know more about this fellow before considering inviting him in?"

Juliet leveled a censuring look at him. "I realize he's a stranger, but so were we not long ago."

She had a good point. The sisters took him in even though they knew absolutely nothing about him.

"Besides," Juliet continued, "I'm a good judge of people and can tell he's a kind man."

Tabitha exchanged a look with Livy. "For him to live here is a big undertaking. We've already added you and Gray to our household."

Juliet ran the length of her headscarf through her clenched hand. "Perhaps Mr. Kelly can stay in the carriage house for a spell. It's dry and shields the wind nicely."

Livy's brow was now wrinkled. "Tabitha, what do you think?"

"Let's you and I chat over there." Tabitha nodded toward the room's far end. Whispering, they strolled in the specified direction.

First, Juliet had rescued him, and now she was championing Mr. Kelly. "I'm impressed by your nature to assist those less fortunate. Do you recall when I mentioned how we need to help each other?"

"Of course." She grinned. "I'm not the one who lost his memory."

He laughed. "Touché. I never expected you to find me a carpentry instructor before you realized I needed a tutor." He lowered his voice and returned his tool to the wooden box. "I cannot remember my so-called expertise with a hammer."

Wet stray hairs from her pulled-back tresses clung to her face's sharp angles and planes. "Do you think that means you're not Alex Sherwood?"

"It certainly begs the question. However, perhaps I do not recall the specifics due to my amnesia. Far too often, I question what is real or my imagination."

"Although it pales in comparison, I sometimes wonder about

that too. For example, will I truly attend a fancy tea party next month, or is it nothing but a dream?"

"Would you feel comfortable at a formal affair?"

She shrugged. "Since I've never been to one, it's hard to guess the answer."

"If I also attend the function, I shall assist you however possible . . . if I can actually build the tearoom in time."

"With Mr. Kelly's help, especially if his gout improves, I wager you'll soon make the sisters' dream come true."

He was far less optimistic than her. Earlier in the day, he had expected to walk into the building and discover peace and purpose. The opposite had occurred.

He heaved a sigh.

Juliet's nose wrinkled with concern. "Are you all right?"

"I am trying to be." The last thing he wanted was to dwell on his troubles, for he had done little else for too long.

She held his stare, the compassion in her eyes warming his heart. Even drenched, she was so beautiful.

His gaze skimmed over her face and then dropped lower. Her wet cloak and garments clung to her body, revealing every curve of her shapely frame. He suspected he had met his share of beautiful women. Yet something also told him Juliet was different, special, and one of a kind, like a rare and precious gemstone. And never any man's dalliance.

Regardless, a flicker of heat flamed to life low in his gut—a flame he would never allow himself to fan but one he probably would not be able to extinguish.

He shifted his attention back to her face, finding her eyes had rounded, and something was glimmering there too. Was it interest? Did she find him as attractive as he saw her?

Her headscarf slipped from her fingers and pooled near his feet. He stooped to retrieve it, and she did likewise. Her warm breath grazed his ear as their fingers brushed, sending sparks along his skin.

"Step back five paces, young people." Tabitha's firm order echoed in the room.

Juliet straightened quickly and hopped back.

He chuckled at the sisters' reaction to his nearness to Juliet. Were the ladies extra cautious, sensing he had developed an attraction to her? If so, they were not mistaken.

Her heart was as beautiful as her face, yet his life was incredibly uncertain. He could not, and should not, pursue anything other than friendship with any woman, at least for a long, long time. If he had committed a crime, his first action would be to turn his life around.

"It's not a laughing matter, Gray," Juliet whispered, snatching up the scarf and retreating at least a dozen paces.

He had the urge to slowly run his forefinger from the middle of her fair forehead to the tip of her exquisite chin. "I hate disagreeing with a lady, but you are wrong."

"Juliet." Tabitha removed the barrel lid next to her and lowered it to the ground before straightening. "Please collect Mr. Kelly and take an umbrella this time. Perhaps we can forge a beneficial arrangement with the man."

"However," Livy added, "we must meet him, evaluate his character, and learn more about his skills before proceeding with any arrangements."

Gray could only pray that the sisters would find the arrangement suitable because he strongly suspected he needed every ounce of help he could find.

Thirteen

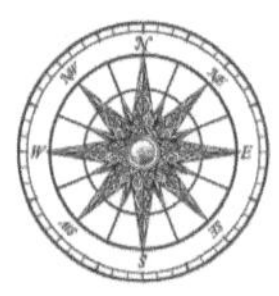

S TANDING BEFORE THE CHURCH, THE
one downtown with the pretty stained glass, Juliet discreetly
covered her yawn with her hand, trying her best to appear
ladylike. Thoughts of Ruby's arrival yesterday had crawled through
her mind nonstop during the service, and she'd barely slept last night.

Gray stood beside her and raised a brow. "Bored beyond belief?"

"Heavens no." She glanced around, hoping nobody overheard
his comment.

Livy and Tabitha conversed with friends closer to the wide front
steps and in the shadows of a giant fir tree. Soon, they'd all trek
back up the hill for the noon meal.

Juliet drew the fresh Sunday morning air into her lungs.

Gray did likewise. "Not that I was studying you, but you appeared a dozen miles away during the sermon. Some might say two dozen."

"I have much on my mind, I suppose." She couldn't tell him about Ruby but wished to confide in someone. Too bad her brideship friends lived elsewhere.

She raised her eyes to heaven. Then toward a noisy group of women on the front lawn, where the sun beamed brightly on their yellow, green, and pink dresses and hats. Juliet smoothed down the folds of Tabitha's borrowed garment without drawing attention to herself. Snippets of the ladies' conversation reached her ears—*tearoom*, *grand opening*, *dance*, and *can barely wait*.

Gray leaned closer and whispered, "You are distracted again."

"No, I'm not." Daydreaming was ill-mannered, according to Tabitha. The sooner she steered Gray's thoughts away from her, the better. "Do you think Mr. Kelly can teach you all you need to know about carpentry?"

"Based on my conversation with him before bed, I believe so. But we shall have to wait and see."

Cy had been relieved and overjoyed when she'd returned to him yesterday and invited him back to the house. The sisters met with him in the drawing room for a while before finally coming out and announcing they had hired him for room and board.

"Quite the shame his gout kept him from church this beautiful morning." Since Cy's ailment prevented him from climbing the staircase, Gray had temporarily relocated to Tabitha's bedchamber after much deliberation. And Tabitha moved into the empty room next to it, placing herself between Juliet and Gray. "That was quite the debate yesterday, trying to determine which upstairs room to assign you."

He chuckled, then lowered his voice. "I was surprised Tabitha did not employ a yardstick to measure the distance from doorway to doorway before reaching the decision."

"It is all ridiculous, in my opinion, though I believe Livy is less concerned about keeping you and me apart." From the corner of her eye, Juliet caught Livy drawing closer, the young pastor at her side. Her monstrous fur-trimmed hat almost smacked the poor clergyman's head.

Most likely, Reverend Channing was five years older than Juliet. Freckles dotted his full cheeks and the bridge of his nose. She dubbed his hair an auburn hue, and someone had cut his locks incredibly short. If he stood taller than her, it was only by a whisper.

Livy gestured to her companion as they stopped before her and Gray. "Juliet Dash, please meet Reverend Channing. He is new to town, like you. And Reverend Channing, may I present Miss Dash. Although she is in our employment, she's practically part of our family already."

Juliet's eyes widened. Practically family? What a kind but outlandish thing to say. Somehow, Juliet found her voice. "It is a pleasure to make your acquaintance. Thank you for your lovely sermon this morning."

He smiled, displaying a straight row of teeth. "A distinct pleasure to meet you, as well, Miss Dash. Knowing what part of God's message appeals the most to my flock is helpful. Can you pinpoint something specific?"

"Yes, Juliet." Gray was smirking. "What did you find most illuminating?"

She shot him a narrowed look. "All of it, I believe, especially the ending. I mean the prayer . . . at the end."

Either Gray coughed or laughed, his eyes full of merriment. If she could legally throttle him, she might.

Livy slapped his back as if she believed he had choked. "And this young man, Reverend, is our nephew, Alex Sherwood. He's kindly helping us renovate our tearoom."

The hatless reverend cupped his hand over his brow, avoiding the direct sunshine. "The upcoming event is the talk of the town.

Like everyone else, I'm excited to attend, since I relish a good cup of tea most evenings."

After nodding, Gray shook hands with the reverend. "Good morning, Reverend." He didn't bother to correct Livy by stating he might not be her nephew. It was probably easier than kicking up a complicated discussion on amnesia. "I, for one, particularly appreciated your message on truthfulness." Gray's expression was overly serious, except for his eyes, which still teased her.

Laughter bubbled up in Juliet. This time, she was the one coughing or choking to hold back her humor. And Livy moved to her and slapped her back. "There, there, dear. It's the humid air after so much rain. It makes me cough sometimes too."

Juliet cleared her throat, trying to hold back more laughter. She needed to get away before she embarrassed herself and the sisters. "If nobody minds, I'll return to the house to check on Mr. Kelly."

"Of course, Juliet." Livy beamed. "You're always thinking of others."

Oh, she was thinking of others, all right, namely Gray. And how she'd like to give him a swift kick. "Excuse me, please."

As she turned to leave, Reverend Channing called, "I hope to see you soon, Miss Dash. You as well, Mr. Sherwood."

What? Was Gray returning home, too? Her heart sped as she strolled away from the church, crisp leaves crunching underneath her shoes.

In no time, he reached her side and extended his elbow. "May I escort you back to the house? A proper young lady always accepts a gentleman's invitation."

Snakes alive, she longed to roll her eyes. She gripped his elbow instead. "You're quite the tease."

"Thank you." He sounded proud of the fact.

She chuckled as a gray squirrel crossed their path, its cheeks full of nuts for the winter. The sun beat on her brow, and she lowered her shawl off her shoulders.

With one hand, Gray unbuttoned his boxy knee-length over-coat, another castoff from the late Mr. Sherwood. "Who do you think taught me manners?"

"My first guess is nobody," she jested.

"Touché, which is French for point taken."

"Parents or a governess, I suppose. It must be hard not to rec-ollect your past."

He peered at her, his gaze thoughtful. "And also difficult to recall too much, I assume."

A rush of warmth spread inside Juliet, catching her by surprise. Why did he notice things others didn't? Had God poured an extra dose of goodness into his heart? Most likely. "What a twist that I long to forget a chunk of my memories, and you desperately crave to recall your share."

As they strolled up the hill arm in arm, they chattered and ban-tered the whole way. Juliet's heart grew lighter with each step until it almost felt like it might float away.

Her life now was everything she wanted, wasn't it? That's what she'd told Livy about her goal on her first day in Everly—some-thing about having a roof over her head, feeling safe and secure, and holding a steady job.

But deep inside, didn't she desire more?

Of course, she'd imagined someday getting married if the right man came along. But truthfully, she'd always put off the idea for one reason or another. Even with the fellas who'd come calling on her when she'd lived in Victoria, she'd had excuses for why she didn't want to court them.

Was she afraid of getting married and possibly having children? Afraid to allow herself to dream that she could have a future filled with her own family? Afraid that she'd lose everything again?

That was silly. But Ruby's threats certainly weren't. Juliet shook her head and then stumbled.

In the middle of recounting something funny Livy had done

yesterday, Gray tightened his grip on her arm, keeping her upright and tugging her closer to his side.

As she regained her balance, their hips bumped.

He halted his story mid-sentence.

Suddenly, she was keenly aware of the long, hard length of his body against hers, the grip of his fingers on her arm, and the slightly labored breaths he was taking. She could almost feel his warmth and strength, stirring the memory of their encounter yesterday in the carriage house when she'd dropped her scarf.

She closed her eyes briefly at the remembrance of the dark heat in his eyes and the warmth that had seared through her, making her breathless with a strange wanting. It was a wanting she'd never felt before but liked.

And that wanting rippled through her again.

"Are you all right?" he asked, slowing his steps to match hers.

"Yes, I think so."

"Rest steady, for I shall strive always to keep you safe."

Had anyone ever spoken something similar to her before? Not that she recalled. Nor had she ever expected anyone to do so. Yet, she didn't hate Gray's concern for her welfare. Likewise, she intended to watch out for him. "Thank you, sir."

He dipped his head. "My pleasure."

Although she preferred not to ponder the matter, she couldn't stop wondering if he had a woman waiting for him somewhere. Nobody would want to lose a man like him. The sisters said their nephew wasn't married, but that didn't mean someone special hadn't caught his eye.

Gray ambled even slower. "I think the reverend may set his hat for you."

"Don't be . . . absurd." There had been a glint of matchmaker in Livy's eyes, though.

"If I recall, you mentioned wanting a husband who is decent, kind, and stable."

"Did I? Well, those are admirable qualities."

"The reverend certainly has them all from what I could ascertain."

"Perhaps he does." Should she be more interested in getting to know the reverend? Because she wasn't.

"Not at all unstable like someone we both know." Although Gray spoke the reference to himself in a light voice, he grew morose.

And suddenly, a gloominess embraced her too. There was no denying an attraction was blossoming between them, but clearly, they both understood it could never go anywhere. Not even a little bit of anywhere.

Fourteen

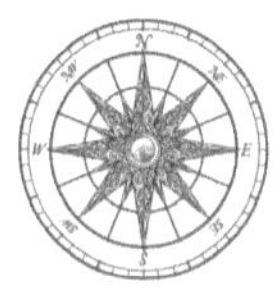

If you wish to be a well-bred lady, you must carry your good manners everywhere with you. It is not a thing that can be laid aside and put on at pleasure.

IT WAS HARD TO PICK WHAT WAS SWEETER— Icala fawning over his lovely wife who was expecting a baby or the slice of apple pie Juliet devoured minutes ago. The sisters had her deliver a care package to the couple on the following lazy, late Sunday afternoon, and now she was eager to return home.

As much as she told herself it wasn't to see Gray, she was having doubts. It was trite to say so, but he made every day brighter. And who didn't lean toward the light? Well, probably plenty, now that she thought about it.

Sighing, she veered off the road and tiptoed to avoid the swampy grass. To the best she could gauge, she headed southeast toward town. Skeletal trees loomed as she hurried down a dirt path, drawing her shawl tighter around her neck.

A large sandbar curved on a horseshoe beach. The sunset of yellows and oranges reflected on the water and beamed on shells and scattered debris. She turned toward the thick, towering woods.

A tall man exited the stand of trees and approached. Juliet paused, squinting at him until he waved his hand high above his head. "Hello." His familiar voice echoed.

Gray. What a pleasant development.

As she waved back, her eyes focused on his form. More accurately, his broad shoulders. "Hello, yourself. Are you coming to fetch me?"

Admittedly, she admired his appearance and liked that he stood taller than her. Not all men did—the reverend, for example. And the scruffy manliness of Gray's whiskers—she liked that too. Not to mention the gleam that sparkled in his lively golden-brown eyes whenever he grinned.

No, she didn't mind that for a heartbeat.

He'd donned a too-short shirt, suit coat, and trousers that rode inches above his ankles. Still, he was the most adorable thing she'd ever seen. Tabitha had ordered him better-fitting clothing that hadn't arrived yet. "Is it not the gentlemanly thing to do?"

When he reached her, she fell into step beside him. "I could have managed on my own. Do the sisters know you came after me?"

"Once I suggested my plan to Livy, she thoroughly supported the idea. How is Icala's ailing wife?"

"She's expecting a baby and can't keep any food in her belly. Poor thing." Juliet had never pictured herself in such a condition. What if she fell in love, wed, and expected a child one day, only to orphan the little one?

The thought made her nauseous, much like Icala's wife, perhaps. No, she couldn't think about that. "What's happening back at the house?"

"When I left, Livy was beating Cy at checkers, and Tabitha was—"

"Reading a book."

"Indeed."

"And you?"

Gray shot her a look. "I was attempting to sketch the lettering on the sign for the tea shop but kept worrying about you."

Her brow rose. "Me?"

"Indeed."

The past week had been busy with construction inside the tearoom. Cy and Gray worked from well before daybreak to after dusk each evening, except on Sundays. Now that Icala had rearranged his schedule, he hoped to start helping with the construction too.

Although it had been evident to everyone that first morning that Gray had not known much about carpentry, he learned quickly under Cy's direction. By midweek, he'd been measuring, sawing, and hammering as if doing so his whole life. Was that the confirmation they had been waiting for that he was really Alex? Or was Gray merely a quick learner?

With him in the lead, they entered the wooded area, the temperature dropping and the light dimming. There were other routes home, though far longer than the one they now journeyed. Gray raised a branch high enough for her to pass underneath before releasing the springy limb.

Before he started forward again, he reached for her hand. "Holding hands . . . for safety's sake might be helpful."

She glanced down at where his fingers encircled hers. His skin was soft, cool, a perfect fit. "For safety, huh?"

"Precisely." Under the canopy of thick brush, his eyes seemed to challenge her, daring her not to pull away. "It is quite dangerous here."

"You're right." She lifted her chin and challenged him back. "I was frightened for my life the whole way to Icala's."

"I am told the raccoons and squirrels are actually vicious in this part of the woods."

"Is that so?" She tried not to smile, but it wasn't working well.

As he started forward again, she didn't pull away from him, but suspected she probably should.

A moment later, when she stepped too quickly down an incline and stumbled, his fingers tightened around hers. "Mind where you step."

"You do the same. We don't need you falling and hitting your head again."

He smirked over his shoulder. "Is that why you haven't tugged your hand free from mine?"

"Partly." Why hadn't she? Try as she might, she couldn't think of a single reason. "Honestly, why are you holding my hand? And don't tell me it's for my safety."

He shrugged. "I did not intend to. But you were so pretty standing there that I acted on impulse."

She was so pretty?

Her stomach fluttered with strange flips. Why had he paid her such a compliment now?

She wasn't the type who went around gripping hands with fellows. But maybe hand-holding was run-of-the-mill for him. With his good looks, he probably always had women eager to connect with him one way or another.

Should she slip her hand free? A part of her said yes, but the other part wanted to enjoy the private moment in the woods together. They seldom had time by themselves. "If we fail to return home in a timely manner, the sisters might hire a native scout, a bounty hunter, or the Royal Navy to track us down."

He chuckled. "I doubt it. Livy knows I came to protect you."

Juliet rolled her eyes, even though it wasn't mannerly. "I've managed on my own for years and years. I didn't need a hero then nor now."

"I am not saying you do." He flashed her a wry grin. "Although

I have no recollection of the occurrence, you rescued me from the woods. So if anyone is a hero or heroine, the title belongs to you."

"That's true."

He was quiet for several steps, then spoke again, this time more solemnly. "Nightfall shall arrive soon. For all we know, whoever stole my belongings and possibly bashed my head still roams the area, intent on robbing others. I want you to promise not to leave the house alone after dark, moving forward."

Slightly dumbfounded, she blinked. The man had a right to his opinion, but she had no intention of promising him anything—not today or tomorrow. And yet she knew he only had her best interest at heart. "It is not your place to tell me what to do. Besides, I can take care of myself. I've been doing just that for a very long time."

"I realize you are capable." Gray held another low-hanging branch as Juliet ducked underneath. "But whoever assaulted me is clearly dangerous. And I would feel better if you did not wander alone, especially in the woods."

"I pray whoever attacked you is long gone and never returns."

"Me too." But something in his voice said he didn't think that was likely.

Was it possible that whoever had harmed Gray in the first place might return to injure him again?

They exited the thick woodland a moment later and dusted pine needles from their shoulders and clothing. The lowering sun filtered through the web of trees, casting Gray's face in light and shadows. Had he ever looked more alluring?

Not in her eyes.

It wasn't one singular feature that attracted her to him. It was the combination of all his best qualities, especially his earnest eyes and how he always treated her so kindly.

Even so, no matter how much she liked Gray, she couldn't give in to her attraction to him. Not with his amnesia. Not while everything about his future was uncertain. Not so soon after the start of her new job. Not when the sisters were investing in her. And not when she was beginning to establish herself despite the threat of Ruby ruining everything.

Alone with Juliet on the edge of the woods, Gray told himself to keep his wits front and center in his thoughts. She tempted and distracted him without seeming to try. He brushed a stray pine needle from her headscarf. "All gone."

"I'm much obliged." Her voice was wry with the humor he loved about her. "I'd hate to return home bedraggled. What would the sisters think?"

That they had frolicked in the woods? Kissed underneath a pine tree? Lost themselves in each other's eyes and arms?

"I cannot imagine." They strode a few paces to reach a carriage pathway winding through Royal Park, across the street from their home. They strode past scattered trees, a cricket field, stone benches, and a wandering stream.

They needed a safe topic of conversation to keep his thoughts off his expanding attraction to her. Of course nothing was wrong with admiring her, but he preferred not to mislead Juliet. He had one primary goal—to uncover his past. Everything else could and would have to wait. "Have Tabitha and Livy relaxed their teaching methods a measure?"

"Mostly, though Tabitha is still stricter than Livy. But no complaints from me, and I am tremendously grateful. Before you know it, I'll be someone better."

His stomach muscles clenched at the word *better*. "Everyone on this side of heaven has imperfections. Becoming well-mannered doesn't make someone better, not deep down."

"You know what I mean."

Did he? "The lessons shall refine you and help you navigate polite society, but you shall always be you."

"Ugh."

His brow arched. "I cannot imagine why you said that. You are . . . wonderfully made."

After an eternity, she spoke quietly. "Are you simply nice to me because I rescued you?"

Was he? Partially, for certain. "At first, I suppose, but I have grown to like you for you."

"For me?"

"Indeed." Some may say she lacked finesse. But to him, her unpolished parts contributed to her character and made her unique. His intuition spoke loudly and clearly—he was not the type of man who gravitated toward sophisticated women who said all the right words at all the correct times.

Why? Perhaps because such a person, male or female, sounded rather dull. But where and when had he interacted with refined women to draw such a conclusion? The answer escaped him like many, many others.

"Before you and I met, my grandfather was the only man who'd truly rallied on my behalf. Like him, you're a decent man, Gray."

"A high compliment." He hoped she spoke the truth, but deep inside, he still felt disappointed, maybe even a failure. Why, specifically? Because he may have broken the law or for another reason? "I have doubts sometimes, but thank you."

"It's true. You are decent—most of the time." Her eyes glimmered with teasing. "Though I wasn't as convinced when we first met."

Despite her playful comment, a hollowness echoed inside him. He had not uncovered one concrete fact to confirm his identity, and far too few memories had sprouted. Questions tangled him in knots. Had he ever fallen in love? Had his heart broken? Did he dare open himself up to such opportunities again or for the first time?

Gray shoved his hands into his trouser pockets. When did a man with amnesia start to look forward instead of backward? And how would he know when to move on with his life? He had no idea, and likely nobody else did, either.

A stone bridge arched over a brook in the middle of the park, and they climbed the short ridge to reach the top. Water gurgled below, and the wind now carried a chill.

"I wish I had something warmer to offer you." He started to shrug out of his suit coat.

She stopped him with a touch to his arm. "I have my shawl and need nothing more since I donned a wool underskirt. It's adorable with red and black stripes, yet I cannot imagine Tabitha ever wearing it. For one thing, it's not brown. If you haven't noticed, that's her favorite color."

He had not. Of course, mentioning her underclothing, particularly to a single young man, was highly improper. But he was not the etiquette teacher, and she was not a student tonight.

They were equals.

She leaned over the bridge's side, her skirt riding higher to reveal her muddy shoes and pretty ankles. "The water isn't frozen yet, and I see a few geese, though they appear asleep."

Dragging his eyes from her hemline, he copied her stance. Their shoulders brushed, and neither of them pulled away. Big and little rocks lined the banks, the slumbering geese tucked between the stones for shelter. "Last night Icala identified these birds as Canada geese."

"Like Tabitha, he knows plenty about this and that." She paused. "From what I can tell, you're becoming good friends with Icala and Cy."

His brow rose. "It is not unlike our friendship. We are good friends too, are we not?"

"I like surrounding myself with a few good hearts instead of collecting too many acquaintances. Only a handful of people have fallen into the slot."

Was she slighting him, uninterested in pursuing a friendship? "I am unsure what else to call us."

"Two people who temporarily reside in the same house. Two lost souls. And two folks who help each other. Dad-blamed, Gray, you're right, though I've never had a male friend before."

He openly assessed her. The longer he stared, the warmer the night turned. He ran his hand over the back of his neck. "Sooner or later, the men in Everly, including the reverend, shall pound on the sisters' front door. After spending time in your presence, I suspect you shall linger on their minds for perhaps . . . forever."

She pressed her hand against her chest, perhaps her heart. "What are you saying?"

Had he admitted he had romantic notions about Juliet or only implied he thought other men might one day? As much as he longed to tell her he would never forget her, he could not. His life was too uncertain.

The best course forward was friendship. "I am simply saying I already count you as my friend, perhaps even more so than Icala or Cy."

They gazed at one another as a current snapped between them. Was he the only one who felt the chemistry, an indisputable tug in the other person's direction? Maybe. Either way, she had the most enticing lips and stood a breath away from him.

A fine-toned bell rang in the evening's stillness, and another chimed in tune, followed by more music. Juliet stepped backward a pace with her chin cocked. "Church bells are always so beautiful."

"I concur."

"Do they play a particular song? I think so." A few more notes echoed. "If I'm not mistaken, the ditty is called 'Home, Sweet Home.'"

In silence, they listened until Juliet sang the lyrics softly.

No more from that cottage again will I roam. Be it ever so humble, there's no place like home.

Juliet retied the scarf's knot underneath her chin. "A sailor on the bride ship sang this tune frequently on our journey, drumming up memories of my grandfather. At the end of his workday, he always said, 'Let's go home to the best place on earth.' And it was."

"A cherished memory, indeed."

"We resided across the road from a church." Melancholy threaded through her voice. "I fell in love with the bells. Grandfather often said on Sundays, 'God is calling us to church, Juliet. Let's not keep Him waiting.'"

Was that a tear in her eye? "I see how much you still miss him."

"Yes." She lightly placed her hand on his sleeve. "But I wonder who you miss."

He waited for a face, a name to enter his thoughts. But nothing resembling a memory arrived. "I shall table your question for a later date."

He glanced toward the sisters' house across from the park, though he could not see it from where they stood. "I hate to leave. However, I suppose we should be on our way."

"Of course. The sisters will want to know that we haven't taken a fancy to one another and lost all track of time." Juliet strode down the bridge's slope, her laughter ringing.

Gray, on the other hand, remained transfixed, then smiled at her cheekiness. As much as he wanted to rush after her and confirm what she just declared, at least on his part, to do so at this point would be unfair to them both.

Fifteen

*Of all the amusements open for young people, none
is more delightful and more popular than dancing.*

A KNOCK RATTLED ON JULIET'S BED-
room door, interrupting her daydreams about Gray and their
time together in the park one week ago. "Ten minutes until
your first dance lesson, dear," Livy called. "Are you excited for tonight?"

"Ugh," Juliet whispered before raising her voice, "overjoyed."

Holding her grandfather's journal, she crossed to the bureau,
reading the first line again. "Just as I am." What did it mean, and
why were the words important enough to record?

If only she could ask him. Instead, she slipped the little leather
book into the drawer and closed it. She wished she could tell him
about her time in Everly, things he'd probably never believe. Especially about all the manners she was learning.

Livy had taken the lead in the etiquette training, which recently included hotel behavior and accepting gentleman callers.

Surprisingly, each lesson had dozens of rules. Most likely, she'd never spend the night in a hotel. And though the reverend had asked to call on her, she'd told him she was too busy getting the tearoom ready.

Ruby still hadn't returned, and Juliet wasn't one speck closer to solving the blackmail problem. Obviously, she didn't have the jewels to hand Ruby. The only way to gather the funds was to steal them. Snakes alive, she'd never do that again.

An expensive teapot had gone missing from a storage crate in the workroom. Was it stolen, or had Livy absentmindedly misplaced the fancy item? She had a knack for forgetting where she placed things.

Juliet plopped on the bed and exchanged her shoes for a pair of black satin dancing slippers, compliments of Livy. Tonight, Gray would serve as her dance partner. She wished she could say she only thought of him as a brother or a cousin, but why lie to herself?

Yesterday she'd emptied a crate of dainty teacups packed with straw in the tearoom. Naturally she'd peeked at him as he stretched for a nail and noted how his biceps flexed when he hammered the little pegs. What young woman could ignore such things? Not any she knew.

She'd carried laundry to the washhouse the day before and observed him cutting firewood. She hadn't meant to gawk, especially after Livy caught her in the act. Juliet made an excuse, expressing concern for Gray's safety with the axe. Instead of a scolding, Livy confessed to falling head over heels for a stable boy growing up.

Fortunately, Juliet wasn't tripping over Gray.

She left her bedroom as he exited his, a long hallway between them. He had donned black trousers and a pale green shirt. Obviously, this clothing hadn't come from the mission or the attic, since the garments fit his form to distraction. She drew a settling breath as he moved to the top of the staircase.

For the record, a woman had the right to admire a man without being infatuated with him.

"Good evening, Miss Dash. I have not had the privilege of seeing you in ages." Gray's brow arched. "Or was it just before supper?"

Aah, the silly little banter ladies and gentlemen often exchanged. She dutifully nodded to acknowledge his greeting. "So formal, Mr. Sherwood, or whoever you are."

He smiled. "An excellent point, and it would be my pleasure to escort you down the staircase this evening."

Of course, she could manage her way to the drawing room on her own. But that wouldn't be ladylike, now would it? What was the proper response to his comment? A moment passed before the perfect reply dawned. "That would be kind."

"I trust you realize how lovely you look."

"It's the new dress. Livy brought it home from the mission for me to wear for tonight's lesson." The blue fabric hugged her curves more than Tabitha's castoffs and featured a lower neckline than she'd ever worn. She tugged a handful of cloth up toward her chin.

"The dress would be unflattering without you."

"I didn't realize you were prone to exaggerations, sir. Have you been nipping at spirits this evening?"

Gray laughed from his chest, a deep, pleasant rumble. "Not a drop. Shall we proceed to the lesson, miss?" He extended his elbow for her to link on to, and she did.

"Let's get this over with."

"Why the hesitation? Where I come from, people dance for amusement and fun."

"Hold on. You said *where I come from*."

"Only a figure of speech."

She nodded. "I've never danced, not even a jig. Thinking about embarrassing myself has me all tangled up."

"Allow me to help untie the knot. Perhaps I'm also unaccustomed to dancing, and we shall both trample each other's feet tonight."

When she glanced at his black shoes, Gray lifted her chin with his knuckle and held her gaze without saying anything. If she were a different type of woman, she might swoon.

"If not by the end of the first lesson, you shall undoubtedly be adept by the second." He lowered his hand. "If I am wrong, I shall forfeit my dessert tomorrow night, and you may claim it."

"I hope it's chocolate cake again."

"And I hope it is not."

Sometimes she wondered if Gray had her all figured out. He had a unique skill for making her more comfortable in uncomfortable situations like this one. "I'll try to enjoy the evening."

"I shall, as well."

He squeezed her hand still in the crook of his arm, and she quivered. Holy Moses. She had to stop acting like a lovesick girl at his slightest touch. Gray was just her friend and nothing more. Yes, he flirted at times and was more than a little handsome. But that was all.

They left the hallway and descended the staircase. Before entering the drawing room, she removed her hand from his arm. Someone had rearranged the furniture, opening space for dancing. Peaches whistled from her cage. Livy, Tabitha, and Cy mingled near the piano.

Grinning, Cy raised his hand in greeting. He'd tucked his shirt into his trousers and removed the gravy stain from his collar. "You remind me of my late wife, Juliet. With your blond hair pulled back from your face and wearing blue. It was her most flattering color, much like on you."

Another compliment, but coming from Cy, the praise had a grandfatherly note. "And you look dapper, as well, Mr. Kelly."

Cy winked at her. "It's sweet of you to notice."

Livy widened her arms, the sleeves of her dress loose and flowy. "Welcome, welcome to dance class. And you do look lovely, Juliet."

"It's kind of you to say so, ma'am. And you sisters spiffed up just right, as well."

Livy waved a turquoise feathered fan before her face. Still, sweat beaded on her upper lip, probably from rushing around searching for her misplaced etiquette book. "Thank you, Juliet. However, 'spiffed up just right' is not only a common term but unacceptable in polite society."

In a nut-brown dress that closely resembled the rest of her wardrobe, Tabitha nodded. "Please refrain from using it again."

"Of course. Thank you for making me aware of such things."

"I'm pleased you find our suggestions helpful." Livy pressed her precious manual against her chest, covering a sapphire brooch as big as a fist. Was the bauble as expensive as it appeared? Juliet sensed the answer was yes and prayed Ruby never got her hands on the jewel.

"Shall we proceed?" Tabitha pulled out the wood-carved piano stool, sat, and tugged the seat forward until her feet reached the pedals. "Livy and Mr. Kelly will demonstrate the dance steps first. Afterward, Juliet and Gray will have their turn."

Gray gestured to his head. "Due to my faulty memory, you may have two students learning to dance tonight instead of only one."

Was he speaking the truth or merely attempting to ease her awkwardness? She hoped for the second possibility and longed for him to recall dance steps and so much more. All the big things—his name, family, and home. And the smaller memories, like his first kiss.

Her trivial worries about making a fool out of herself dimmed in comparison.

Livy turned the pages in her trusty manual. "Thankfully, there is a whole chapter devoted to dancing. Isn't that sublime?"

Unfamiliar with the word's meaning, Juliet simply nodded.

"Let me see here." Livy turned another page, then cleared her throat. "'Dancing is a beneficial and popular amusement. It is to be performed with grace, ease, and modesty of movement.'"

"Wait one minute." Cy rested one hand on the piano. "Nobody mentioned gracefulness when you roped me into this lesson. I said I could dance, but I didn't say I had a lick of talent."

"My sentiments exactly." Gray slipped his hands into his trouser pockets.

"Nonetheless, we shall continue." Livy's cheeks were already flushed, giving her a youthful look. "'Never entertain a flirtation on the dance floor. Never romp. Never devote solitary attention to one individual. Never cross a dance floor alone if you are a woman. And if you only concentrate on your steps and carriage, you may be mistaken for a dancing instructor.'"

For Juliet, such a scenario wouldn't happen in a dozen leap years. "We can't have that, now can we?"

"Bravo, Miss Dash." Livy glowed as if Juliet had uttered something brilliant. "We expect you to learn the following dances— quadrille, polka, schottische, and waltz."

At the daunting task, Juliet's new and improved positive attitude and shoulders wilted. "All tonight?"

"Of course not." Tabitha straightened her music on the piano stand above the keys. "We'll start with the waltz."

"Come along, Mr. Kelly." Livy lowered her fan and manual to the small table next to where she stood before moving to the center of the cleared space. Her stiff crinoline expanded her skirt and narrowed her waist. "Let's show the young people the box step."

"By all means." Cy followed to where Livy stood and faced her, his posture more erect than his usual stoop. Since his gout had improved, he now walked with ease. "Will you allow me to lead?"

Livy smiled up at him sweetly. "Yes, because that is how a lady behaves, Mr. Kelly."

"I'm happy to hear it, Miss Sherwood."

Once they placed their hands in position for the dance, Tabitha's fingers stroked the piano keys. An unfamiliar yet pleasant tune filled the air. Cy waltzed Livy around the room as she continuously counted. "One, two, three, one, two, three." They rose onto their toes slightly, then dipped again as they glided around the open area.

The dance struck Juliet as easy enough, at least from the sidelines. The couple's movements and the music flowed until the song's crescendo and final note. She glanced at Tabitha and Gray. Should they applaud the stellar performance? When nobody else clapped, she clasped her hands instead.

Far too soon, she followed Gray onto the makeshift dance floor, now abandoned by their predecessors. Juliet considered nibbling on her fingernail but doggedly fought the urge. Gray's eyes lit with anticipation or amusement, and she wasn't sure which one.

"The leader shall now place his right hand on the follower's back or near her shoulder blade," Livy instructed. "Go ahead, Gray."

Even before his hand connected with the back of her dress, Juliet's silly heart increased to a wild beat.

"Now, follower, place your left hand on the leader's right shoulder or upper arm." Livy raised her hand to an imaginary partner to demonstrate.

With a shaky breath, Juliet placed her hand on Gray's shoulder. Unless mistaken, his muscles rippled under her touch. He had a handsome neck, thick and sturdy. The wound to his temple had left behind the start of a jagged scar, mostly hidden by his wavy hair.

"Superb," Livy continued. "Next, clasp your free hands at the chest or shoulder height."

Meeting her gaze, Gray cradled her hand. "Or you could say at the height of my heart."

Heart, for heaven's sake? Tonight had nothing to do with romance. If Gray thought to lighten the mood with his little quip, he'd fallen woefully short. Or was she the only one wrongly pairing heart and romance together?

And was she alone in thinking the sisters were practically shoving her into his muscular arms? Society had more illogical rules than logical, in her humble opinion. Besides, other than the dance after the open house, how much waltzing would she perform in the days to come? "How often does the average lady ordinarily dance in a year?"

Tabitha's brows knitted. "I'm certain it varies from woman to woman, though it's a fundamental skill for all young ladies. You must learn now because our dance won't have enough partners."

"I suspect you shall have a full-roster of men longing to dance with you, Juliet," Livy added.

Leaning his hip against the piano, Cy leafed through the music sheets. "Definitely."

Gray frowned and squeezed her fingers tighter than necessary before releasing her hand. What was wrong with the man?

Livy proceeded to explain the specific dance steps. They'd move in a square. Hence, the name box step.

They practiced the movements for several turns, and she was surprised by how much fun it was. A delightful surprise, to say the least.

Afterward, Gray released her. "I believe you are a natural, Juliet. I only hope I keep pace with you."

"False, and I look forward to savoring every crumb of your chocolate cake." Still, a small thrill of excitement warbled inside her.

Tabitha clapped her hands twice. "What is the first rule for dancing?"

Cy rested his elbow on the piano, his chin on his palm. "Somebody needs to say it, and I volunteer. The first rule Livy read is rubbish. No flirting on the dance floor takes away half the fun. Or perhaps all the fun. Am I right, Gray?"

Tabitha pursed her lips even more than she usually did.

"Completely." Gray's mouth quirked up into a playful smile.

The sight sent her heart into a tumble. His grins were always so charming. *He* was so charming. And too blamed good looking.

Tabitha began playing again, calling Juliet to straighten her carriage and ease back into Gray's waiting arms. Soon, they leaned into the rhythm and waltzed, though perhaps not as perfectly as Livy and Cy. The pulse of music led their steps.

"Gray, you're very good at this." Not for a minute did she think tonight was his dancing debut.

"I'm as surprised as you." His whisper tickled her ear.

She supposed dancing was far from horrible with the right partner. And Gray was definitely the right partner. He was patient, careful, and gentlemanly. She felt him studying her face from time to time. Whenever she gazed up at him and their eyes connected, her blood stirred with warmth.

The man knew how to hold a woman with strong hands and make her feel coveted and priceless. The closeness, the growing intensity, the feel of his hands on her—it all excited and scared her at the same time, so she kept her eyes mostly on his chest.

When the song ended, they broke apart, and Cy applauded. "It's almost as if the waltz was made for the two of you."

"Balderdash." Juliet swallowed hard, her eyes darting between Livy and Tabitha before turning to Cy. She swooped into an awkward curtsy before straightening. "Please forgive me. I meant to say, *Thank you, kind sir*."

Tabitha stood and covered her lips with her fingers, perhaps to hide a smile. "On that note, tonight's lesson draws to a close."

"Yes, indeedy." Livy tucked her manual under her arm. "Thank you, everybody, and I shall see you in the morning." With a nod, she crossed the room, humming.

"I look forward to it." Cy's eyes twinkled as he watched her depart, or maybe Juliet imagined the glint. Was he flirting with his dance partner?

Livy glanced over her shoulder, smiled enthusiastically, and resumed her exit.

What was happening? Regardless, it wasn't Juliet's concern. She had enough to tend with. Especially her climbing attraction to Gray, which swirled her thoughts as much as her heart.

Sixteen

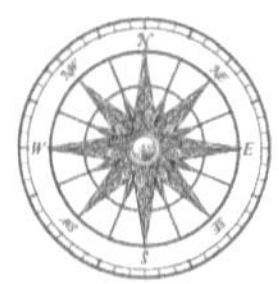

GRAY SPRANG OUT OF BED, HIS HEART pounding in his ears. A memory or a dream placed him in the middle of a confrontation. He closed his eyes, recapturing the image—sand, waves, the swing of a gun ramming his temple. Excruciating pain followed. And he recalled nothing more.

Real or a nightmare?

He dropped his face into his hands. If a genuine memory, did the image confirm he was a scoundrel, consorting with men who wielded guns? Heaven, please help him.

Wide awake and with dawn not far away, he lit a lantern and dressed. Thoughts of dancing with Juliet had kept him from falling asleep in the first place. Holding her in his arms was unforgettable. At least, he hoped it was.

He departed the room, then quietly descended the front staircase, starlight shining through the wide window above the door. There was no reason to rouse anyone else at the early hour, and his mind was still on Juliet. Her silken hair had carried a citrus scent, her skin felt breathtakingly soft, and her brilliant eyes were as enchanting as a fairy tale.

And her form . . .

When his foot touched the foyer floor, an envelope slid underneath the front door. Startled, he paused a moment. What in the name of heaven was going on? And who stood on the other side?

He rushed forward, picked up the paper, and quickly unlocked and opened the door. A cold December breeze rushed inside. He held up his lantern to find a small-built woman starting down the front step.

She paused in the darkness of the early morning hour. A dark hood enveloped the stranger's hair and much of her face. "Where is Juliet?"

"Juliet?"

"You heard me."

A warning bell clamored inside him. "Who is asking?"

"An old friend from Victoria." She pointed at the envelope in his hand. "Give her that and tell her it's urgent."

His muscles tensed, wary of the stranger. "What's your name?"

"You don't know me." She clearly had an American accent, so she couldn't be Willow or Daisy, the friends Juliet had made on the bride ship. Or Willow's sister Sage. Juliet hadn't talked about any other friends. But that didn't mean this woman was lying about the friendship.

Squinting, he peered deeper into the darkness and only spied a cat creeping in the yard. "Are you alone?"

"You don't see anyone besides me, do you? Come on, fella. I don't got all night."

Although he hesitated to involve Juliet, she brimmed with compassion and would offer aid if required, especially for a friend. "Proceed to the rear of the house, and I shall determine if she desires to converse with you."

The stranger cocked her head and studied him in silence. "You do that."

Gray watched her stalk away before he shut and locked the door. Then quietly climbed the staircase. The sisters' doors remained dark and closed—two small blessings. No need to awaken them and deprive the ladies of sleep.

In a few steps, he reached Juliet's room, where a soft glow came from underneath her not fully-closed door. The inappropriateness of going to her bedchamber jabbed at his chest, yet he ignored the stab. "May I speak with you a moment?" he whispered.

Footsteps pattered before she opened the door a notch more. "What's wrong?"

The intimacy of Juliet in her bare feet and cream-colored night-gown perked up his pulse. Her hair hung loose, falling over her shoulders and landing near her waistline. Her heart-shaped lips, a perfect cupid's bow, locked his attention until he raised his gaze to her blue eyes.

"Perhaps nothing." On the dance floor, she had smiled like an angel one minute, a vixen the next. She had fit perfectly into his arms as they waltzed around the drawing room.

Gray shook his head, regaining control of his wayward thoughts, and handed Juliet the envelope. "This is for you."

"Me?" Her brow cocked before she reached for his wrist and drew him more fully into the room.

"I am surprised you are awake."

She collected a shawl from a hook on the wall and tossed the knitted garment over her shoulders. "Why are you passing me a message? If you have something to say, go ahead."

"The correspondence is not from me. A woman came to the

door and wants to speak with you. She waits behind the house, though you need not go to her. If you wish, I shall ask her to leave."

She drew a sharp breath before cupping her hand over her mouth. Then she unfolded the paper and read the message, her lips silently moving.

A small fire and a lantern combined to light the room, her bedding in disarray. Had memories of dancing also kept her from slumber? Or was his notion nothing but vanity?

A fuzzy memory surfaced inside him—a letter, a room with a blazing fire in the hearth, and sadness. Nothing more. What did it mean? He had no clue and would need to postpone his pondering until later. Juliet required his full attention now.

"Holy Moses," Juliet whispered.

"What is happening?"

She tightened her shawl over her shoulders and hesitated for a moment. "Her name is Ruby O'Reilly. She swiped something from our old employer, hid it, and it went missing. Wrongly, she blames me." Squinting, she reread her correspondence before lowering the letter. "I can't understand all of her scribbles, but I puzzled out the main points."

He extended his hand. "Let me read it. Perhaps I can make sense of the message."

"No."

"Why?"

"It has nothing to do with you."

Their eyes locked. Then Juliet refolded the paper, tucked the slip down the front of her neckline, and lifted her brow to a challenging degree.

He blinked, not anticipating her hiding place. The odds of him hunting for the scrap stood at one and an infinite number. Unsure what to do with his hands, he stuffed them into his trouser pockets. "I insist on accompanying you."

"All right, but you can't listen to our conversation." She looked at the floor. "All of this, in a sense, is tied to my past, and I'd be ashamed if you ever knew the truth."

"I shall not judge you."

"You might."

He sighed. "I accept your terms, though you shall remain in my eyesight."

"So be it."

Their discussion had the faint ring of a negotiated business deal, but their agreement was more than a transaction. Juliet's safety and welfare were potentially at stake.

He waited in the hallway as she changed, and then they tiptoed down the back staircase, across the kitchen floor, and outside through the back door. He held his lantern up to find Ruby leaning against the trunk of a barren oak tree, as a sliver of light brightened the eastern horizon.

"I'll talk to you there." Juliet started across the grass, pointing toward the tearoom.

"Who's the fella?" Ruby straightened, and her stare remained brazen. "Your guard?"

"Never mind him." With the shawl slipping off her shoulders, she advanced toward her foe on determined steps. "He's no one."

No one? The knot in Gray's stomach tightened to a painful degree. He did not want to be a *no one* to Juliet.

He had been trying so hard to keep his growing feelings for her at bay, but at her easy dismissal, all those feelings rushed in to swamp him—desire, protection, and need. They swirled inside, hard and fast and strong.

How could he deny that she was becoming important in his life? The simple truth was, he could not.

Juliet's pulse pumped at full force. Had Ruby remained in Everly since they last saw each other? More importantly, was she about to seek revenge since Juliet hadn't located the money or the jewels?

Juliet paused near the teahouse and spun to face Ruby. "First of all, I don't have what you seek. Your letter mentioned your vengeance. Whatever it is, spit it out."

They locked gazes, and the tension grew heavy enough to pour into a pitcher. Finally, Ruby spoke again. "I ain't hair-brained. The jewels got to be somewhere."

"True, but they're not here."

"Iff'n you tell me where the Queen's brooch is, I'll leave you be."

Juliet released an exasperated sigh. "Just go away, Ruby. Please."

"Can't." Ruby's voice dropped to a menacing tone. "Fact is, if you don't hand over the jewels, then next time I'll be coming with my man. And he ain't happy with you."

From the fresh bruises on Ruby's face, he clearly wasn't happy with Ruby, either.

"He said to tell you he knows those ladies you're working for are rich, and he won't mind raising trouble for them."

Juliet winced. This was precisely what she'd dreaded—bringing danger to the sisters. "Please don't harm them. They've not wronged you."

Truthfully, neither had Juliet.

"Don't matter. I'm gonna have a young'un in the spring and need that money now more than ever."

Was it true? Ruby's cape hid her belly. Juliet wasn't so naïve to think a woman had to be married to find herself with child, but it undoubtedly helped. "I'm not offering to steal for you, but can I help you another way?"

Ruby stepped a pace closer, fire in her eyes. "You'll be helping me by fetching the money or the jewels. That's all I need from the likes of you. And don't go warning anyone or running to the constable. It'll only make matters worse."

"Worse? What could be worse?"

Ruby rapped her knuckles against the tearoom's wall. "Such a shame if this joint burnt until crispy."

Juliet gasped, and chills raced up her spine. She tightened her shawl to her neck. "You wouldn't dare."

"Watch me."

"Are you mad?"

"According to some folks, I suppose."

She could try to reason with Ruby, but her gut told her not to bother. Little by little, her strength seeped away, and she wrapped her arms around her shivering body. Tears threatened, but she fought to hold them back. "Leave."

Juliet turned toward the house, unable to look at Ruby a moment longer. Or to even breathe the same air.

"Next time I come, have it or else. . ." Ruby's hiss followed her.

Juliet didn't look back, only picked up her pace. A scrawny tabby cat sauntered through the yard, drawing closer until Gray stepped toward Juliet. The animal fled.

Had Ruby run off as well? Please, let it be so.

The first pastel shades of dawn had inched over the horizon, daylight ready to devour the darkness. Why couldn't the same scenario occur inside her? All she wanted was a better life.

Gray reached her, the brightening sky capturing his worried face. "What is happening?"

He guided her toward the back door, but instead of entering the house, she sat on the hard stone step, hoping the cool air would chill her feverish thoughts. What a disaster. It was like being homeless again after her grandfather died, not knowing what to do next. How would she solve her impossible problem this time?

Gray lowered himself to the spot beside her. "Are you sure you don't want to go inside where it is warmer?"

"Not yet." She couldn't return to her beautiful, shiny bedroom. She'd sit on the step and sort through her king-sized worry instead. There had to be a solution, didn't there?

"Shall we discuss what just transpired?"

"I'd rather forget it forever, forget her forever."

"How may I assist you?" Warmth radiated off his body.

She sidled closer to him. "I'm unsure anybody can." Silence gathered for a minute or two as she mustered her courage. "She's still accusing me of taking jewelry *she* stole. In particular, there was a brooch that once belonged to the Queen. Her man wants it and is threatening her over it. So now she's threatening me . . . and said next time she comes back, I need to have the jewels or the money they're worth. If not, she intends to steal from the sisters. She even threatened to burn down the tearoom."

Gray pinched the bridge of his nose. "You have to tell the local constable."

"Ruby warned me not to. But. . ." Juliet sighed. "You know how I feel about the law. Besides, the constable would probably take her word over mine."

"You do not know that."

In her gut, she did. Juliet loved that Gray believed in her innocence. But her association with Ruby left behind a dirtiness, something Juliet had tried to banish since her pickpocketing days. "I'm afraid you think less of me now, although you may not realize it yet."

"Absolutely not." Gray reached for her hand and clasped it firmly.

Warmth spread through her insides. From their first touch, he had awakened something inside her. It was almost an invitation to be vulnerable. And oddly, she nearly wanted to comply.

"If I am Alex Gray Sherwood, I am a criminal. Will you change your opinion of me after my identity is revealed or confirmed?"

"Of course not."

"Exactly, and you have not done anything wrong, Juliet."

The warm sting of tears hit the backs of her eyes, and she blinked them aside. But she had done a million things wrong in the past.

The stray cat returned and crept closer until it rubbed against Juliet's shins. Then leaped into her lap. Its rotting rubbish scent twitched Juliet's nose. Still, she petted the animal's mangy fur, a patch missing on her hindquarters. Was the cat unkempt because nobody had cared enough to shelter her?

Between not enough sleep—due to Gray waltzing through her thoughts after their dance—and the confrontation with Ruby, fatigue swept over her. She released another weary sigh. "I feel stuck. I try to improve myself but can't get a good footing."

"Until my amnesia abates, I am stuck as well, trapped between the past and present. Maybe I shall dwell there forever."

Now that he mentioned his dilemma, Juliet realized she had wedged herself into a similar slot—between long ago and the future. "I'm sorry."

He raised her hand and kissed her knuckles.

Hard to miss tingles climbed her arm. *Calm down.* Everyone knew gentlemen kissed the back of ladies' hands regularly. The intimacy probably meant nothing to him, yet it meant nearly everything to her.

"And I am sorry Ruby is trying to draw you into her troubles."

"*Trouble* happens to be my old friend." She absently rubbed the cat that now purred. "After my grandfather died, his landlord shooed me away. I slept in an alley at first, then in someone's cellar, though the owners didn't notice for months. In time, I moved to a church."

"A wise decision, was it not?"

"You'd think so, with the Bible preaching to help the downtrodden, but they forbade me from staying there."

Gray winced, then cupped her hand in both of his. The tenderness was like a healing ointment to her scarred soul. He was thoughtful, caring, and perhaps the type of man she could fully bare her soul to.

"Always I scrounged for food. Then one day, I stole an apple from an old merchant's full cart. In my mind, he had plenty to spare. Like most folks, he paid me no mind and didn't notice."

"You had to eat." His tone was matter of fact, not judging in the least.

"I told myself that same thing. Soon I met a girl who introduced me to a Mr. Lanker, who offered shelter and safety."

Gray stiffened. "In exchange for what?"

"Pickpocketing. I had a knack for nicking things, big and little—everything from food to jewelry. The night that ended my career, I'd chosen an elderly lady as my mark, and for a good reason. Her flashy necklace sparkled like a million stars at midnight. I could almost hear Mr. Lanker praising me after I handed him the goods."

Juliet's muscles tensed as she pictured the incident. A dusting of midsummer moonlight. Guests moving like cattle toward the street after a night of dancing. A kindly woman smelling like apple blossoms. "I pretended to fall and cry, and the gentle lady bent to assist me. It was sweet of her, really."

"Indeed."

"I snagged her emerald in two seconds flat. As I dodged the crowd, a fistfight broke out. One man's right hook sent his opponent hurling against my shoulder, knocking me into a constable."

"Then what happened?"

The lawman hauled me to the orphanage. I attempted to run away twice, but I was caught, beaten, and broken both times."

Gray hugged her shoulders as the door behind them creaked open, and they sprang to their feet, the cat jumping down.

Cy stuck his head outside, his hair still unruly from slumber. Stocking-footed, he held a magazine under his arm. "You two better get inside. Tabitha is up for the day."

Gray nodded at Cy. "Thank you for the warning."

Once alone again, Gray reached for Juliet's shoulder and

squeezed. "You are not alone, Juliet. We shall solve this problem together."

She hadn't intended to confess so much, not for a minute. But he was a good listener. Somehow, he offered reassurance and safety, exactly what she needed most.

"I shall distract Tabitha while you slip up the back staircase." Gray opened the door and headed inside.

She tarried outside a moment longer. Her hands had grown cold and stiff, so she stuffed them in her skirt pockets. As her fingers brushed Ruby's note, her heart sprinted. She'd shoved the tattered paper inside after changing out of her nightgown.

What she touched was more than a scrap of paper.

She possessed evidence.

Seventeen

Politeness is very essential to the right transaction of that great business of a woman's life, shopping.

HOW DARE RUBY BLACKMAIL JULIET? Ever since the upstart had left the lawn at dawn, Gray had thought of little else while laboring in the tearoom.

He slammed his hammer against a nail, driving the little piece of iron into the floor. Then he leaned back on his haunches and reached for another. When his fingers found nothing, he turned for a closer examination, wiping his brow with his sleeve. "Are we out of nails?"

From the top of a ten-foot ladder, Icala examined the new ceiling. "You'll have to ask Cy."

"Where is he?"

Icala twisted around, a wrench poking out of his shirt pocket. "It is three o'clock. Therefore, he is in the library for mid-afternoon tea with the sisters." Icala wriggled his brows and grinned. "My hunch is he's sweet on Livy."

What? Not in a dozen years would Gray pair the two. Perhaps their waltz had sparked a romantic interest in one another. Dancing with Juliet had nearly started a wildfire inside him. But Livy and Cy? "Some claim opposites attract."

With his eyes on the ceiling, Icala said, "Are you referring to Cy and Livy—or you and Juliet?"

Gray smiled at the good-natured jesting but refused to admit or deny anything. As much as his attraction to Juliet had grown recently, he continued to rein it back as much as possible—which truthfully grew more challenging with every passing day. Not even reminding himself of his ready-made life somewhere awaiting his return helped to contain his feelings for her.

Was he to live in limbo forever? Merciful heavens, he hoped not. But if his memories never returned, when was the right time to move on and build a new life? And what would such an endeavor resemble? Would it include Juliet? Had she meant what she told Ruby this morning, stating he was *no one*? Or was she merely trying to protect him from the wily thief?

He stood and dusted down his trousers, then scrounged for nails, lifting a tarp and digging through a barrel. After searching the entire room without success, he paused to assess their progress with the conversion. The place was transformed a little more with each passing day.

The walls were in place, a new floor was nearly complete, and Icala hoped to finish the lower ceiling by tomorrow. They had designated a location for the new stove, attached a sideboard to the far wall, and added a door to the back storage area. Next, they'd paint the walls. But only if the sisters finally agreed on the color.

The satisfaction of working with his hands and building something out of nothing had seeped into Gray's bones. Whether Alex Sherwood or not, he had discovered a profession to love and a direction to follow. But would he change careers if a different livelihood awaited his return one day?

Icala descended the ladder and set it against a bare wall. "Find what you seek?"

"Not even a broken one. I shall ask the boss, though I hesitate to interrupt his tête-à-tête."

Icala laughed, squatted, and riffled through the box's assortment of tools. "Better you than me, my friend."

Chuckling, Gray left the tearoom and followed the cobblestone path to the house as the sun rolled toward the western horizon.

Ahead, Juliet placed a saucer of milk on the back step and waved at him. "How is it going in there?"

"Making headway. How is your day?" As much as he wanted to discuss Ruby's early morning visit, specifically the part where Juliet needed to inform the constable, he had to ease into the conversation.

"Fair to middling." She rose and glanced around the yard scattered with dried and dead leaves. "Have you seen Bells?"

"Who?"

"The stray cat."

"Not since she sat in your lap this morning." He glanced at Juliet's fingers, so small compared to his, and recalled kissing the back of her hand hours earlier. Was he a fool for doing such a thing? If so, he could tolerate the moniker. What he had hoped to do was offer comfort and help her feel less alone.

Thoughts of her tragic childhood still consumed him. How had she not fractured under the strain? And now Ruby lobbed another threat to the life Juliet had painstakingly established. One way or another, he had to protect his friend.

"No doubt Bells is scared and hungry." Juliet reached for the door handle. "Hopefully by the time I return from the emporium, she'll have lapped up every drop."

"What draws you to the shop?"

"I'm fetching a teapot the sisters ordered all the way from China."

He held open the door and waited for her to proceed before him. "I am on my way to consult with Cy regarding the lack of nails. I understand he converses with Livy in the library."

Juliet grinned. "I'm starting to think something brews between them."

"You sound like Icala." He followed her inside and down the hallway, the sway of her hips a little too mesmerizing. When he reached the library, he almost continued to follow Juliet to the foyer, where she was gathering her coat and hat. But he stepped into the inviting library of bookshelves and green plants, including a row of bluish African violets on a stand before a corner window.

Livy and Cy conversed on the sofa, their backs to him. No sign of Tabitha.

Gray cleared his throat, and they turned in his direction, nearly bumping noses. Livy hopped to her feet, her teacup clattering as she set it on the table. Her cheeks had pinkened. "Tabitha just left to fetch her reading glasses from her room. She'll be back any minute."

Had the couple developed tender feelings for one another? Everyone deserved happiness. "Pardon me, but I believe we are out of nails."

Cy placed his delicate floral teacup on the saucer in his hand, biscuit crumbs on his chin. "Give me a minute or two, and I'll head out and fetch more from Haney's Hardware."

"Stay and enjoy your tea while I collect them myself." Was it not a perfect excuse to speak privately with Juliet as they traveled in the same direction?

He excused himself, hurried to the foyer, and claimed a bowler from the coat tree, perching it on his head. Tabitha had cited having accounts at businesses downtown, eliminating the need for cash transactions—an ideal scenario since he had no coin to toss in the air.

Outside, he chased after Juliet in a gentlemanly yet hurried clip down the long hill leading to Main Street. A panoramic view sat before him—the city, the river, and primarily trees on the uninhabited other side. Near the wharf a half dozen men unloaded goods from a paddle wheeler. Trees overhung the riverbanks, and fringes of green sedge skimmed the edges. The town's new sawmill buzzed in the distance, the heavy scent of pulp floating in the air.

Quickly, he closed the gap between Juliet and himself, matched his stride to hers, and tipped his bowler. "Greetings, miss."

A large maroon hat with a wide brim covered her head, most likely a cast-aside from one of the sisters. Yet it was too plain for Livy's taste and too large for Tabitha's.

"A cautious lady would think you followed her."

"Goodness, no. I am merely on an errand for nails. You are a happy coincidence." Was she really, though? Of course not.

She laughed, the sound soft and warm.

Lately, he'd been finding one excuse after another to seek her out. There was no sense denying it, at least to himself.

"I'm suspicious of your motives."

"I cannot imagine why." He reached for her elbow to guide her around a divot in the road, then released her arm.

"What's on your mind, Gray? You have that look about you."

What look? Could she read him that well? "I believe telling the legal authorities about Ruby's threat is in your best interest. The constable should hear the truth from you before she fills his head with lies."

Halfway down the hill, she halted, her brows furrowed. "Dealing with constables is tricky. Plus, who has had more run-ins with the law? You or me?"

As far as he knew, she only had one encounter. "Me, perhaps."

She patted his sleeve. "I'm sorry. That was thoughtless of me. But at least I have the note Ruby wrote me."

"Aah. Evidence."

"Maybe." They resumed walking. "I'm thinking about telling the sisters tomorrow."

"Why not today?"

"Usually, I rush forward willy-nilly, and it's time to stop behaving rashly." She paused, then heaved a sigh. "The truth is, I'm afraid I'll lose my job over this."

"Tabitha and Livy adore you. They would never fire you over something that is not your fault."

She nodded, though not convincingly. "Either way, I don't want to put them in danger. And that's exactly what my presence in their home will do."

"We do not know that for certain." Yes, Ruby had made threats, but surely they could find a way to stop her if they worked together. "When you speak with the sisters, I shall gladly accompany you."

They had reached the bottom of the hill, and she softly smiled. "Thank you. This is where we part, and I will see you later."

He tipped his hat and watched her approach the emporium, a stand-alone structure across the street. The white two-story building featured black trim and three empty benches beneath the same number of windows on the front porch. Huckleberry Emporium was written across the upper level in bold print.

A wide, weed-filled footpath to the shop's right led to the Fraser River. The words Haney's Hardware scribbled on a board leaned against the outside wall of a square log-built building next door.

After entering, Gray requested the nails from a friendly shopkeeper on duty. They conversed about the mild weather and the price of hammers before he reentered the sunshine with his purchase in tow. When he glanced at the emporium, he discovered Juliet sitting on a front wooden bench, her shoulders slumped with apparent dejection.

His muscles tightened with the need to comfort her and make everything better. Suddenly, a new memory flashed through his thoughts of a girl crying. No, she was sobbing, and he was ignoring her. Another fellow knelt beside the girl, trying to ease her pain while shouting angry words at Gray.

His heart raced at the vividness of the memory, even if the faces were blurry. The same strange despair he had felt previously pulsed to the surface. Who was the sobbing girl of his past that he had ignored? Had she been a sister? A friend? And the fellow? A brother? Or another friend?

He did not know, nor could he place them. But one thing was quite evident—that he had been a selfish and insensitive cad in his former life. Although he had sensed this possibility before, he could no longer deny the truth.

Nor could he ignore Juliet, who required his full attention now as she wept. He would have to ponder the new revelation about himself later.

Juliet stood and tried to drag in a breath that would chase away her insecurities, but with the fancy new teapot in the basket at her side, she could only think about Ruby's threat to torch the tearoom.

It was one thing to face danger herself. She'd confronted it often enough throughout her life that it was no stranger. But she couldn't bear to bring harm to the sisters. Should she move on before she did so?

Yet the thought of leaving this place and the ladies wrenched Juliet's heart, bringing a sharp pain to her chest. She had already lost so much that she'd loved in her life. How could she bear to lose more?

"Juliet?" Gray's call drew her attention. Concern etched his handsome face. "Is something amiss?"

Gray. The pain in her chest radiated, and she nearly wobbled. She couldn't leave him, either. Absolutely couldn't. Her heart wouldn't survive losing his friendship, at least not easily.

"It is obvious that something troubles you." He gestured toward a footpath running between the emporium and the hardware store. "Let us find a private place to talk, shall we?"

Even though sweeping and mopping the kitchen before supper still waited for her back at the house, she followed Gray down a well-trodden route to the water, a chilly breeze swaying the long weeds. Soon, they sat side-by-side in the dried and withered grass on the riverbank in the shade of a paint-peeled fish shanty. The basket with the new teapot, the nails, and the borrowed hats sat beside them on the ground.

A steamboat chugged past. Alongside and behind it, natives paddled two canoes. Had Ruby left town this morning on a vessel? Or did she still linger in Everly?

"Will you tell me what is discouraging you, though I assume the answer is Ruby?" Gray leaned back on his elbow, the breeze teasing his thick hair as he ran his splayed hand through the dried grass.

She'd lost people and homes before, and she'd survived. If she had to move on, she would survive again, wouldn't she? She leaned back into the grass on her side next to him. The loamy earth filled the air as she propped her head with her hand.

"Tell me." His voice was soft and pleading and much too hard to resist.

"Has anyone informed you that you are good at issuing orders?" She tried for a lighter tone.

"Has anyone ever told you that you excel at diverting the subject when it suits you?"

She smiled, already starting to feel better. "Has anyone informed you that you're good at helping distract people from things they don't want to think about?"

"I can be quite distracting, can I not?" He smiled in return, laying on all the charm she'd grown to love about him. "I think I am the king of distractions, if I may boast."

"You may."

Even though he was sprawled out beside her with his legs crossed casually, he still had an aura of power and authority that seemed inborn to him. She loved the way he carried himself with confidence and determination. Even now he watched her as though he had every right to look at her for however long he wanted.

"Would you like me to continue to distract you?" His gaze danced across her face and landed on her lips.

Was he insinuating that he would kiss her? Certainly not. He wouldn't be so brazen, would he?

Her gaze fell upon his lips—his fine, fine lips that looked both impossibly hard and soft at the same time. How might they feel brushed against hers?

She was suddenly breathless. "What distraction do you have in mind?"

"What distraction would you like?" His lids lowered just a little, and he smirked as though he knew exactly what she'd just fantasized about.

Her heart tapped faster. "Perhaps you can sing me a song? Or tell me a story?"

"I could." He rolled onto his side before leaning closer so their bodies were now parallel, not touching but close. "Or I could distract you with something I am more exceptionally skilled at."

This game they were playing was sending sparks through her belly. "And what is this exceptional skill?"

"Let me show you." His gaze landed upon her lips with a finality that nearly made her swoon. He leaned in even more until his mouth was only an inch from hers, close enough to feel the warmth of his breath. He waited, clearly allowing her to back away.

She closed her eyes and angled toward him.

In the next instant, his mouth surged against hers. Deliciousness swept through her. His kiss was just as powerful as she'd imagined, but gentle too. She tasted the spiciness of cloves and the sweet taste of possibilities.

She suddenly wanted to explore his neck and cheek with her fingers, but they had to stop. It wasn't proper. And after all her training on the topic, she couldn't fail now.

She broke away, wanting to shove him playfully and bring their relationship back to what it had always been and where it belonged. But he held her arms and pressed his forehead against her brow, each of his breaths labored and filled with a desire that almost made her tremble.

Slowly, he dragged his hand down her sleeve before they sat up and straightened their clothing silently.

After a moment, he cleared his throat. "I am sorry, Juliet—"

"Please, don't be." She scooted away from him, closer to her hat. What was more awkward—talking about their kiss or ignoring it altogether? Probably, even odds. "Let's forget what happened."

"Highly impossible. For all I know, that was my first kiss."

She smiled. He had known precisely what to do with his lips a moment ago. "Highly unlikely, is what I'm thinking."

Something told her he'd kissed his share of young women in ballroom shadows and on quiet moonlit strolls. But she liked the idea and the sweetness of being his first. Hers was forgettable and with a boy she never saw again afterward.

Juliet examined the river's bend, where a fallen log trapped everything in its path, making it impossible for the wedged debris to change course and break free. As much as she hoped God would intervene in her life, would He?

She barely knew how to ask for help anymore. Without practice, a person turned rusty, even with prayers. Was it time to start praying again? Could God help her clear out all that was broken in her life so she could be free from the debris?

Whatever the case, she couldn't linger on the riverbank with Gray. If someone had spotted the two of them kissing and the news reached the sisters, they would be mortified. In fact, she was mortified just thinking about how appalled they would be.

She stood and wiped the grass from her garments and shifted her messy skirts into place with a wiggle. When she glanced at Gray, he was grinning. "You look happy."

"For good reason. Your state of disarray and your apparel adjustment method deserve a smile."

Unsure how to reply and all fluttery inside, she collected the basket and hat from the ground, wheeled around, and worked her way back toward the road. Her poor heart was in trouble. Big, fat, unstoppable trouble. As much as she'd liked the kiss with Gray, it couldn't happen again.

Eighteen

DON'T PANIC. YET JULIET SIZZLED LIKE lit fireworks, ready to explode inside the library. She fanned her face with her hand. The proper words to explain Ruby's blackmail still eluded her, and time was running out to capture them.

Seated on a floral sofa, she and Gray occupied one side of a long, mahogany coffee table, and the sisters lounged on a matching settee on the other. Tabitha held a book in her lap, and Livy recited a long-winded report on various teas worldwide.

Cy had retired to the sitting room with a head cold. Or he'd heard enough about tea for one day—or a lifetime.

Livy paused her recitation and looked at them. "More tea?"

Everyone declined.

A hearty fire in the hearth sizzled, the curtains drawn for the evening. Every inch of Juliet longed to postpone the upcoming conversation. But the sisters deserved the truth, especially since Livy had called her *almost family* that day after church.

And family looked out for each other, didn't they? Anyway, that's what she'd heard and somewhat remembered.

Her pulse refused to slow, even a notch. She'd thought of little else since Ruby's arrival early yesterday. Well, she'd also relived Gray's unforgettable kiss over and over in her mind, even though she'd tried not to.

Again, he sat beside her, ready to proclaim her innocence to anyone within earshot. Not long ago, he'd stated he wasn't a hero, an evident mistruth. What more could a woman want from a . . . friend?

When Livy drew a breath between sentences, Juliet spoke. "I have something important to share."

Tabitha closed her thick book and rested it in her lap. She removed the glasses perched on her nose and set the wire-framed pair atop the book. Were they new? Did it matter? "Then I suggest you go ahead."

Juliet opened her mouth to speak, then clamped her lips shut. More hot guilt crackled through her, and she shoved up her sleeves. Maybe it was due to her thieving past, or was it because Ruby's accusation cast doubt on Juliet's character? Probably, both reasons were correct.

Praying her voice wouldn't wobble, she forced herself to open her mouth again. "I believe Mrs. Moresby explained the troubling incident at the Firth residence, where I previously worked."

"I assume you're referring to the—" Livy's gaze shifted from Juliet to Gray. "Is this conversation for everyone's ears?"

"He already knows everything I'm about to say, or mostly, anyway."

If her announcement surprised either lady, she couldn't tell, based on their straight faces.

Gray crossed his knees and leaned forward. "Indeed, I do. After

Juliet speaks, I would like to help formulate a plan. Naturally, we all desire what is best for her."

The sisters exchanged worried glances.

Undoubtedly, she was on the brink of upsetting the ladies. If she could spare them the distress, she'd gladly do it. But how? "Ruby O'Reilly, my former roommate, blames me for a crime I believe she committed."

"Juliet is innocent," Gray blurted.

"Completely innocent," she added. "If you want me to swear on a Bible, I will."

He sent her a quick, encouraging smile. "Your word is enough. No reason to take a sacred oath."

"Indeed." Tabitha pursed her lips. "I recall our letter exchange with Mrs. Moresby before we hired you, but I don't believe we've heard why Miss O'Reilly blames you, Juliet."

"It's hard to know for certain. We were roommates, and I caught her stealing and tattled on her. Plus, I've seen her with a black eye several times. I think she works for her man, who pressures her to steal a certain number of valuables. When she doesn't, she's in big trouble."

"Oh my goodness." Livy fell back against the cushion.

"Plus, she's expecting a baby, which is a whole other kind of predicament."

Wide-eyed, Tabitha sat stiffly.

"If I don't give her what she desires or an equal amount of money, she'll seek revenge."

The sisters said nothing, probably stunned into silence. But Livy's face had turned two shades paler, and Tabitha had barely moved a muscle. Then she raised her chin. "Did this Ruby character send you a letter about her plans? Or have you known about them since you arrived in Everly?"

The grandfather clock struck ten o'clock, reminding Juliet she'd put off this conversation as long as possible. Too bad she couldn't have postponed it forever. "She delivered her message by hand shortly before dawn yesterday." Juliet dug into her pocket, then handed Tabitha Ruby's note.

"Miss O'Reilly was here?" Livy's voice brimmed with disbelief as she leaned closer to her sister, trying to read over Tabitha's shoulder. "At our home?"

If Livy thought Ruby's trespassing on the property was worrisome, wait until she learned the blackmailing details. Juliet wiped her hands on her skirt. "We spoke outside, and Gray stood in the yard the whole time."

"In the middle of the night?" Tabitha stood, and the items in her lap clattered onto the floor.

Gray quickly retrieved the book and eyeglasses. "Daylight was breaking, and nothing untoward occurred." He then set the items on the coffee table as they returned to their seats.

Juliet could feel Gray's eyes upon her, but she didn't look at him. She'd purposefully avoided gazing at him directly since the kiss yesterday. Although most of their interactions had been casual and as teasing as she could make them, she sensed something had shifted between them—something charged and intense.

Instead, Juliet forced herself to keep going despite her insides trembling. She feared she was about to lose everything in Everly. And she desperately wanted to hang on to every last bit. "I don't know what *untoward* means, but Cy saw us out there, and he will vouch for Gray and me."

"Cy is involved with this . . . mess too?" Livy's voice screeched. Surprisingly, the man didn't come rushing in from the sitting room based on her high-pitched voice.

Tabitha waved the tattered paper in the air. "According to this message, Miss O'Reilly came specifically to unveil her threat. Now would be a good time for you to tell us exactly what that looks like."

This was it, the moment Juliet dreaded most. She inhaled twice.

"If I don't do what Ruby wants, she'll steal your valuables." She squeezed her eyes shut. "And maybe torch your tearoom."

Someone gasped, probably Livy, or maybe the woman had fainted. Juliet opened her eyes and found the sisters holding hands, staring at one another. "Go ahead and fire me if you want. If I was you, that's what I'd probably do."

Gray shook his head firmly. "How could you leaving possibly help this situation, Juliet? It would not, and again, you have done nothing wrong."

Her chest had grown so tight it was difficult to breathe. "I brought trouble to the sisters' doorstep. If I disappear, maybe the Ruby problem will too."

Tabitha rose and moved to the secretary against the wall, speaking over her shoulder. "Not for a minute do I believe Miss O'Reilly will get away with her scheme. Although this news is alarming, I respect that you trust us with this information, Juliet. You could have fled and not said a word."

A pinch of relief stirred inside her. The last thing she'd expected was Tabitha to express gratitude. But had the elder sister ever held a grudge? "How could I not tell you? She threatened your home and your livelihood. It's . . . wrong."

Livy sipped her tea, undoubtedly lukewarm by now. "How shall we proceed?"

"Step one," Gray said, "is to alert the legal authorities." When Juliet opened her mouth to protest, he extended a feather-light touch to her sleeve. "Now that you have informed the sisters, it is time to involve the law. Shall I collect the constable or accompany you to his office in the morning, Juliet?"

"Shouldn't we all be present for this conversation?" Livy asked. "At this point, we're all involved."

Tabitha returned to stand beside the sofa, holding a brass magnifying glass. "Why don't you and I speak with Mr. Blake first,

Liv. He has a firm hand and reputation for upholding the law, and people consider him fair."

The good Lord knew she didn't want to accompany the sisters to the law office, but maybe she should. "Won't he want a description of Ruby?"

"Most likely," Tabitha said. "However, you're our charge, and I prefer we speak with him first." She bent over Ruby's note and examined it more closely.

"Whatever are you doing, Tabby?" Livy was watching her sister with wide, curious eyes.

"I'm intently examining Miss Ruby's note. I'm hoping to find a clue, perhaps."

Livy nodded. "The good news is we have a gun on the premises, should anyone need it. It's cleverly tucked inside our piano stool."

Odd, but so be it. Juliet leaned back, but relief refused to flow. Telling the sisters about Ruby had gone better than she'd expected. As usual, they were understanding and kind, almost too good to be true . . . Yet they were genuine through and through.

It might kill her to put them in harm's way. But how could she keep them safe? Should she leave and never return? Even if that was the best plan, how could she walk away from them forever, not to mention Gray?

Nineteen

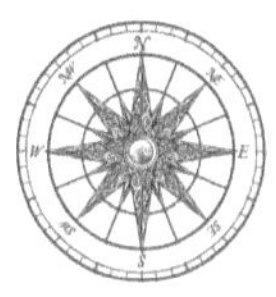

"Juliet, you're spilling tea." Livy hopped up from her chair at the kitchen table and stepped back a pace.

Unaware of her terrible aim and caught daydreaming about kissing Gray three days ago, Juliet jerked her hand to raise the spout. Then she spun and deposited the china pot onto the sideboard before grabbing a nearby towel and sopping up the mess. "I'm sorry, and I don't know what's gotten into me."

That wasn't entirely true. She had too much on her mind, but now wasn't the time to let her thoughts spin in all directions. Livy was teaching her to pour afternoon tea properly, and it was disrespectful not to pay attention.

"It's fine, dearie, and you didn't spill much." Livy carried her matching cup and saucer to the sideboard. "Sometimes I dribble tea down the front of my dress. It's a nuisance."

Juliet's heart warmed at Livy's attempt to minimize the mistake. She wiped her hands on her skirt as she turned around. "Thank you for trying to make me feel better."

The sisters had spoken with the constable yesterday and told him everything they could. Then he came to the house as she'd expected. They all met in the drawing room, including Cy and Icala. With Gray at her side, she'd described Ruby's appearance and relayed everything else memorable.

The incident wasn't as horrific as she'd expected or feared.

"No harm done, and we'll have another lesson tomorrow." Livy removed her deep rose cape from the back of a chair and tossed it over her shoulders. "I'm off to check the men's progress this fine afternoon. They're finally painting the walls a lovely pink today."

They could have done so sooner if someone hadn't taken forever to select the color. "An exciting step."

A new shipment of cups with a dozen broken handles had arrived, though everything else in the delivery remained intact. However, there wasn't time to order replacements, with the tearoom's opening less than a week away. The recently installed stove in the carriage house failed to produce heat, and a window broke when the head of a hammer flew through the pane.

The celebration would arrive before she knew it, and she hadn't determined what to wear. To purchase a ready-made dress was frivolous, and she'd have to wear one of Tabitha's castoffs. But it would have been a pleasure to wear something special to the party. It shouldn't matter, but it did.

Livy hastily donned her hat. "It's all just so lovely, so lovely. So much more than I ever imagined. A dream come true, really."

When the door closed behind the sweet sister, Juliet slid into the nearest chair and slumped. With every passing day that the tearoom neared completion, Juliet worried that might be the day

Ruby returned and set the place on fire, destroying the weeks of labor and the sisters' dreams. With every passing day that the sisters continued to make Juliet a part of their family and showered her with their kindness, she only felt guiltier for the danger creeping closer to their doorstep.

"Oh, God." She lifted her prayer heavenward, hoping it wouldn't get stuck this time. "I don't know what to do."

Would it be better for everyone, even her, if she snuck away before it was too late?

A loud knocking resounded on the front door. "Please, don't let it be Ruby again."

Juliet stood, tugged down her cuffs, gave her skirt a good fluff, and hurried to answer the call. She summoned her best ladylike smile and swung the door open.

Two men she failed to recognize stood before her. "May I help you, gentlemen?"

The taller man wore a brimless black hat and an open smile. The other fellow gripped a shiny ebony walking cane in one hand and a satchel in the other. A gray, moody sky dribbled rain over their shoulders.

"And you are . . . ?" The first fellow asked.

"Juliet Dash. And your name, sir?"

"Alexander Sherwood."

Holy Moses. She reached for the door to hold herself steady. Gray was Alex Sherwood, wasn't he? They all believed it true—or perhaps wanted to believe it. He was building a new life here, and now the walls threatened to crumble if this stranger was who he claimed.

But why would this fellow lie?

"This is my business associate, Mr. Nashua." Alex motioned at his companion.

Juliet nodded to the man, yet he remained stoic. Now that she thought about it, neither fellow had doffed their hats for her. How ungentlemanly.

"May I speak with one or both of my aunts?"

"Of course. Tabitha is next door visiting a neighbor, and Livy is in the tearoom. Would you care to step inside?"

"Yes, and I have no preference on which one you collect. One aunt is as good as the other, but please hurry. I have a ship to catch."

Juliet retreated a pace as the men entered the foyer. They chose to keep their hats and walking stick in their possession as she led them to the drawing room. Why had the supposed nephew not commented on the carriage house renovations or mentioned his regrets for not lending his carpentry skills?

Had he never intended to assist with the project?

If so, how rude. Gray made a better and nicer Alex. Maybe they should keep him and get rid of this fellow. If only they could.

The men had barely settled into side-by-side chairs, and she was about to offer them tea when the front door creaked and opened again. Was the wind to blame? "Excuse me, please."

Juliet retraced her steps to the foyer, where Tabitha was hanging her overcoat on the hook. "You'll never believe who came to the door, and he's in the drawing room."

"Then you certainly should tell me."

"He says he's the real Alex Sherwood."

Slowly, Tabitha turned, her bluish-green eyes wide and full of surprise. "Oh my stars."

"Uh-huh. Another man is with him. Should I fetch Livy or offer them refreshments first?"

"I'm slightly in shock." Tabitha tapped a finger against her pursed lips as if deep in thought, then she gazed into the wall mirror and tamed her windblown hair with her hands. "Please collect Livy, and we'll proceed from there."

"Absolutely." Juliet didn't bother to run upstairs for her shawl. Instead, she headed directly outside toward the tearoom and let the cold, misty air nip at her skin, which was good because she was suddenly hot and riled.

Poor Gray. How would he feel when he learned the identity foisted upon him might belong to someone else? Of course, that possibility had always existed, but over the past week or two, they'd all seemed to accept that's who he was. Undoubtedly, the discovery would upset him. The news would fluster everyone.

Would Tabitha and Livy kick him into the street since he wasn't their flesh and blood? Of course not. They'd allowed her and Cy to reside under their roof. Then again, Gray might think living elsewhere would be best.

Juliet's heart beat furiously as she hurried up the cobblestone, raindrops tumbling. Bells darted out of a shrub, mewing and begging Juliet to scoop up the furry creature, which she did. The cat purred with pleasure, and the affection was mutual.

The tearoom door flew open, and out darted Livy. Her face was alarmed, and her hands fluttered as she dashed up the pathway, her heels tapping on the stones. The pheasant feather in her hat quivered. "Oh my. Oh my. Oh my."

Juliet rushed toward her, ignoring the rule that a lady never runs. "Whatever is wrong?"

Livy halted and cupped her hand over her mouth, her eyes tearing. "Mr. Kelly tumbled from the ladder. It's the most frightful thing. The way his arm is bent, I fear . . . it's broken. He prefers I don't make a fuss, but I am fussy to the bone."

Indeed, she was.

"I am off to collect Doctor Pooley and pray he's back in town." Livy bustled forward.

Juliet stopped her. "Let me go on your behalf. You stay here . . . with him. Having you near will offer comfort." Juliet glanced over her shoulder then turned back around. With Livy already in a fret, should she mention what transpired in the house? Maybe only share a snippet. "Your sister would like you to join her in the drawing room when you can. Guests have arrived."

"They'll have to wait. Cy comes first. And bless your blue eyes, Juliet, for going after the doctor." Livy ran her finger over the beaded pattern that trimmed her cape at the neckline. "Please hippity hop. I hate to see him in pain."

"Of course you do."

Livy nodded and bustled back toward her man. Another round of "Oh my. Oh my" accompanied her steps.

Juliet lowered Bells to the ground. As she straightened, Tabitha exited the kitchen then opened an umbrella. Why had she left her guests so quickly? In a few steps, they met on the cobblestone. "I told Livy you wanted her, but Cy took a tumble, and she's worried about him. I'm off to fetch Doctor Pooley."

Tabitha released an exceedingly large sigh for a lady. "Maybe it's true that trouble comes in bunches like grapes."

No fooling. "I've never heard the expression, but I agree."

"After answering several of my questions, I do believe the young man claiming to be our nephew is truly who he says he is."

"I see." Juliet's chest tightened. For many reasons, she wanted Gray to be the sisters' nephew. She couldn't imagine a better family for him or how he'd feel when he learned the truth. He would be utterly confused again. And maybe utterly empty.

"He informed me that his father sent a letter insisting he return to England posthaste. Alex has already left to catch the next steamer bound for home. Oddly, he also requested money from me for the trip, but I find it hard to believe his father wouldn't have supplied the necessary funds for his travels."

"Huh. I mean, that is puzzling indeed." What a dunderhead. The fellow hadn't seen his aunts in ages, came begging for money, and left again when he didn't receive his handout. Or maybe Tabitha gave her nephew what he sought. As much as Juliet wanted to learn the answer, it would be impolite to inquire, so she swallowed her nosy question.

Tabitha handed Juliet the umbrella, and they crowded underneath it, shoulder to shoulder. "Take this, and please run your errand before my sister ties herself into a tizzy, but perhaps it's already too late."

Juliet shrugged, not about to say anything negative regarding Livy. "I will."

"Unless you strongly disagree, I'd like you present when we tell Gray the truth."

She was honored to be included in the conversation. As Gray's friend, she wanted to be at his side for the announcement. "I'd like that as well."

"I thought you might."

As she spun to leave, Gray's image slid into her thoughts. If he wasn't the sisters' nephew, who was he?

A rural setting. A pond, horses, and a spreading oak tree. Gray tightened his grip on the paintbrush and tried to capture the full memory before it disappeared.

His recollection was like before, only broader, with an auburn-haired girl reclining in the grass after tumbling from her horse. A faceless boy kneeled at her side and held her hand. Instead of rushing to offer aid, Gray hesitated.

Why was he callous toward her, and why did the same specific memory resurrect again while countless others remained hidden? The temptation to fling the brush across the tearoom beckoned. Instead, he drew a deep breath.

Cy's fall earlier had undoubtedly triggered the recollection. But Gray had also fallen in the woods behind the house before Juliet found him. Was that occurrence not more significant than the one from his youth?

"It's time to baste the salmon." Icala wiped his hands on a rag near the door, drawing Gray from his thoughts. A patch of pink paint stained the cook's white sleeve, and another splotch graced his chin. "I'll be back. Then we'll compare which of us did better on our tasks."

Gray raised his brow and tried to focus on the present instead of the past. "Has your nature always leaned toward the competitive side?"

"Has yours?"

"I'm going to say yes because a man with amnesia gets to make up whatever he wants about his past."

"True enough." Icala chuckled.

"When you go inside, check Cy's condition."

"Planned on it."

After Cy's fall, they'd helped him to the sitting room and settled him in his bed. He had insisted he would survive and needed nobody to fuss over him. But Gray had waited until the physician arrived before returning to the tearoom.

Icala cocked his head to the side, studying the wall. "I think we need to add a second coat of paint."

"I thought the same thing, then changed my mind."

Icala reached for his coat on the floor near the door. "My father was full of advice. For example, he said to follow my instincts and not to second-guess myself, a rule I've tried to follow ever since. Usually, I have no regrets."

Regrets—what a heavy word. Gray could not say how he knew but sensed he had a few. Perhaps many. "Any other wise advice from your father?"

Icala finished tugging on his long leather overcoat and then tapped his eye patch. "As a child, my brother and I played swords with sticks. Somehow, I accidentally poked myself hard enough in my eye that I lost my vision."

A painful tragedy, yet his friend had notably risen above his affliction. Had he always accepted the situation or slowly adapted to his new limitations and reality? "No doubt, that was an adjustment for you."

"My father claimed mistakes are merely part of living. I've never forgotten those words." With a nod, Icala exited, the door banging behind him.

What mistakes had Gray made over his lifetime? Too many to count?

With every passing day, Gray pondered whether it was time to quit dwelling on his restricted memory and stop trying to figure everything out. The truth was his memories might never return. Instead, should he move forward with this new life and strive to become a better man than he was in his nebulous past?

He had held himself back from establishing roots to a degree because he expected to leave eventually. But maybe his lot in life was as a carpenter with the sisters in Everly.

Could such a future also include Juliet? Was it time to stop holding himself back from her and start pursuing her more seriously?

After their kiss, she had rarely left his mind. Thoughts of her filled him whether he was awake or asleep, whether working or resting, whether with her or not with her.

He supposed she had consumed much of his thoughts even before the kiss. But something about how she responded to him had sealed their connection, made it permanent, and confirmed that she was the perfect person for him.

Of course, he still struggled with the need to kiss her again. There were intense moments around her when the temptation was entirely too strong.

He stretched and glanced around the nearly completed room

as a strong sense of accomplishment settled inside him. Hopefully, despite Cy's injury, they would finish in time. But now they needed to paint the walls twice.

With no time to waste, Gray bent to dip his brush into the paint, the strong linseed oil fumes rising around him. With a swipe of his hand, he added another streak of pink. Only one-third of his wall remained unpainted with the first layer.

Juliet backed through the door, carrying a plate with bread, cheese, and orange slices. Today, she wore her hair high in a bun, almost like a crown. "I'm delivering a treat, and Tabitha will join us momentarily."

"Thank you, and I shall finish this last section of painting if you do not mind."

"Go right ahead." She balanced the nourishment onto the seat of a nearby weathered chair before straightening. "Unfortunately, I don't have an update on Cy yet."

"Icala left to check on him too." Gray changed his strokes from horizontal to vertical. "I had a memory after Cy fell off the ladder."

"Good news, indeed. The memory part, I mean. I hope it was a pleasant one."

"Not exactly, and it is still hazy around the edges, though less so than before."

She helped herself to a piece of yellow cheese. "Did the recollection confirm your identity?"

He added more paint to his brush, ensured nothing dripped, and straightened. "No, but I am accepting that I am Alex Sherwood. After a slow start, I now believe carpentry is my calling and I harbor a kinship for Tabitha and Livy. If not their nephew, where is my counterpart?"

Her face fell, but then she regained her composure. Or had he misread her reaction? "That's something Tabitha and I want to discuss with you."

He cocked a brow at her. "What do you mean?"

"I prefer to wait until she comes before I say more." She glanced at the door, which opened as if she willed it to obey her wish.

How odd. Juliet generally spoke freely in his company.

Tabitha whisked into the tearoom, the sheen of raindrops on her overcoat. "Doctor Pooley confirmed Cy has a broken forearm. Fortunately, his pain is not severe, and Livy has calmed herself but wishes to remain by his side. Therefore, we'll hold this discussion without her."

Intrigued, Gray lowered his brush to a rag, ready to focus on whatever was about to unfold. "Please continue."

Juliet drew to his side, her face wreathed with concern. "Most likely, you'll find this news unsettling."

"Just tell me."

"Of course." Tabitha slowly removed her coat. "A young man came to the door this afternoon. He presented himself as Alex Sherwood. After answering multiple questions, I believe he is our nephew."

Gray felt the blood draining from his face. *The* Alex Sherwood had come to the house. Their nephew. The real nephew.

"I'm sorry, Gray." Juliet reached out a hand to comfort him but then dropped it. "I know that might be disappointing, perhaps even frustrating."

It was both of those emotions and more.

"We completely understand if you're overwhelmed. Please know"—Juliet's voice broke—"that we all care about you and your welfare."

"Indeed we do." Tabitha stepped closer, her forehead puckered and her eyes filled with kindness and concern. "Our nephew is sailing back to England soon and has already left for Victoria to catch a steamer. You are welcome to stay under our roof for as long as you choose, Gray."

Did he want to remain in Everly? Perhaps for now. If he left, where would he go? It would take time to determine his next steps, wherever they led.

"Are you fine, Gray?" Juliet asked.

"Caught off guard, I admit."

He swallowed hard, trying to digest the revelation. He had allowed himself to believe this might be where he belonged, that he would forge ahead with a new life and forget the old. Maybe he had not entirely convinced himself he was Alex, but he had decided to live that role.

Suddenly, he was more lost than ever before. Now what?

Twenty

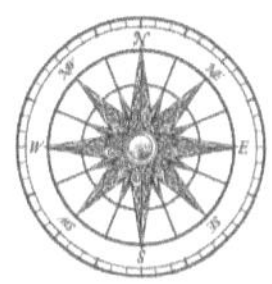

*Be careful, unless you wish your name
coupled with his, how you dance too often
with the same gentleman.*

NOBODY COULD HAVE PREDICTED that Juliet would mingle with high society at a fancy party, especially not her, even if she only worked at the tearoom's grand opening.

But everyone who resided under the sisters' roof had a job tonight. Tabitha and Livy were greeting the guests. Gray was busy assisting Icala with the food, and Cy was showing the new arrivals where to hang their overcoats and hats in the cloak area in the back corner. They were in agreement, determined to meet each guest's needs and whims.

Juliet admired the crocheted snowflakes decorating the pink walls as she repeated her serving instructions in her head. Add the cool cream to the cup before the hot tea to avoid cracking the porcelain. Pour tea from the right, never the left. Always ask if the guest desires a lemon slice. And so on.

"More tea?" She stopped at a table of four ladies, all dressed in perhaps their Sunday best. A long-tapered candle served as the centerpiece atop a lace-trimmed tablecloth.

"Yes, please." A young woman approximately Juliet's age wore a light lavender satin wrap draped over her shoulders, glistening in the candlelight. Would she and her friends become regular customers in the tearoom? Juliet hoped so.

Tabitha approached to stand beside Juliet. A thin weave of gold thread trimmed her belted sage green dress at the high collar, cuffs, and hemline that swept the floorboards. "I'm uncertain if you've all met Juliet." She made the introductions, and everyone smiled like a person might expect. "She's not our niece or daughter, but that's how we view her."

Much like Livy's flattering comment after church a few weeks ago, the surprising praise warmed Juliet's heart. The sisters viewed her like family, like a niece, even a daughter. How was that possible?

She hadn't been part of a family in a very long time, and the idea of being in this particular one was more than she could have anticipated or imagined.

Was this her goal—the dream she'd been too afraid to voice to Livy on the first day she arrived in Everly—that she'd have a home again and a family one day? Was it too much to hope that this place, these people, this life could really be hers?

A longing swelled in her chest, one she hadn't allowed herself to feel in years, one she'd stuffed deep. The desire to belong.

She hadn't belonged anywhere or with anyone since her grandfather's death. And she'd given up hope that she ever would. She'd failed to fully fit in wherever she'd lived since then—at the orphanage, with Molly, even with the Firths. What made her think she could belong here? In this lovely place?

Her hand shook, and she struggled not to spill what remained in her teapot, forcing herself to settle the container with two hands.

She finished serving the ladies, excused herself, and asked a fellow servant to offer a plate of sandwiches to the foursome. Then she wove around scattered tables to reach the sideboard in the bustling tearoom. Still trembly, she carefully lowered the empty teapot to the shelf built into the wall. The scents of tart lemon and smoky salmon eked a growl from her stomach, though she'd have to wait until later to sneak into the back room for samples.

The smile she'd pinned on her lips earlier in the evening had seldom faltered, but it slid away now. She took several deep breaths and tried to silence the qualms that were swirling inside, doubts that shouted she wasn't good enough to belong anywhere. That no one wanted her, and that she'd end up disappointed again. She refused to think about all of that now. Not on this special evening for Tabitha and Livy. She had to focus on them.

Juliet paused to steal an extended peek at the room. She'd never seen Tabitha and Livy beam brighter than while hosting the open house. So far, everything was streaming perfectly.

A hired violinist performed in the corner, and chatter flowed in the room along with the music. Women in full-skirted dresses in every hue conversed with men in evening wear or military uniforms. The new cast-iron stove and fireplace pumped warmth into the space, and multiple lanterns added the perfect lighting. According to Cy, no expense was spared.

Gray was no longer helping Icala with the food. She didn't see him anywhere in the room. Where had he gone?

They hadn't conversed as often over the past week since the final preparations for the tearoom had taken so much time and energy. They'd even worked into the evenings instead of sitting together in the drawing room like before.

If completely honest, she missed him. She missed their bantering, their conversations, and the games. And she missed not talking to him more deeply about how he was doing, especially since learning he wasn't Alex. Now that he'd had the past week to think about the startling news, how did he feel?

Maybe later, during the dancing, she'd spend time with him and learn the answer. How many dances would they share tonight? Was a dozen too many to hope for? Dare she forget her worries for one night and enjoy the celebration? Whether she embraced the evening or not, her concerns would undoubtedly greet her in the morning.

Tabitha approached as part of her rounds. "You look pensive."

"Not at all, only full of thoughts. Your night is a success."

"Indeed. Everyone appears sated for now. In about ten minutes, I'd like you to change out of your uniform while the room is prepared for dancing. Earlier, Livy and I left a surprise on your bed."

Juliet blinked, her mind whirring. The sisters hadn't purchased her a new dancing gown, had they? No. For heaven's sake, they weren't mind readers and couldn't have guessed how much she desired something special for the dance. "Thank you kindly."

"Our pleasure." Tabitha nodded before turning and speaking to guests as she worked her way to her post near the front door.

The next several minutes buzzed past before Juliet returned to the empty house and raced up the back stairs. She burst into her bedroom and halted abruptly. Draped over her bed was a crimson tarlatan dress with a double skirt, the upper one looped up with delicate silver rosettes and velvet trim. A wide, almost off-the-shoulder neckline and capped sleeves added flair to the elegant gown.

Filled with awe, she approached the bed to ensure her imagination hadn't stirred up the image. Her fingers explored the dress. Silky, soft fabric. Delicate, dainty trim. Perfect in every way. A new crinoline rested beside the garment and a pair of dyed matching satin slippers waited on the carpet next to the bed.

How had the sisters gone from strangers to almost family, or even fairy godmothers, in such a short time? Nobody had ever extended such kindness, except perhaps, her flesh and blood family long ago.

She drew an excited breath. Maybe all her fears about belonging again were unfounded and unnecessary. Possibly, she didn't have to worry about being rejected again, left alone, or pushed aside. Maybe she really could believe everything would work out fine.

Was it possible to have more than friendship with Gray one day? Of course, life remained uncertain, even more so now that they had no idea who he was or where he'd come from. But that kiss had meant something, and neither of them could deny the attraction growing between them.

She wiggled out of her black uniform and into a pair of silk stockings and the dome-shaped, caged crinoline. With care, she gently donned the gown, then shuffled the dress into place with a shake of her hips. Satisfied, she slipped on the dainty slippers.

Almost ready to return to the celebration, she gazed into the full-length mirror, her long hair shimmering in the lantern light. The lonely orphan girl with a broken heart was gone. In her place stood a lady with dear, generous friends. "I wish you could see me now, Grandfather," she whispered.

Blinking back a tear, she exited her room and descended the staircase at a stately pace. As she stepped out into the crisp evening air, the tinkling music from the tearoom beckoned to her. She strolled over the cobblestone path lined with lanterns and past the male guests clustered under the trees to smoke and wag tongues.

Bells mewed and threaded between her slippers, begging for attention. Although chilly without a shawl, Juliet bent and scratched the cat's head. "As much as I would love to pick you up, little kitty, not tonight. I don't want cat hair marring my dress. But I promise to cuddle you twice tomorrow."

As she straightened, she glimpsed Reverend Channing sidling toward her through the nearby men. The glow of lanterns glinted off his tall black hat and revealed the eagerness on his face. After she'd started focusing during his Sunday sermons, she'd spotted stirring points each week. Next time he asked about her favorite part of his message, she'd offer a ready answer.

He halted in front of her with a wide smile. "Please allow me to tell you how stunning you look this evening, Miss Dash."

"Thank you, Reverend. However, good manners prevent me from pointing out that it's difficult to see clearly in this light."

"And yet the darkness cannot hide your beauty."

Oh my goodness. The reverend was a charmer too. She ought to be flattered, even flustered by his compliment, but she felt none of the same fluttering that had happened with Gray's compliments.

"May I escort you to the festivities to avoid stumbling?" He extended his elbow to escort her.

She hesitated.

She'd learned he was a widower and childless. By all accounts, he was also a decent, God-fearing man. Once upon a time, she would have been thrilled to have a fellow like him interested in her, someone unattainable.

But he wasn't Gray . . .

It wouldn't be fair to the reverend—or anyone else, for that matter—to lead him on when the truth was that she wanted to spend the entire evening with only one man, and it wasn't the fellow in front of her.

"Thank you, Reverend. However—"

"Juliet, there you are." Gray's voice carried from behind her.

She turned to watch him draw closer. He'd donned a dark suit, and his white shirt and cravat added an elegant touch. Never had she seen clothing fit a man as it did now, the sole reason her stomach wildly spun. Of course, the lighting was poor, but she stood firm in her opinion.

"You promised me the first dance, if I recall."

Had she promised him such a thing? She didn't remember

doing so. Still, she wouldn't mind opening the evening in his solid arms and ending it there.

Juliet nodded to the reverend. "I will see you inside."

"Most assuredly, you will." He tipped his hat at Gray, then headed back toward the gathering of men under the trees.

Juliet looped her arm with the dashing man at her side, alone with him on the pathway.

He bent closer, and the fresh scent of soap with cinnamon filled the crisp air. "Finally, the man of the cloth makes his move."

"What move? All Reverend Channing did was ask me to dance."

"Should I be jealous?"

"Are you angling for a compliment?"

Gray laughed and squeezed her fingers before growing serious. "Speaking of compliments, you are as pretty and elegant as a princess tonight."

"Really? Have you seen a princess before?"

"Not that I recall, but anything is possible."

Indeed, more flattery. Yet Gray's praise touched her center, and his soulful eyes called to her like a beacon in a blizzard. "And you are very, very elegant yourself. Your jacket isn't two sizes too big, and your britches cover your ankles."

Gray's chest rose and fell twice before he spoke. "If you look at me in the same fashion on the dance floor, I may forget every move of the dance and turn into a bumbling idiot."

Her brow arched. "And incur the sisters' wrath?"

"An excellent point. We could never cause a scandal at the grand opening."

Of course, they would never hurt or embarrass the sisters. Not in a dozen decades. Which was why she'd worried all week about Ruby's return. Yes, the sisters, Gray, and the constable were all aware of Ruby's threats. But that didn't mean anything. Ruby could still stir up problems. Hopefully, her old roommate's absence meant she'd finally accepted that Juliet didn't have the Firths' stolen jewels and moved on to other endeavors, whatever they might be.

Arm in arm, Gray led her toward the tearoom door and inside. The crowd from earlier had diminished by half. Maybe thirty people remained, and the slimmed-down number suited her fine. In her opinion, the fewer bell-shaped skirts to maneuver while dancing, the better.

The long sideboard now displayed another round of refreshments for guests to help themselves as they mingled. The bright lighting from the previously scattered lanterns had dimmed, adding an air of romance to the setting.

At the sight of Juliet, Livy rushed forward, dragging Cy. Her shiny pink gown matched the walls, and her surplus of white feather adornments reminded Juliet of a downy swan.

"You are dazzling." Livy puffed Juliet's sleeves. "Against my instincts, I allowed Tabitha to choose your gown. Thankfully, she picked wisely."

Heavens, if Livy had selected her dress, it might resemble the fancy French cream puffs once served at the Firth mansion. But Livy was Livy, and Juliet had grown to appreciate her style. All the same, she had no intention of copying it.

"Thank you for your kindness," Juliet said. "I owe you a tremendous amount, and I fear I'll never be able to repay you in full."

Livy's hand had moved to Juliet's arm, which she patted. "That's unnecessary. You're a fine young lady, and I'm proud of you. And you are very dapper tonight, Gray."

Gray bowed with a regal flourish. "You are too kind, my lady. You and Cy both look charming, as well."

Cy smiled, his eyes crinkling in the corners. "A first for me, but not Livy, who is always divine. Do you like my arm sling tonight?"

Juliet examined the white cloth harnessing his injured arm. Someone, and no doubt Livy, had embroidered red hearts near his wiggling fingers. "I do. I adore it."

The pianist stroked the ivory keys, introducing a dance. The violinist and the cello player were primed to join in on the tune. After a moment, Livy smiled and grabbed Cy's unhampered arm. "Shall we dance, Mr. Kelly? I fear our guests are bashful."

"Dance? Even in my current state?"

"I'm quite certain we'll manage." Livy led him toward the room's center, drawing every eye in their direction. Attendees fringed the open area, talking amongst themselves. Others had congregated on chairs lined up against the back wall.

Some guests might have never learned to dance, like Juliet, not long ago. After a half dozen lessons, she still fumbled with several steps. But what if she and Gray joined Livy and Cy? If she botched her movements once or twice, the guests might realize perfection wasn't expected or required. She turned toward Gray, ready to ask him to dance as Livy had done with her partner.

"May I have the honor of this dance, my lady?" Gray held out a hand to her. She could admit her bias, but he was the most handsome man in the room. And she'd dare anyone to disagree with her.

"My pleasure, good sir." She offered her best curtsy, low and exaggerated. Seconds later, a lively polka had her focusing on the quick steps. As she hoped, others soon joined in on the merriment, and happy laughter accompanied the music.

The jaunty song ended, and a romantic waltz took its place. Gray leaned forward. "Please dance one more number with me. Then I shall allow the eager swains to woo you."

Juliet's breath quivered. Dare she dance with him twice in a row? What if this was the night's only waltz, and they would never have another chance? "Perhaps I don't want to dance with any eager swains but you."

Dark, swirling emotion filled his eyes before he touched her hip and took her hand. It was an emotion she couldn't read or understand. Nonetheless, her insides trembled. After tripping over him in the woods, she'd kept falling for his charm every day since. And now, was she finally falling in love?

Her pulse skipped to a flourishing beat, but it was time to calm down. Better yet, they should have done it two minutes ago.

She reluctantly focused on anything and anyone but him. Livy and Cy had disappeared from the room. Tabitha stood near the door, nodding to the beat. Icala was transferring an empty dessert platter to the rear workroom.

As the song tapered to a halt, Gray seemed reluctant to release his hold on her as his eyes held hers captive. "Would you care for a breath of fresh air?"

Breath of fresh air? Or did he seek something more? Like a kiss? And was that what she wanted, too?

Twenty-One

HE COULD NOT KISS JULIET TONIGHT. At least not until he had the chance to talk to her about everything on his mind since he had learned he was not Alex Sherwood.

But heaven, blessed heaven. He wanted to kiss her desperately. He had longed to pull her into his arms from the moment he had stepped out of the house and witnessed her talking to Reverend Channing. Her beauty had taken his breath away, and he still was not sure he had recovered it fully.

"So..." She leaned against the back of the tearoom beside him. Sparse starlight filtered through the long-limbed branches draped overhead. Even though the December night was cool, the air was refreshing after the stuffiness inside and after all the dancing.

"So. . ." He imitated her posture and tone.

"Are you thinking the same thing I am?"

"I highly doubt it." All he thought about was her. Dancing with her had been a form of sweet torture, holding her near but having to restrain himself. Even talking and bantering over the past week had been more difficult than usual as he tried to pretend that their kiss had not altered his world. It had rattled him to his bones.

He slid a sideways glance at her.

She cocked one elegant brow at him. Even in the dim lighting, her face was as expressive as always. A face that meant more to him than anything else. *She* meant more to him than anything else.

But was that true by default because he had lost everything else he esteemed? Or would he feel as strongly about her even if he had met her at another time and place when his life was normal and full?

He suspected the man he had once been would not have cherished her as she deserved. But did his past mistakes matter anymore? He was becoming a better man. At least, he hoped he was.

Yet, how did a man without a past make his way into the future? Stumbling, no doubt.

He had pondered his identity daily since learning he was not a Sherwood. On the one hand, he was relieved he had not committed the crimes in Barkerville. On the other hand, he was back to knowing almost nothing about himself except for the few sparse feelings and memories that had come to mind.

All week, he had wrestled with the fact that he might never recall his actual name, his birth family, or any of the years of his life up to this point. Indeed, it was a dreadful thought with the power to plague him forever.

Yet he had no means to restore his memories. Was it finally time to dedicate his life to living in the present? And was the first step establishing himself as a carpenter under the name Gray . . . whomever?

Evidently, he would need a new last name sooner rather than later.

At the movement of an embracing couple within the shadows of the nearby trees, he stood taller. They were likely just another pair who had stepped out for air . . . or more.

Beside him, Juliet locked in on the couple too. She stiffened briefly, then released a soft chuckle as she leaned against the tea-room again. "Fancy that. Livy and Cy canoodling."

Gray peered through the darkness and tried to see the pair more closely, this time catching sight of Livy's feathery white gown, which was difficult to miss. "I saw Cy leading Livy away earlier. And now I know why."

"Do they need chaperones?" Juliet's voice held teasing. "Shall we go over and offer our services?"

"Maybe we should," he teased back, although he was happy for the two and would never begrudge them a moment of privacy. "The other day, I returned a book to the library and caught them reciting poetry to one another while Tabitha read silently in the room's corner."

"Dreamy poetry, I assume."

"Shakespeare."

"Snakes alive, of course it was."

He smirked, suspecting no amount of etiquette lessons could thoroughly shake free all of Juliet's unvarnished tendencies. Thank goodness, since she constantly charmed him. "Tell the truth. I expect you are pleased the pair are fond of each other."

"Thrilled, actually. Since I deem them a sweet couple, does that make me a romantic?"

"Yes, and I am happy to hear it." He shifted to face her and drew her long hair behind her ear before running a silky lock between his finger and thumb.

"Is that so?" She met his gaze with an unflinching stare as the moonlight's glow captured her delicate face like a picture frame.

Her blue eyes matched the African violets in the library's window. He desperately longed to trace her perfect jawline with his finger, yet reluctantly refrained.

He paused for a heartbeat, knowing he needed to say something about their relationship. From the beginning of his amnesia, her presence had anchored him amidst all the tumult. She may not have been a part of his past, but she had been there for him when he needed someone the most. She was here with him now, and he wanted her in his future. But was it too soon to tell her such a thing?

He expelled a tense breath, rousing a round of frosty air to swirl between them. "I have had much on my mind this week."

"I figured so." She lifted a hand to his arm and squeezed. "I'm always here if you want to talk. I hope you know that by now."

"I do." He loved that about her, that she listened so well and understood him. "Now that we know I am not the sisters' nephew, I am simply a nobody with nothing to offer anyone."

She released a huff of protest. "You're not a *nobody* and have *plenty* to offer."

"You know what I mean."

She grasped his arm more firmly. "All I know is that you are among the most charming and giving men I have ever met. You aided the sisters in completing the tearoom, though you had nothing to gain."

"Even so, I do not know if I can ask any woman to be a part of my life when I have nothing but who I am here and now to give her." He could not keep his breath from snagging in his chest as he waited for her response.

"What if a woman didn't care about anything except who you are here and now?"

He attempted to read the emotions playing across her lovely face in the faint light. "Does such a woman exist?"

"I believe she does."

Staring at Juliet, with her close enough to kiss, a memory jabbed into his brain—more words than images. *Never kiss anyone unless your intentions are pure and honorable.* Who had spoken the sage advice? A parent? A grandparent? An older sibling? A sense of yearning swelled inside him as his hand grazed her waist, igniting a current too powerful to ignore.

She softly gasped, her eyes now on his mouth.

Gray leaned forward. He met her warm, willing lips as a bonfire burned in his middle, rapidly spreading. He drew her into an embrace, her body pressed snugly against his. Merciful heavens.

Slowly, his hands roamed her back, up and over her shoulders, to finally delve into her loose hair. Soft, lush, and as irresistible as expected. The pad of her thumb caressed his neck, shooting dizzying energy through his veins. All the while, her lips teased, tantalized, and clung to his like snow on a mountaintop in spring.

He tightened his grip, his breaths short and rapid, and they kissed like it might be their last opportunity. But it was not, was it?

Even though he had no direction or compass pointing him toward a specific future, all he knew was he craved Juliet's smiles, her excellent opinion, and their conversations. Was he falling in love with her?

The first church bell chimed for the town's weekly musical show, a reminder to slow his ardor. Yet he clutched her a minute longer, hating to return to reality. Using all the self-control he could muster, he transferred his lips to her cheek, then trailed kisses to her temple. He held her close until she raised her head to peer at his face.

"I forgot it was time for the town's musical show." Her voice had become airy, and her eyes were darker than before.

"Kissing you made me forget everything but you, even my name." He smiled. "I suppose that is a falsehood. I have not known my name for weeks."

A grin curved her lips in the most becoming fashion. "I'm glad you can joke."

"As am I. The more I contemplate the future, the more committed I am to change my mindset. I cannot waste my life waiting for memories to return. It may take forever."

"A big decision, indeed. I'm proud of you." She rose onto her tiptoes, captured his cheeks with cold hands, and softly kissed his lips much too briefly before pulling back.

Barely trusting his voice, Gray reached for her hands, cupping them between his. "Will you dance with me the rest of the night?"

"A lady never dances with the same man more than twice in a row." Her voice sounded like Livy's when quoting from the etiquette book. "And she must sit out every other number, or she'll grow weary."

He laughed, the sound echoing in the trees. "Sayeth Livy, the Queen of Etiquette."

"It took a while, but I like that about her." Juliet shivered and then wrapped her arms around her chest.

"You are cold." What had he been thinking, staying outside until she developed a chill? He quickly started to shed his suit coat.

She shook her head and began to walk away, the music from inside faint but beckoning them. "We've been gone long enough and should return to the dance. I don't want to worry Tabitha or cause a scandal. Not tonight." He trailed after her, still attempting to shrug out of his coat. He should have been paying better attention to her needs and how cold it was.

As Juliet turned the corner, she stiffened.

What was it? He hastened his steps and stepped out from behind the tearoom's wall to find an incredibly tall man and a petite woman peering into the tearoom's large window. Why did they not join the party inside?

"Ruby." Despair laced Juliet's voice.

When she turned toward them, the short woman's dark cape

hid every part of her except for her small, round face. "There you be, Juliet."

The unsmiling and bewhiskered man wore a too-tight dusty gray sack suit that showed his muscular build.

Gray braced himself for a confrontation. He would do whatever was necessary to protect Juliet from Ruby and this man. Even so, he needed to send Cy or Icala after the constable.

The lawman and his wife had attended the tea party but departed before the dancing. If only the fellow had stayed longer. He might not have been able to arrest Ruby based on her previous threats alone, but his presence may have frightened her and, at the very least, dissuaded her from causing problems.

Juliet raised her chin and glared at Ruby. "Go away."

"I ain't here for the reason you think." Ruby's narrowed eyes scrutinized Gray, traveling from his shoes to the top of his head. "I came because of your fellow and his past."

"Mine?" Gray stepped forward. How could Ruby know anything about his past? Nobody else did.

"His?" Juliet asked.

Ruby retrieved a wrinkled, tattered paper from her pocket, unfolded it, and stabbed an image with her finger. "Seems a Mister Henry Graighton disappeared from Victoria a month or so ago. After staring at your face during my last visit and then seeing this here notice tacked up to a building in Victoria, I snapped the puzzle together."

Henry Graighton. Gray's mind raced. Was that why the name Gray had resonated?

Ruby scrutinized his face in the light from the tearoom window and then glanced at a picture on the sheet. She grinned, looking proud of herself. "Yep. Just like I thought. You're Henry Graighton. Me and my man have come to haul you back to your royal ship in Victoria."

Juliet sputtered. "Royal . . . ship?"

Ruby's cohort nodded.

Gray longed to grab Juliet's hand and leave Ruby far behind. After their kiss, one that held the promise of a future together, he hated the idea of anything upsetting the start of something new between them.

But his heart was pounding hard and demanding that he discover exactly what Ruby was talking about. He strode toward the young woman and snatched the tattered paper from her hands. Then he held it up in the light, turning the sheet so Juliet could view the grainy image that filled it. One big-lettered word stood out: *Missing*.

For a long moment, he and Juliet studied the picture. A man with an angular, cleanly shaven face peered back. One with similar features and the same eyes, although the hair was neater and shorter and the clothing far fancier.

"I can admit I resemble the photograph, though the man's name stirs no distinct memories."

Ruby raised her chin to a haughty tilt. "That's because your noggin ain't working right."

"I am uncertain what to think." Gray examined the sheet again and read the few sentences this time: *Prince Henry Graighton of Bascandy went missing on November 7th. He is six feet one inch tall, narrow in build, with wavy brown hair and brown eyes. Any information regarding his whereabouts will be generously rewarded.*

The description fit him perfectly. And the timing for early November when he'd arrived at the sisters' home was also perfect. How could this not be him?

But a prince? Of Bascandy? That was absurd, was it not?

Wordlessly, Juliet continued to stare at the picture, her eyes wide.

"The thing is," Ruby said, "Henry Graighton is a genuine prince, and there's reward money for the taking. I'm guessing it's a heap of cash. As soon as I haul you to Victoria, it'll be mine."

"I shall go nowhere with you." Gray folded and stuffed the picture into his pocket, then reached for Juliet's hand, tucking it into the crook of his arm.

Ruby widened her feet as though to block him, and the fellow at her side regarded him with narrowed, serious eyes.

At the same time, the reverend and another man stepped out of the tearoom. Surely Ruby and her burly companion would not try to abduct him with witnesses present. If they did, it would be a mistake.

"You're the missing prince." The music inside had ceased, and Ruby's declaration rang out in the now-quiet night. "And I aim to get my reward for finding you."

Reverend Channing and his companion started toward them. "Is everything all right here?"

Before Gray found the right words to explain the bizarre unfolding—something he did not fully understand himself—Ruby and her fellow darted toward the woods.

Juliet watched their departure, then stared at him as if he were a stranger.

"Miss Dash?" The reverend drew nearer, his voice filled with concern as he gazed at the two disappearing into the dark woodland. "Are you fine?"

"Yes." She kept her eyes on Gray. "Please tell me everything is all right, Gray."

He wanted to offer reassurance that Ruby had only spouted falsehoods. But he could not. Deep in his soul, something told him she may have spoken the truth.

Twenty-two

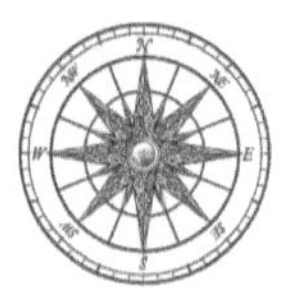

Politeness forbids any display of resentment.
The polished surface throws back the arrow.

U NABLE TO SLEEP, GRAY HAD SPENT the last hour staring at Henry Graighton's image and the word "Missing" until his eyes blurred.

If Ruby had spoken the truth, why had the mention of his birth name not shaken loose the missing parts of his brain? Indeed, he resembled the image on the paper. But a prince? He still could not fathom the prospect.

At first light, he would investigate the notice without Ruby's help.

His stomach growled, and he rose, dressed, and left the bedroom. Surely, he would find something delicious left over from the party. Halfway down the rear staircase, a soft clatter rose from the dark kitchen below.

Voices. Male voices.

Gray froze as his pulse accelerated. Thieves, or had Ruby returned with reinforcements?

For all he knew, a weapon remained tucked inside the piano stool. Although a strange hiding place, he was grateful for it tonight. Silently, he returned up the staircase and down the hallway. As he reached the top of the front stairway, he peeked down. A rattling emitted from below, and he flattened himself against the wall.

With a movement beside him, he startled, finding Juliet.

She'd copied his action and had flattened herself to the wall beside him. "What's wrong?"

"Why are you awake?"

"Too much on my mind. Why are we pressed against the wall?"

"Two men in the kitchen. Thieves, or possibly tied to Ruby. Awaken the sisters, then bar all three of you in one bedroom. Don't come out until I return."

Juliet reached for his fingers and squeezed. "Let me help you."

"It is too dangerous, and I refuse to place you in peril."

"But—"

Of course she would resist staying behind. But he could be as stubborn as Juliet. "Please do not argue with me."

Amazingly and without complaint, she rose onto her tiptoes and kissed his cheek. Then she crept toward Livy's room, looking over her shoulder at him one last time before slipping through her door.

He hadn't spoken with Juliet since she returned to the tearoom after Ruby's appearance. Too confused and agitated to join her, he had paced instead for a short while, saying Henry Graighton and Bascandy repeatedly, hoping the words would alert something in his brain.

But no such luck.

By the time the dance ended, midnight had come and gone. The sisters had insisted on waiting for the morning to clean up the tearoom. Thus, everyone had gone directly into the house and readied for bed. So he hadn't spoken privately with Juliet about the matter, and he suspected she hadn't told the sisters about Ruby's visit or the revelation of his identity. If so, they surely would have mentioned the fact.

Gray crept to the top of the front staircase. The starry night sky shone through the window above the door, and he strained to listen. Only the grandfather clock striking four times delivered a sound. With silent footsteps and tensed muscles, he descended.

On the last step, he paused and gazed around. He planned to secure the gun and then investigate the premises. He would keep the trespassers from reaching and frightening the ladies at all costs. Something crashed onto the floor, originating from down the hallway. The dining room, perhaps, or—

"I said, get!" Cy shouted.

A chill dropped down Gray's spine. He shot toward the drawing room. Through the darkness, he raced into the room toward the piano and was stopped short by slamming into something solid. No, someone solid, with enough force that they both crashed to the floor. Peaches released a piercing whistle.

His opponent bore the brunt of their fall and grunted. The man was similar in size to Gray and reeked of body odor. Where was the other one? Still with Cy? Or were there more than two trespassers inside the house?

Gray jerked his opponent sideways, trying to gain an advantage. Then they rolled in the other direction, bumping into a side-table leg and sending it careening to the floor with a crash. The deacon's bench sat to his right and the piano to his left. If he could only reach the weapon, he could end this tussle and hopefully assist Cy.

In theory, it was a decent plan. But now for the execution.

Gray twisted enough to free his arm, then jabbed his elbow into the man's face with a driving force. Immediately, his foe released him, allowing Gray to break free. He quickly scrambled to the piano stool.

"Stop. I have a gun." A deep male voice carried a bite and a vague familiarity.

Gray stiffened, but his mind whirred, trying to find a way out of his bind. Slowly, he turned toward the shadowy figure in the doorway. But then the air whooshed, and the body collapsed, followed by a thud. The outline of a slender person stood over the man with the weapon—a large rod of some kind?

"Cy?" Gray asked.

"Look out behind you." It was Juliet's voice.

Merciful heavens. What was she doing down here? His first instinct was to run to her and ensure her safety. But apparently, she had control of the situation.

Instead, he flung open the stool lid and felt for the firearm.

No gun.

He spun around, his opponent on hands and knees as if searching for something, likely a weapon dropped in the scuffle. Quickly, Gray pounced on the man's back, collapsing him to the floor. Then he pinned the intruder to the carpet. Though the fellow writhed, straining to free himself, Gray held tight.

Faint lantern light seeped into the drawing room. "I got a weapon," Cy said, his voice growing louder as he drew closer. "And I love shooting it."

The man beneath Gray cussed and quit resisting.

With sweat on his brow and labored breaths, Gray rose and glanced at Juliet. She knelt beside the unconscious man, who was sprawled face-first on the floor. Lantern light glinted off the blade of a knife in her hand and the abandoned iron poker beside her on the floor.

Where was the motionless man's weapon? Did he lay atop his firearm, or had he bluffed?

Gray's body ached from the brawl, especially his ribs. The man he had grappled with now sat, his back against the leg of the deacon's bench. Blood flowed freely down his face into his lap and onto the floor. Was the fellow's nose broken?

Stepping around the toppled side table and destroyed lamp, Cy handed Gray his revolver. A sling held his injured arm, and his hand gripped a lantern. "I fooled the one trespasser into thinking he knocked me out."

Gray pointed the revolver at his attacker.

"Are you both all right?" Juliet stood by the door, the poker stick now ready for another blow, which hopefully would not be necessary. Her voice and brow expressed concern. Yet, throughout the ordeal, she had remained unflappable.

"I'm dandy," Cy said.

"As am I." Gray offered her a slight grin. "I must say you are quite handy wielding a makeshift weapon. Thank you for not staying upstairs like I requested."

An impertinent smile landed on her lips. "Anytime, Gray."

"Gray?" The man sitting beside him raised his head, blood smeared on his face and bushy hair. "I thought your name was Henry Graighton. The prince."

Had he heard the rumors attached to Ruby's claim last night? By now, the entire town had probably caught the news that had unfolded hours ago.

Gray stepped closer to the trespasser and examined him more closely. The man's front teeth were missing. His heart slammed against his chest, and he tightened his grip on the gun. This man— no, this thief—had stolen his memories, a part of his soul.

"Gray is Gray." Juliet's voice rang out defiantly. "He's not the missing prince from far away."

Clearly, that was what she wanted to believe, though the evidence said otherwise.

Cy said nothing.

A memory streaked through his thoughts—awakening on a

boat ride from Victoria before his escape. The recollection had a genuine roundness, almost as if he could touch the steamer's cold floor. Smell the hay and feel the icy water rushing over his head that day.

Deeply, he longed to be alone to sift through his recollections and prod a few more. But not yet. Only after they finished securing the trespassers—his kidnappers—tying and locking them up until they could go for help.

Sutton's image flew through his brain, and a raw ache squeezed his heart. Mother had sent him a letter explaining his brother's death and killing all hope of ever forgiving each other and restoring their bond. It was not fair.

Who else had Gray forgotten? A picture of his straight-shouldered father dropped into his brain. Like train cars following an engine, the images of his four younger sisters—Amanda, Charlotte, Nora, and little Maureen—rolled through.

He could picture his home, a stately palace on a hill, complete with a moat and drawbridge. He captured the beauty of Bascandy. The ragged coastal cliffs, the sandy beaches, and the flowering vegetation joined in calling him back to his birthplace.

And what about Dobbin? The last time he saw his friend, he was unconscious on the ground. Had God spared his life? Merciful heavens, he hoped so. Soon, he would leave Everly to learn the answer.

His eyes strayed to Juliet. What would she say when he revealed he was one hundred percent a prince?

Twenty-three

I ASSUME YOU HAVE HEARD THE CHATTER regarding my identity." Gray stood beside the constable on the front walk outside the sisters' house in the dawn light. He had changed his clothing and donned shoes but neglected to add an overcoat in his haste to catch the lawman before he left with the kidnappers.

Mr. Blake straightened his top hat, shaky in the stiff breeze coming off the mountains. "Apparently, word spread after the tea party last night. Some say you're a prince. Is it true?"

Without a shadow of a doubt.

"Yes, and the two men you arrested kidnapped me last month." Gray glanced at the cart in the street, ready to deliver the bound villains to jail. "They brought me here on a ship from Victoria. While docked at the harbor, I escaped before suffering amnesia."

"Any idea why they kidnapped you?"

"For a ransom. They mentioned a boss in Hope, though I have no name to hand you. From what they said earlier, they searched for me the past few weeks but thought I ended up back in Victoria. They had only returned to Everly a few days ago but had nearly given up on me for dead."

"All this time, everyone thought you were the sisters' nephew."

"I realize that." An early-morning owl hooted a lonesome cry.

Slowly, the constable ran his hand over his mouth. "I'll try and squeeze what information I can out of these two, then head over to Hope to investigate a ringleader. I'd keep an eye open in case their boss arrives to finish the job these two failed to complete."

A wrinkle Gray had not yet considered. He nodded.

The lawman moved toward the conveyance with a hand on his hat brim as Gray turned toward the house. He drew fresh air into his lungs. It was the start of another wintry day. What would it bring? Last night was a whirlwind, one Gray hoped never to live twice. And yet, the incident had finally resurrected his memories. What he needed now was time alone with his recollections. He climbed the stairs, a large Christmas wreath gracing the front door as he entered the house.

Juliet stood in the foyer, resting her elbow on the banister and her ankles crossed. "Are you sure you're fine, Gray? I hate being a pest, but you look troubled."

Fine? Not exactly. Overwhelmed was a better description. "Yes, though I am full of thoughts and on my way to bed. Good night or good morning, whichever you prefer."

She delivered a caring smile. "What a relief. I was worried about you."

A rush of tenderness passed over him, and he kissed the top of her head before climbing the staircase. Was she still in denial about who he was? Soon, he would tell Juliet every startling detail about his identity, but only one aspect would spin her head—his royal status.

He continued to his room, closed the door, and lay on his bed, folding his arms beneath his head. Sleeping was not on the agenda. Only quiet to welcome the return of his memories.

Once again, his life had changed in a blink. What did he know about himself? He was christened Henry Phillip Graighton to honor two of his maternal uncles.

More memories arose—visions of horseback riding, Christmas gatherings, dancing in the great hall, swimming in the pond. Even his first kiss with a girl named Gabriella.

One Christmas Eve, he and Sutton had a knockdown brawl in the fencing room. Why? He had no recollection. But he had blackened his brother's eye. Sutton had shoved him into an old suit of armor that crashed to the floor, bloodying his lip and delivering a gash to his thumb. He rubbed the scar that still lingered all these years later.

Finally, their father intervened by pulling them apart. A massive scolding followed, the root being that his sons had better behave and mature or else. How old were they? Eight and nine?

One son immediately took their father's words to heart. The other followed a slower, more meandering path. Nonetheless, could he and Father finally make amends? Gray scrubbed a hand over his face. He would soon return to Bascandy, and Everly would become a memory.

A lump lodged in his throat. But what about Juliet?

Holding her on the dance floor had solidified his plans to build a future with the woman of his dreams. How could he leave her? Not when he'd already pictured her as a part of his future. Not when he had formed so deep a connection with her as a friend but also as more. Not when he had come to rely upon her to anchor him through the storms. What would he do without her?

He shook his head. No, he refused to think about life apart from her. Not yet. And not ever.

The sisters' footsteps pattered in the hallway. Soon, their doors closed. Were they returning to their beds or getting ready for the day? Had Juliet also retired to her room, or had her day of chores already commenced?

He doubted there was a perfect time to tell her about his past, but perhaps now was as good as any, especially if they stole a few minutes alone. After he rose, he left his room, crossed the hallway, and peered into Juliet's empty bedchamber, the door wide open. Not locating her, he continued down the staircase and into the kitchen.

She stood at the washbasin, her back to him. She had changed into a dress and added shoes and stockings to her attire, but her bundled hair still sat atop her head. "I am happy you are still awake," he said.

Juliet whirled around, drying her hands on her apron. "It'll be a full day cleaning up the tearoom and the incident down the hallway. Plus, I'm too worked up to rest since the scuffle."

"Can you squeeze in time for a conversation? There is something I wish to tell you."

"If you can walk and talk at the same time? It'll be the dickens to remove that man's blood from the carpet, and I'd like to get started."

"Fortunately, I possess multiple talents, including walking and conversing simultaneously."

"You could add holding your own in a tussle to the list." She picked up a wet, wadded cloth from the sideboard. "I was thoroughly impressed."

"That is what it takes to impress you?"

"It takes very little." Her eyes held a teasing glimmer as she led the way from the kitchen.

When they reached the drawing room, he moved to the settee,

sat, and patted the cushion beside him. "I changed my mind and request your rapt attention while I tell you something vital."

She pulled her eyes from the dark bloodstain before joining him on the cushion. Someone, probably Juliet, had already righted the end table and removed evidence of the broken lamp. "You are acting quite mysteriously."

"If you recall the day we met, I told you I was a man of mystery."

Juliet lowered her damp cloth to the carpet near her feet. "That's right, and it's a good memory to hold tight."

And now he had a million more. "Brace yourself for a shock."

Her chin rose to an adorable tilt. "There is little that truly surprises me anymore."

"My memory has returned."

Wide-eyed, she reared back and grasped his hand. "Holy Moses. That's . . . grand."

An overwhelming need to embrace her wrenched him forward, and he tucked her into a warm hug, his chin resting on her head. Holding her now was different than before, maybe because he understood himself better, realizing he had wanted someone genuine like her all his life.

There was no doubt about it any longer. He loved Juliet wholeheartedly.

But could he bring her back with him to Bascandy? Would she be willing to go? The daily scrutiny at the palace would be magnified compared to Tabitha's. Could she withstand the pressures? Maybe and possibly not.

Her warm breaths stroked his neck, then she leaned back and placed her hands on his shoulders, studying his face. "Did your memories suddenly slide back into your head or slowly trickle into place?"

Earlier, he had allowed Juliet, Cy, Livy, and Tabitha to assume that the two trespassers had come in hopes of a reward after hearing the rumor about him being a prince. And of course, he and Juliet had no choice but to report the earlier encounter with Ruby at the party and her declaration about him being missing royalty. He had failed to admit his identity at that point. Still, they had been shocked by the possibility, to say the least.

"I recognized the men who broke into the house. Immediately afterward, my recollections surged into place."

Her quizzical brow rose. "Recognized them from where?"

"They kidnapped me from Victoria last month."

She blinked, then shook her head as if unable to believe his claim. "I'm not following you. More details, please."

"Ruby spoke the truth last night. I finally, and fully, understand who I am, and that person is Henry Graighton."

Emotions flitted across her lovely face. "Are you sure?"

"Yes, completely. My amnesia is gone, and I recall my family, my home, and everything else."

Juliet cupped her cheeks and stared at him unflinchingly. "If you are Henry Graighton, you are also a prince."

"And in line to the throne of Bascandy, my country. It is north of France, but we have more in common with England." He was rambling. No doubt, her head twirled like the spindles at the textile mill where she'd previously toiled.

"You kissed me. Twice."

He softly smiled. "And desired to kiss you two dozen times, or more accurately, two hundred."

"But . . . you're a prince."

"And still your friend."

Juliet added space between them. Then she laughed almost recklessly, evidently unconcerned that anyone might hear the disturbance. "I had hoped we might share a future one day. What an absurd notion."

"I desire the same thing."

"Because of my past, the palace wouldn't hire me to change the bed sheets, let alone allow me to be your . . . friend." She appeared to shudder. "I'm thrilled your memories have returned for your sake. But for my sake . . . I am shockingly . . . shocked."

"Of course." How would he respond if Juliet claimed to be a princess? Fall off the sofa, most likely. "My life is abundantly complicated back home, and even more so since my older brother's recent death. I had received a letter with the information only a short time before my kidnapping."

Her beautiful eyes brimmed with empathy. "I am terribly sorry."

"The worst part is that Sutton and I never forgave each other." He struggled to name the monumental grievance that had caused their wide rift in the first place. Yet he recognized that a mountain of little complaints had expanded the barrier ever since.

She patted his hand before her eyes widened again. Then she yanked her hand to her lap. "Do you have other older brothers?"

"No."

"So, you'll be King one day?" Her voice shrieked.

"Yes."

Juliet jumped to her feet. "I need a moment to myself, Gray." Anguish strangled her words. "Umm, Henry. Or Your Highness, I guess." Spinning, she fled the room, and her footsteps soon pounded up the staircase.

Sighing, he leaned against the settee and gazed at the ceiling. "What am I to do?" he whispered. His family expected him to make an advantageous match with Faith in Sutton's place. Even if he could free himself from his betrothal to Faith, the King would never permit him to marry a servant.

Nobody questioned the ruler's edicts, especially his only living son.

But having tasted freedom during his voyage and since coming to live with the sisters, he had shaken loose the shackles that had trapped him back home. He was his own man now, and if forced to choose between Juliet and the crown, he would always choose her. Wouldn't he?

Yet before making too many plans, he had to determine if Dobbin still lived and breathed. If so, his loyal friend would never return to Bascandy without him, even if that meant toting Gray's dead body home. Fortunately, he had dodged that outcome.

However, before he boarded a ship bound for Victoria, he had to tell Juliet of his plans to leave Everly temporarily. As Cy entered the drawing room, straightening his shirt collar, Gray stood. "What's all the racket?"

Obviously, Cy was referring to Juliet storming up the staircase.

"I barely know where to begin with my explanation."

"May I suggest you go straight to the heart of the matter?"

The heart belonged to Juliet.

Before he replied, the sisters arrived in the drawing room. Livy patted her curls, and Tabitha carried a thick book underneath her arm.

Tabitha halted abruptly and pinned her severe gaze upon him. "Is anything amiss?"

Gray nodded to acknowledge both sisters. "I shared surprising news with Juliet moments ago. As a result, she raced to her room, but we still need to finish our conversation before I leave Everly for a short stint."

Worry lines creased Tabitha's brow. "I can ask if she'll come down and talk with you."

"Please," he said.

As Tabitha departed, Cy hobbled toward the hallway. "I'll heat water for more tea. Seems like all we do some days is drink the brew."

Livy wrung her hands. "Does the surprising news have anything to do with your identity, Gray? I have a hunch it does."

At his core, he knew he would miss living in the sisters' home. They had nursed, sheltered, and treated him like a cherished family member. "My amnesia is over, and I recall who I am. Exactly who Miss O'Reilly claimed."

"Oh my. That is indeed a blessing. A blessing and a curse, I suppose." Livy had a wisdom he had grown to appreciate and would indeed miss.

"Incredibly so, and the news has understandably shaken Juliet." Though they had pondered his identity for weeks, this scenario about him being a prince had never crossed his mind, nor hers, undoubtedly.

"It is evident you care deeply for her."

"I hope always to have Juliet in my life. But my existence is overly complicated, and I do not know how to reconcile what we have now with what must come in the future." Especially because he was technically betrothed to another woman.

Livy ran her finger over the velvet frippery on her cuff. "She has made great strides in becoming a lady, but a princess might be a stretch, in her opinion. I wonder if the prospect overwhelms Juliet."

All too well, he understood the crown's burden. "Perhaps, but in my eyes, she is perfect as she is and always has been."

"Indeed. You have always accepted Juliet. I pray others, including your parents, will see her for the wonderful person that she is."

Most likely, his father would not because they rarely agreed on anything in recent years.

"Gray, can you come here, please?" Tabitha called from upstairs.

After bowing to Livy, he left the drawing room and climbed the front staircase like a well-mannered royal. Tabitha stood before Juliet's slightly ajar door. In a few steps, he reached Tabitha's side.

"She prefers not to leave her room. However, you may converse, provided you remain in the hallway. Is that acceptable?"

They could speak through an open window if that enabled them to finish their conversation. "Yes, ma'am."

Tabitha nodded, her eyes full of concern, then departed.

The next few minutes could set the course for his future, their future. With a deep breath, he leaned closer to the opening and whispered, "Juliet?"

Only silence answered.

Twenty-four

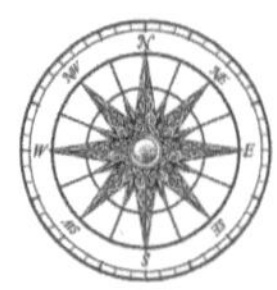

A ROUND OF GUT-WRENCHING TEARS had left Juliet drained, and her face was undoubtedly red and blotchy. She preferred not to open the door until she had time to compose herself and sort through everything that had transpired—the good, the bad, and the befuddling in between.

She hadn't wanted to believe Ruby's news last night. She'd tried hard to deny the truth about the paper with Gray's picture. She'd made up one excuse after another for why it couldn't be him. And she'd tried to act like nothing had changed between them. But it had.

It had been selfish of her. After all he'd gone through, he deserved to have his memories back. It's just that she wished he had different memories of a different past. But they confirmed every aspect of what the poster had detailed. Gray was the prince of Bascandy.

As a result, the fragile start of a future together now lay broken and scattered between them. Even though Juliet loved him, there was a literal kingdom to consider. Yes, she loved him. It was time to admit the truth to herself fully.

But look where that love got her. She finally opened herself up to the possibility of a bright future, to belonging, to having everything she'd once lost, only to lose it all over again.

Wouldn't she be better off having never met Gray and falling in love with him?

Sniffling, she leaned into the door's crack with her hand on the latch. "I need more time before we continue this conversation."

"But I shall leave soon to check on my friend and valet Dobbin to let him know I walk among the living. Afterward, I shall return."

Already his old life called to him. "You don't need to come back."

"Please open the door, Juliet."

If she widened the opening, he'd see her vulnerable side. She wasn't ready for such a thing and might never be again. "I'm sorry, but I'm . . . numb." The sensation would fade, unlike her heartbreak. "It's wonderful you recall your family and your home, Gray—I mean Henry."

"Call me what you prefer. I have grown fond of the name and you."

Juliet drew her hand to her chest, heart pounding against her palm. What she felt for him shined brighter than *fondness*. It was like comparing the moon's glow to the sun's brilliance.

"While in Victoria, I shall speak to the constable about my kidnapping and Ruby's blackmailing attempt. One way or another, we shall stop her before she steals one item from the sisters."

"I hope you're right, and please don't worry about me."

"An impossible request." His long, slender fingers wrapped

around the door's side, a sliver of his white cuff showing. "You mean everything to me."

Between the agony in his voice and the emotions barreling against her chest, she considered yanking open the door and throwing herself into his arms. Instead, she tried to rouse her strength, toughness, and good sense with a few sturdy breaths.

She'd learned plenty since her first etiquette lesson, but not enough to court a prince. He deserved the best wife—an actual princess who curtsied on cue and chose the right fork at the dining table on her first try—someone who understood the difference between a spoon bonnet and a cottage bonnet. And a proper young lady who never uttered *Holy Moses*, *dad-blamed*, or *snakes alive*.

His bride would be gentle, soft-spoken, and elegant, unlike her. If he didn't realize that yet, he eventually would. And although he may profess that he was fond of her and she meant everything to him, that was now. Once he returned to his normal life and routine, he'd soon see her for who she really was—an orphan maid who didn't belong in his world.

If they stayed together, he'd eventually grow tired of her, resent her, and find a way to cast her aside, just like everyone else in her life had.

Besides, the prospect of mingling with royalty other than him tangled her stomach into a messy knot. She'd forever be judged. And who wanted a lifetime of being condemned?

Nobody in her circle of friends. "I'm not being a martyr, but you deserve someone better than me. Someone familiar with your royal world. Someone polished."

A thump, which opened the door a smidgen wider. Did his head hit it? "There is nobody better for me than you. However, you deserve to know that my life is full of rules and rigors. A person could wilt under the censure of not feeling good enough. I have multiple times. Yet, I believe together you and I can conquer anything."

What a sweet and far-fetched claim. Also, who had deemed

him inadequate and how dare they? "Do you want to discuss the disapproval you received? Because I find it hard to believe anybody could find fault with you."

"That would be a long conversation, and I admit I am partially to blame. Another time, perhaps. What is important now is that you realize we belong together."

Belong? Did she belong anywhere? Even with the sisters? Would they accept her if they knew everything about her, especially the deepest secrets about her past pickpocketing days? Maybe she'd been foolish to think she could finally have her secret dreams come true. And perhaps she would be better off if she locked such a dream away again, keeping her free from more hurt and disappointment.

"Even though my memories are back, I want to keep being the person you have come to know."

Although his heart and soul had not changed, being royalty set him miles apart from everyone else. "But a carpenter is approachable. A prince . . . is not."

"I am me at my foundation, and you are you. It is as simple as that."

She scoffed. "I find it hard to believe you truly think our situation is simple."

"My royal status is admittedly a large bite to swallow, but it does not need to separate us." Frustration had crept into his voice.

How could it not? The monarchy was a giant, unmovable wedge slammed directly between them. From where she stood, it appeared insurmountable. "We will miss each other greatly. In time, we'll undoubtedly agree our parting is for the best."

He adjusted his grip on the door. "No."

His opinion wasn't the final say-so. Her decision counted as much as his. "What do you mean *no*?"

"I love you, Juliet."

Warmth and tingles rippled through her, top to bottom. His

honeyed words stuck to her heart as she stared at his fingers, longing to kiss each knuckle. *I love you, too* was what she wanted to say. But she had to set free the charming and almost too-good-to-be-true prince of a man. He deserved a kingdom of happiness, the precise thing she wanted most for him.

Other than for a brief span, they had led vastly different lives and were woefully incompatible. "I don't fit into your world anymore." A soft chiding in the back of her mind told her she was spouting excuses. But it didn't matter. She had to let him go.

"I disagree and believe you need more time to ponder the matter." After a moment, he added, "If I could give you one thing, it would be for you to see yourself as I do."

Tears welled inside her, and she swallowed what she could. The remainder leaked onto her cheeks. The old Juliet would have rolled her eyes in disbelief. Now, a lovesick fool and practically a lady, she refrained.

"When I return, we shall discuss this, along with our fu—"

"Don't say it." Her throat tightened.

"Why?"

"It's too much," she whispered, her voice trembling with the weight of her emotions.

He was silent for several long heartbeats. "Speaking of too much, there is one additional matter I feel obligated to mention before I depart."

What? That his family had two kingdoms instead of one? "I'm listening."

"I am betrothed to another." His words hung heavy in the air. "Though I shall end the arrangement immediately once I reach Bascandy."

She gasped and then lightly pressed her head against the door. As tears flowed, she mopped them with her sleeve. She would never divide a man and woman, whether already wedded or on the brink. Wasn't that why she had left Manchester, to not come between Molly and her husband?

She closed her eyes. It was easy to picture Gray's handsome face—winsome brown eyes, a regal nose, and perfectly full lips. Any minute, thanks to her, his expression would crumble. She couldn't bear to see it, not even in her imagination.

Still, in her heart, she knew what to do—beckon her strength and walk away. One day, he'd understand. "I'm incredibly sorry, but don't come back, Henry. Ever."

"Wait—

Juliet closed the door.

After he rapped on the door twice and called her name, she moved to the bed, buried her head under a pillow, and wept.

Twenty-five

MINUTES AFTER ARRIVING AT THE hotel in Victoria where he had previously stayed, Gray primed his fist to knock on Dobbin's old room when the door opened, revealing his oldest friend. His heart beat wildly. "Merciful heavens. I was worried about your welfare."

The color drained from Dobbin's face as he drew a stack of paper against his chest. "Henry?"

Neither spoke for a moment, only stared at one another. Dobbin's face was as familiar as his own. "So, you were not overly injured after the seashore incident?" he asked.

"I'm fine, but . . . you've been missing for weeks. Where have you been?"

"I shall explain it all. But first, I would like to don something dry." Rain had accompanied him from the dock to the hotel. Gray glanced over his shoulder before turning back around. "Are my belongings still in the same room?"

"Everything is as it was. I never stopped believing you'd come back." Dobbin heaved a shaky sigh. "I was just on my way to distribute more missing-person papers."

Gray smiled. "I saved you a trip."

Dobbin fetched the room key before opening the door across the hall for Gray, who exchanged his wet garments for a dry set. Then, Dobbin started a fire in the hearth as Gray provided an abbreviated summary of what had transpired since they last saw each other.

All the while, Juliet's last words before he departed from Everly eight hours earlier still echoed in his soul. *Don't come back, Henry. Ever.*

Their conversation left him with one monumental regret—not telling her that Faith had been Sutton's love, never his. Initially, he blurted out his betrothal without rehearsing how to explain the complex situation gently. He had tried to fix his blunder, but she refused to open the door and listen to his clarification. If Juliet knew the truth, could she be persuaded to change her mind about traveling to Bascandy with him?

He was unsure. From the moment he had started speaking with her through the crack in the door, she'd seemed to have made the decision to separate from him. What was he to do?

Mid-afternoon rain pelted the windowpane of his room, and a fire now sizzled in the hearth. "You stare at me as if I am a figment of your imagination. It is unnerving."

Standing near the window, deep worry lines etched Dobbin's forehead, his jaw tight. His fair hair had grown longer since the last time they had seen one another, and his blue eyes carried a wariness. "Apologies, sir. You've been absent for weeks, and I'm still absorbing that you were kidnapped and suffered amnesia. It's much to comprehend."

"Were you badly hurt the night of our attack?"

"A headache for a few days. I never saw anyone sneak up on me. When I came to, you had disappeared. Please forgive me."

"No need to apologize. I was also completely caught off guard, and the waves were thunderous if I remember correctly."

"Still, it was my job to protect you, Henry."

Henry. He should probably start thinking of himself by his proper name. "Let us talk no more of it. What is done is done."

He had caught the first steamer out of Everly to Victoria. Between a barrage of memories and thoughts of Juliet, he had pondered on a bench for the seven-hour ride, except when he paced for long stretches. He also contemplated his relationship with his father, realizing that amnesia and Sutton's death had taught him a valuable lesson—among many—about not taking others for granted.

How could they resolve their differences? A wholehearted conversation? More time? Whatever the answer, Henry intended to put in the work to make changes. Surely, the King desired the same outcome.

Dobbin hung Henry's coat in the wardrobe, turned around, and drew a deep breath. "An official correspondence arrived a week or so after you vanished. When you didn't promptly return, I read the missive in your absence, sir."

Henry moved to a plush chair beside the fireplace and gestured toward a matching gold chair for Dobbin to sit. "Go on, but first, stop calling me sir. It drives me a little mad. Today, I only need a friend."

After Dobbin angled the furniture so they could view one another, he sank into the seat and rubbed his palms down the front of his trousers. "The King has died, Henry."

"No!" The jolt hit him with bullet speed, directly punishing his heart. Everything inside him squeezed as memories marched through his mind—Father on his beloved steed, then at the head of the table, and finally next to Mother in their private sitting room.

First Sutton, now Father. Undoubtedly, the double heartaches must have shattered his mother and sisters. Bascandy, as well. A hollowness burrowed inside him, a raw space he knew not how to fill. He drew a deep breath to gather himself "Had my father taken ill?"

"Chest pains one evening, then never awoke in the morn." The same ailment had shortened Henry's grandfather's life, though he had lived much longer.

Unsteady, he gripped the chair's arms as the magnitude of the King's death slowly bled into his skin. He was no longer just a prince. He was the ruler of his country. He was the new King.

Merciful heavens. He had thought he would have more time to adjust to the prospect, to learn to accept the duties that would one day be his, duties he had never wanted and a role he had never coveted.

"You will do exceedingly well succeeding your father."

Would he? It was too late for the King to offer even a whisper of wisdom regarding how to rule Bascandy. When Henry left home, he never expected his family to decrease by two so rapidly. "Time will tell, I suppose."

"During our youth, do you recall how my mother bribed us with desserts so we would listen to her Bible stories?"

A bundle of gratitude multiplied inside him because, once again, he recalled big and little pieces of his past. "Yes, and I also remember her apple cake." He was swept back to the warmth from the kitchen hearth, the never-ending cinnamon scent, and Mrs. Taylor's spirited voice as she shared the Scriptures. Characters from Abraham to Zacchaeus had sprung to life.

"Then I suppose you also recall how she used to say a person's true identity was in Christ, not in being a king, a pauper, or anyone else."

Mrs. Taylor's words were as vivid today as when she recited them at her table long ago. "I did not understand her message back then, but I do now."

Dobbin leaned back and crossed his ankles. "I suspect your amnesia and leading a life as a commoner has molded your character and prepared you to rule Bascandy. Of course, it's merely a guess."

Henry had always believed that leading an ordinary life far exceeded one full of pressures, expectations, and rules from the palace. Then God answered his earnest prayer, dropping him into the role of a simple carpenter who faced hardships and heartbreak—the same as everyone else.

Cy had trained him to be patient and to start each day with a plan as they renovated the carriage house. More than once, Icala had relayed the importance of trusting his instincts, of not hesitating to try a new endeavor, and that mistakes were inevitable. The sisters had repeatedly embraced him as a beloved family member.

And then there was Juliet, the best person he had ever met. Throughout her life, she persisted and carried hope in her heart. She had a gumption he respected, and she always treated others with compassion, even the stray cat.

Was that not what God also preached—kindness and charity toward others?

Could he take fragments of what he had learned and lead Bascandy with integrity and empathy?

His time in Everly had shown him he was capable of all those things and more. In fact, he had matured and changed, and he was better suited now to the kingship than before he started his journey around the world.

Why, then, was he opposed to those duties and that role? What was wrong with him? Why did he still balk at filling his father's spot?

"I am not Sutton. He was born to rule. And me? I have always made mistakes, causing problems and earning Father's censure."

Dobbin was silent a moment before speaking again. "Do you remember what your father told you on the dock as you were leaving for your voyage?"

Henry closed his eyes and tried to recall his father's farewell. "'I pray you grow into the man God created you to be.'" Although wise words, Henry had not reflected on the poignant message since leaving home.

"You may have thought he wanted you to be like Sutton." Dobbin's voice was earnest. "But he only ever wanted you to be the man God designed *you* to be, someone different than your brother, to be sure, but still a worthy and noble man who was admirable in his own right."

Henry opened his eyes and met his friend's sincere gaze.

Was carrying on his family's legacy without too many missteps possible? What if God had even allowed his amnesia to prepare him to be a better ruler?

But who would reign beside him? A sharp pain stabbed his temple, and he rubbed the sore spot with his fingertips.

"What specifically troubles you, Henry?"

His stomach burned with dread. "It may kill me to leave my beloved behind."

Dobbin's eyebrows climbed high as he leaned forward. "You have a beloved?"

One day, he would share the unbelievable tale of his Everly days with his friend, perhaps during their long journey back home. But two pressing matters elbowed that conversation to the side for now. "Yes, indeed. I have fallen deeply in love with Juliet Dash, who discovered me unconscious behind her workplace. She is everything to me."

After blinking, Dobbin's eyes still held a dazed stare. "In a matter of weeks, you met and developed deep-rooted love for Miss Dash while having amnesia? And she works for a wage?"

"Correct."

"I don't mean to question you, but are you certain it's not merely an infatuation or gratitude since she saved your life?"

Dobbin's skepticism failed to surprise, offend, or deter Henry. Naturally, he would forever be thankful for Juliet's rescue, but love had shoved appreciation to the side. "My sentiments for Juliet are sincere. She is kind, charitable, and a genuine angel of mercy. At a tender age, she took responsibility for her life and faced many hardships, then traveled here on a bride ship."

"She is searching for a husband and set her sights on you." Although he failed to say *rich husband*, Henry caught Dobbin's inference.

Juliet cared about him as a person, not as royalty. "Actually, I gather she preferred me as a carpenter to a prince. Still, I intend to wed her if she agrees."

"Forgive me for playing devil's advocate, but what about Faith?"

Henry drew a labored, frustrated breath. "A fair question that I cannot answer, though I shall speak with her immediately upon arriving home."

"Have you already proposed to Miss Dash?"

"Not yet. I realize I need to break my engagement with Faith first. For all I know, a wedding date is set, a dress is sewn, and invitations are mailed. Yet even if Juliet refuses me, I cannot wed another."

"Faith must miss Sutton dreadfully."

"Indeed, and I assume she is unwilling to wed so soon after his death. Perhaps I shall remain single forever." The idea held a measure of merit should Juliet ultimately refuse him, and she certainly could.

A royal life was not for everyone.

Dobbin's brow arched. "What about an heir?"

Henry groaned and slumped as silence built around them, sleet lashing the windowpane. "How long until we can sail home?"

"A few of your men continue to search for you and have ventured into the wilderness. We'll need to round them up. Since your disappearance, we've explored the area between here and Seattle and recently ventured to the mainland."

"Including Everly?"

"I am unsure exactly where on the mainland, but we continue adding additional places up and down the coastline daily. Someone reported seeing you near Port Alberni, north of here, but obviously, it was a false finding."

Everyone serving the crown swore oaths, agreeing to sacrifice their lives for the royal family. Their devotion humbled Henry. Now that he thought about it, Juliet had acted similarly, offering to step aside as he chose a better bride. Except none existed, and he refused to give her up without mounting his best arguments.

"I also sent a letter to the palace explaining the situation, which was excruciating," Dobbin said.

Henry winced. As soon as possible, he must return home. "I shall write Mother yet today."

A sharp knock sounded on the door, and Dobbin moved to answer the beckoning as Henry stood. "Who is there?" Dobbin called.

"The chief constable. I understand Henry Graighton is inside this room, and I must speak with him immediately."

Dobbin's blue eyes swam with deep concern as they met Henry's. "One moment, sir."

Ruby had traveled on the same steamer to Victoria, though she had the good sense to refrain from speaking to him. Had she run straight to the constable, dragged him to the hotel, and now expected a reward? Juliet had explained that the poor woman had a child on the way, so why not give her the money to help her provide for the baby?

"Bid him inside. He has saved me a trip. After he leaves, we shall go to the harbor, address our men, and instruct someone to find those who search for me. And you shall accompany me to Everly to meet Juliet in the coming days."

Chuckling, Dobbin reached for the latch. "By Jove, you sound like a proper king, full of instructions and plans for the future."

Henry grinned before growing serious again. He was ready for justice to reign, even in a frontier town perhaps newer than his borrowed coat hanging in the wardrobe. It was time to reveal the truth to the constable—Ruby had stolen her prior employer's jewels and now blackmailed Juliet.

With Ruby no longer a threat, Juliet could move on with her life. But on what path? With him or without?

Twenty-six

JULIET HAD PUT OFF THE CONVERSATION regarding her past long enough. If Henry hadn't left, he'd buck her up for the upcoming heart-to-heart, then sit beside her as a pillar of support. But he couldn't help her now. He'd been gone for three days.

Juliet's stomach lurched as she poked her head into the drawing room. Musical notes floated in the air. Positioned on the piano stool, Tabitha's fingers roved across the silky keyboard. Livy knitted in a spindle-backed rocker, half of a rose-colored blanket draped over her lap.

Couldn't she postpone the chat until Tabitha finished playing the piano? Even better, why not tell the sisters about her wayward pickpocketing days tomorrow over breakfast?

But then Livy raised her hand before Juliet ducked out of the doorway. "Please join us, dearie."

Tabitha stopped playing, turned toward Juliet, and softly smiled. She didn't waste her grins. Offering one now was almost like an embrace between friends. "Would you like a warm cup of tea on this snowy night? It's jasmine, and you'll find all you need on the cart."

"Yes, ma'am, and thank you."

Well, this was it. There would be no more stalling with the dreaded conversation. Juliet moved toward the double-tiered wooden cart with two large, spoked wheels in the back and two little ones in the front. Tonight, it was positioned in the corner near Peaches's cage.

After reaching the cart, she picked up a teacup and slowly poured her tea, in no hurry to rush about. Then she returned the pot to the cart.

The piano playing resumed, and the bird whistled. Juliet wouldn't have stumbled over Gray in the woods if not for the parakeet. So much—and especially her heart—had vastly changed since then. Did Gray think about her half as much as she pondered him?

She yearned for his smile across the room and missed challenging him at chess, even though he always let her win. The sound of the town's chiming bells was a painful reminder of their shared moments, and the absence of his warmth in every room was a constant ache.

And she missed kissing him. She missed that a lot. But she craved more than intimacy. His loyalty made him irresistible, not to mention his kindness and wit.

Tears welled in her eyes, blurring her vision. She sipped her tea as the evening wind creaked the rafters. Even the house mourned and complained about his absence. Who could blame it? Certainly not her.

Finally, she rejoined the sisters and settled onto the deacon's bench beside Livy's chair. Then she shifted her head to the left.

Did the Currier & Ives hand-colored lithograph hang crooked? Yes, and she'd straighten it later.

Too bad her cockeyed life wasn't as easily fixable.

As another hymn began, Tabitha sang along. Her alto voice was warmer, smoother, and sweeter than heated syrup over Icala's flapjacks at breakfast. Wound tight, Juliet slowly relaxed to the soothing music until Tabitha crooned:

> *"Just as I am, though tossed about,*
> *With many a conflict, many a doubt;*
> *Fighting within and fears without,*
> *O Lamb of God, I come, I come!"*

Just as I am? The exact four words that graced the first page of her grandfather's journal. What a peculiar coincidence.

"Whatever is wrong, dearie?" Livy lowered her long knitting needles to her lap.

Juliet blinked aside the tear caught on her lashes. Pesky thing. "It's nothing. This song reminds me of my grandfather, is all."

"It is lovely and poignant. Did he sing it to you once upon a time?"

"Not that I recall, but he wrote 'Just as I Am' in his journal, which I still have. I always wondered why he opened his diary with those words."

After Tabitha finished the song, she rose and moved toward the shiny deacon's bench. Her much-loved slippers shuffled across the floor, offering a sense of coziness that even Juliet felt. "That song always makes me weep, and I never weep." She released a little lady-like sigh as she sat beside her. "I suppose I'm convicted to stop carrying around my strife and lay my worries at God's feet."

Juliet half-heartedly nodded and set her teacup and saucer on the carpet. Whether from the tender song or rattled by Henry's leaving and Ruby's possible return for the jewels, she contemplated talking to Him again. What did she have to lose?

Tears swelled inside her, and she swallowed the bundle. She refused to turn into a blabbering idiot in front of the sisters. Or even God. How precisely did someone place their worries at His feet, anyway?

Her stomach spun, and she pressed her hand against the constant motion. She'd already lost the man she loved. Was she about to say goodbye to the two women who'd become the closest thing to a mother she'd known since infancy?

Heaven knew she didn't want to. They had sheltered her, taught her to be ladylike, surprised her with a fancy dress for the dance, and treated her like a . . . daughter.

But she'd lived as a criminal for almost two years. Some folks might hold the fact against her, yet the sisters had gracious natures. Whether they would or would not, it was time to learn the answer. "Once upon a time, I was a thief." She hung her head, examining the geometric shapes on the carpeting as she awaited the sisters' reaction.

"In Victoria?" Livy asked, her voice high and screechy. "Mrs. Moresby said you didn't steal from the Firths."

"That's true. I wasn't a thief then and will never be again." The sisters deserved her respect, and Juliet raised her chin. "But I was as a girl in Manchester after my grandfather died and before I landed in the orphanage. Based on his Bible teachings, I understood the wrongness of it, yet I pickpocketed anyway."

Juliet pursed her lips before spitting out the remainder of her sour recitation. "Until now, I questioned if I had the nerve to tell you about my unflattering past."

Livy clutched her ivory cameo dangling on a black ribbon around her neck.

Silence hung in the room before Tabitha patted Juliet's arm. "And the song prompted you to do so?"

"Partially. I've considered telling you for some time because Livy said a true lady has a pure heart. The good Lord knows I don't have that, but I'm working toward it. Then the song's lyrics mentioned being tossed about and many conflicts and doubts. Well, that describes me, especially since Gray left."

Livy leaned forward, concern in her eyes. "Because you miss him?"

"It's far worse. I love him, and he also loves me. But he's a prince, and I'm a pauper. We don't belong together any more than I belong here with you."

Also, Gray had a fiancée back home, but Juliet hesitated to mention that nagging detail. A piece of her wanted him to sweep back into the house, promising his undying love and plans to remain in Everly forever. But that story was only a fairy tale.

If Gray intended to return and was eager to see her again, he would have arrived by now. Then again, she had told him never to come back.

Livy smiled gently at Juliet. "My dear child, you are beautiful inside and out. And you were that way even before we started the manner training."

The old skepticism spinning inside Juliet for years refused to abate. If she was beautiful inside and out, why had so many people left and rejected her over the years?

Tabitha reached for Juliet's hand and squeezed. "You belong here, Juliet. And you belong with Gray. That's easy to see."

"Not for me. I've never belonged anywhere." Tears once again threatened the backs of Juliet's eyes. "And I wouldn't blame you now that you know about my thieving if you want me to leave."

Tabitha leveled a severe gaze upon her. "It almost sounds like you want us to do so."

Juliet's ready response died. Did she?

"Do you think you're pushing us away because you fear we

might eventually reject you?" Tabitha asked. "And do you think you're doing the same with Gray?"

"No, I don't think so—"

"If you're afraid of getting hurt and losing people," Tabitha continued, "then you might be distancing yourself before it can happen."

Holy Moses, what if Tabitha was right? What if she was letting her fears from her past keep her from staying in one place and finding a new home? Maybe she had come into the drawing room just moments ago trying to sabotage her job and her relationship with the sisters to leave them before they left her.

Tabitha squeezed her hand again. "Whatever the case, you're our family now. And you can't get rid of us that easily."

"That's right, dearie." Livy's eyes filled with tenderness. "Besides, everyone makes mistakes. Don't you think it's time you forgive yourself? I do."

Hoping not to cry, Juliet leaned back and focused on the Currier & Ives framed scene again. Could she forgive herself? A sense of unworthiness had trailed her forever. If she'd known how to stop the shadows, she'd have banished them long before now.

Livy resumed her needlework. "Ages ago, and I won't tell you how many years, our poor mother abandoned my sister and me on a rich man's doorstep."

"We were three and five," Tabitha added. "Not to mention dirty, ill-mannered, and didn't trust a soul."

Juliet touched her parted lips. The revelation answered why the sisters failed to resemble the oil painting of their father in the dining room. Perhaps also partially why they'd offered her a job despite the incident at the Firths'. "I never suspected."

"Why would you?" Tabitha gave Juliet's hand a final pat before releasing it. "Our dear adopted mother, with the help of a governess and a finishing school, taught us manners, elegance, and refinement. Sadly, she died shortly before we debuted in society."

Glassy-eyed, Livy nodded. "Tabitha and I thank God we landed on Mr. and Mrs. Sherwood's doorstep long ago. And every day, we thank God you landed on ours."

Juliet swallowed the impossibly large lump stuck in her throat. She hadn't believed God heeded her calls for help for so long. But hadn't He spared her life and given her Tabitha and Livy? And Gray?

Gray claimed to love her just as she was. And so did God, according to the song's lyrics. Therefore, why not extend grace to herself? Was it as simple as handing the load to Him through prayer and trust? Maybe. She could at least try.

With her eyes closed, she silently prayed, mentioning her gratitude and the troubles in her heart.

When Tabitha rose, Juliet reopened her eyes. She didn't feel entirely different. Maybe it would take longer to unstick all the debris that had built up in her life to choke off her prayers. But she did feel better for having laid her worries at His feet.

"I am tremendously curious how the next week will unfold." Tabitha moved to the teapot to warm her drink. "I wonder who will return first, Miss O'Reilly or Henry."

Livy's knitting needles again clacked as her hands moved in a soothing rhythm. "Perhaps Miss O'Reilly is too busy counting her reward money to bother with us anymore?"

Juliet drew a deep breath and slowly released the air. Knowing Ruby, she'd probably come back eventually despite receiving a heap of money for finding the missing prince. And what about Gray? Would he even want to return after their time apart, now that he had reexamined the future and what was at stake?

For goodness' sake, the man had a fiancée, which utterly ruined everything.

Twenty-seven

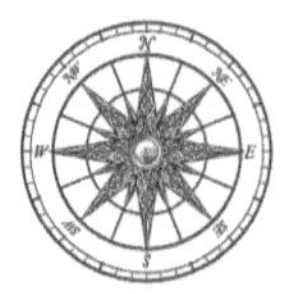

GOOD DAY TO YOU, SIR." HENRY BOWED
after finishing his business with the Everly constable before leaving the jail.

Afternoon snow flurried in every direction as he moved toward the rented carriage parked in the street, where Dobbin dutifully waited. Their steamer had arrived in Everly forty-five minutes prior.

With one pressing conversation complete, another more significant one followed—explaining to Juliet the details of his pending arranged marriage. He still kicked himself for not giving her all the facts immediately after his amnesia faded. His only excuse was having a brain heavy with memories, questions, and the driving need to check on Dobbin.

Now he had to make Juliet understand he had only ever loved

one woman—her. And to convince her they belonged together. As the new King, could he not continue to smooth the way for Juliet in Bascandy, like in Everly?

He would do his very best.

Ruby's recent incarceration was another matter to discuss. According to the constable in Victoria, she had committed many crimes, not counting the theft of her former employer's jewels, including the Queen's brooch. Henry alerted the lawman of Miss O'Reilly's blackmail attempt, which would lengthen her imprisonment.

Henry quickened his pace, eager to see Juliet. As much as he longed for a bride of his choosing—someone full of life, kindness, and charity—did she want him? Certainly not before he broke his engagement to Faith.

"Henry!"

At the sound of Tabitha's voice, he turned and drew his collar tighter around his neck to ward off the wind. She approached from the bank, a tall whitewashed structure in the backdrop. He tipped his hat. "Good afternoon. I was on my way to pay you a call."

She smiled in that familiar way of hers. "Me or Juliet? Either way, we are delighted."

"You are on to me. How is she, by the way?"

"Well, indeed." Tabitha's voice dropped. "Yesterday, she informed us of her hardships and misdirection after her grandfather's death. Fortunately, she persevered."

Juliet's admission of being a pickpocket, a well-buried secret, was monumental. His chest swelled with pride on her behalf. "May I offer you a ride? I need help with a plan, and you are the perfect person to assist me."

Her brow cocked. "How intriguing, and I'd appreciate a lift. Not a snowflake in the air when I left the house earlier."

He offered his arm, and she linked with him before they moved toward the carriage, snow crunching beneath their boots. Few pedestrians or conveyances traversed the sidewalk and street, likely due to the disagreeable weather.

Dobbin, standing by the door, assisted Tabitha into the coach. She sat on one side, with him and Dobbin on the other springy red cushion. The combination of black walls, drapes, and dreary sky forced him to squint in the dimness.

Introductions followed as the carriage jerked forward, the road bumpy beneath the wheels. After exchanging pleasantries, Henry leaned back against his seat. "I had a long talk with Mr. Blake moments ago. Apparently, a man named Victor Thayer coordinated my kidnapping to receive a handsome ransom."

"He is under arrest, is he not?" Dobbin asked, his fair brows knitted.

"Yes." There was no reason to tell Tabitha or Dobbin the remainder of what Mr. Blake had said. Henry's ruse had worked, fooling his kidnappers into thinking he had hidden on the second steamboat after his escape. The steamer left the dock for Victoria with the men still on board, searching high and low for Henry, who had jumped into the water.

Eventually, the pair returned to Everly, the last place they had seen him. Not until after the tearoom open house, with everyone whispering about a missing prince at the local saloon, did the kidnappers find Henry's trail again.

"You know, Henry," Tabitha said, "it is good you did not leave Everly with Miss O'Reilly during the open house. Otherwise, the kidnappers may have followed you to Victoria and captured you a second time."

Or perhaps not. He doubted his entourage, mostly Dobbin, would permit him to wander away for a similar plot to unfold. "Do you honestly believe Juliet would have permitted me to leave town with her foe, even if that meant sitting on me to stop the departure?"

"Never in a million years." Tabitha chuckled.

"I can barely wait to make Miss Dash's acquaintance." Dobbin grinned. He usually remained stoic when in public, but Everly had a way of changing people.

"You'll adore her as we do," Tabitha said.

When the carriage driver stopped before the sisters' home, Dobbin quickly exited and waited at the door to assist Tabitha.

The northern wind whipped inside through the opening and sprinkled snowflakes onto Henry's trousers, which he brushed aside. "Will you please give us a moment, Dobbin? I want to speak privately with Tabitha before we leave the carriage."

"Of course." After bowing, Dobbin silently closed the vehicle's door.

Henry met Tabitha's gaze directly. "May I financially compensate you for expenses incurred during my stay?"

"Heavens no. We were happy to assist you however possible."

"Thank you."

Tabitha nodded. "You might be interested to know that I received a letter from my brother this afternoon."

"All is well back in England, I hope."

"It is." A moment passed before she added, "I don't believe I told you, but when Alex stopped by the house, he asked me to help fund his upcoming trip home."

Henry raised his brow. "No, you did not mention that detail, though it was none of my business."

"My nephew's request perplexed me at the time. I couldn't imagine Nolan not providing for his son. Especially since he requested Alex return home directly. My brother is known for his generosity."

"I am sorry." Although they never learned what specific crime Alex had committed up north, swindling seemed like a strong possibility. "If only our family members behaved exactly as we preferred."

"Yes, because we know best."

He smiled. "Indeed."

"Now what was this plan you desire my help with?"

Ah, a much better topic. "There are critical matters I must discuss with Juliet and prefer to do so privately. And perhaps romantically."

"Intriguing. Leave the details for Livy and me. But I must ask, are you intending to propose marriage, young man?"

"Ideally, yes, but sadly, not today. I still need to convince her that we are well suited, though I fear she would abhor the acute attention she would receive at the palace. It is stifling, to say the least."

"Understandable, though Juliet has a sturdy backbone."

"That is true." Not for the first time, he admired Tabitha's faithful support of her charge. He also appreciated that she treated him as an equal, with no indication that his royal status made a fraction of a difference in their relationship.

"I suspect you'll easily persuade her."

He was less convinced. "Except there are two things you do not know about me."

"Then, by all means, do tell."

"I am the new King of Bascandy and engaged to another woman."

"Oh my stars."

"Juliet, it's time for another lesson." Tabitha's smile was vast, and her eyes were as bright as the lantern she gripped.

"You look pleased this evening." Juliet rose from her knees beside a new shipment of tea from India, the spicy scents spilling from the crate she had unpacked. The shop had closed an hour earlier as dusk had settled.

"Do I?" Tabitha's grin faltered a notch. "I suppose I am. Though my afternoon started poorly due to the surprising snow, it vastly improved."

"Some days definitely follow that pattern." The night of the open house sprang to mind as Juliet reached for her shawl draped over a chair and tossed the garment over her shoulders. "On what topic is my next lesson?"

"Hmm . . . I don't know the specifics. You'll have to ask your instructor."

What had Livy planned this time? Probably something essential, such as what jewelry to wear in season or out. Never mind that Juliet had nothing of that sort. Yesterday, Livy spent two hours reciting personal care recipes, everything from cold creams and the cure for chapped hands to tooth powders and rose lip salve.

All important, perhaps. Yet less than riveting.

They exited the tearoom and crossed the slippery cobblestone pathway, the ice momentarily slowing their steps. Juliet gripped Tabitha's elbow to keep her from falling. Stars had replaced the earlier snowflakes, dotting the sky with sparkly diamonds.

As they entered the back door to the kitchen, Icala turned away from the stove and revealed a wide grin. The scent of roasting meat also offered a warm welcome. "It is a good day, is it not?"

Fairly run-of-the-mill, in Juliet's opinion. She stomped the snow off her shoes onto the braided rug and started to shed her shawl. "I'm glad you think so."

"I'll take your wrap." Tabitha extended her arm, her overcoat still buttoned to her chin. "You go on ahead to the library."

"Enjoy your lesson." Icala shooed her toward the hallway with his wooden spoon.

Juliet glanced at the floor near his dark shoes to ensure he hadn't dripped a droplet. Satisfied he hadn't, she nodded and left the kitchen. Why all the smiling and enthusiasm about Livy's instructions? Of course, there was nothing wrong with their keen interest and support. However, a suspicious person might wonder why they were almost giddy.

Juliet would have preferred to take a minute or two to tidy herself, but apparently, there wasn't time. She freed her hair from the binding, stuffed the leather piece into her pocket, and threaded her fingers through the strands before entering the library.

She halted abruptly at the sight of lit candles everywhere. On the mantel, the coffee tables, and scattered on the bookshelves. And there was Gray, standing before the fireplace, his back to her, flames licking the hearth. A dark blanket and wicker basket were splayed on the floor behind him. An intimate picnic. Had she ever seen anything more romantic and lovely? No and then he turned around.

He was as handsome as she remembered, maybe more so, if possible. Hungrily, she drank him in, from his cleanly shaven face to the tips of his shiny black boots. His brown waves were tamed and shorter than before he left Everly. But his golden-brown eyes hadn't changed a tinge. They still had the power to weaken her knees.

"You're back." She said the only thing that came to mind, which ended up being the obvious.

He chuckled that masculine laugh, deep and throaty.

The sound of it, along with everything about him, sent shivers tingling up her spine.

"You look beautiful."

She tucked his sweet compliment deep inside her heart, where she stored all his others. "I've worked all day and am likely a mess."

Shaking his head, he approached her. Was there wariness in his eyes? "Trust me, you are the best thing I have ever seen."

Her hands grew clammy, and she swiped them on her uniform's stiff skirt. What about the two unmentioned matters that loomed large in the library—he was still a prince and engaged to somebody else? "I was to report here for a lesson. Does that make you my instructor?"

"Not at all, and the lesson was mine to learn, never yours."

What in the tarnation was he talking about? Was she the instructor? No, she had no wisdom to impart. She glanced at the wicker basket. "I assume Icala is to thank for our private meal."

"Yes, he, Tabitha, and Livy helped with this little surprise. Shall we investigate what he has prepared?"

It was almost as if Gray wanted to court her. But he'd leave town soon, and the man had a fiancée. Not one thing since Tabitha had entered the tearoom minutes ago had made a speck of sense.

When she nodded, he reached for her hand and led her to the blanket where they sat. She tucked her legs beneath her skirt as the fire sizzled over his shoulders. "I'm surprised there isn't a chaperone on duty."

"Cy and Livy, along with my friend, wait around the corner in the drawing room. Later, I would like for you to meet him."

"I'd like that, as well." It wasn't every day she met someone from his past. In fact, she had never experienced the pleasure.

He unpacked the hamper—slivers of rare roast beef, deviled eggs, thick rye bread, cheese squares, and a currant-and-nut pudding in individual tureens.

After Gray blessed the meal, he filled his plate. Oddly, Juliet had no desire to eat, only to sit and stare at him instead. A notable cleft dented his chin, something she'd missed when he wore whiskers. She fought the temptation to fit her finger into the groove.

His attention swerved from his full plate to her face. "Your gaze is quite intent."

"I'm curious what is on your mind."

He wiped his mouth with his napkin. "Two critical items. First, the chief constable visited me the day I arrived in Victoria and reported Ruby was already under surveillance for additional crimes. She is now locked in a cell, awaiting trial."

Holy Moses. Emotions bombarded Juliet, everything from relief to sympathy for her tormentor. "I am tongue-tied."

"The good news is she cannot hurt you anymore. Perhaps her

captivity is the push she needs to change her life. For the child's sake, I did ensure she received the reward money."

"Thank you." Juliet's heart squeezed. Her old roommate was a tried-and-true criminal. But then, so was Juliet, once upon a time. Childhood pickpocketing was still stealing, no matter how a person twisted the facts and made excuses. Starting today, she would pray for Ruby and her baby. Would someone kindly help raise the little one, much like Mr. and Mrs. Sherwood had taken in Tabitha and Livy? *Please let it be so.*

Juliet reached for the pudding tureen and sampled a delicious bite. "I told the sisters about my past. They reminded me God loves me as I am."

The intensity of Gray's stare sent her stomach spinning. "How true. That leads to my second point, my lesson, if you will," he said. "I made a monumental mistake when I left before explaining my relationship with Faith."

"Your intended?"

"My temporary intended. She and my brother loved each other fiercely. After his death, my parents moved me into the groom role."

"Without your permission?"

"That is how my world works back home. But rest assured, I intend to break our betrothal as soon as I arrive in Bascandy."

Was ending a royal engagement that simple? Juliet suspected not. "But if the King has decreed the wedding, is that not an un-breakable contract?"

Gray's eye twitched before he drew a deep breath. "Unfortu-nately, when I was in Victoria, I learned my father has also died."

"Oh, Gray." She reached for him and wrapped her arms around him in an embrace. First, he'd learned of his brother's unexpected death. Then he waded through his amnesia, and now this. What an onslaught of woes in a short span. "I am immensely sorry for your loss. You must be eager to return to your family."

"It is complicated." With one final squeeze, he broke their embrace to capture her hands and held them tight against his chest. "Now that my father is deceased, I am no longer Prince Henry. I am King Henry."

"King?" The word carried a stuffy, unrelatable ring. Rulers belonged in fairy tales and the Bible, not sitting on the library floor, for heaven's sake.

"I am heir to a throne I never wanted. More than anything, I long to propose marriage to you, but alas, it is impossible until I break my engagement.

Juliet fought the urge to nibble her fingernail. But it wasn't ladylike, and someone had hold of her hands. "By refusing Faith, you'll go against your parents' wishes."

"I believe Mother shall change her mind after meeting you."

"Meets me?" Juliet's voice squeaked. Had she ever had more questions arrowing through her thoughts than now? Granted, Gray's royal world was more foreign to her than a pickle fork on the day she first arrived in Everly. "Is she nearby?"

"No, but I propose you travel to Bascandy with me to meet my family. I shall talk to Faith and explain the situation. Afterward, you and I shall wed if that is agreeable."

She released his hands and clutched a handful of skirt. Could she believe Gray had her best interest at heart? A tiny voice inside her whispered no, that eventually he would tire of her and reject or leave her.

"I see your hesitation. It is not unheard of for an heir apparent to abdicate and give up the throne for one reason or another. Perhaps that is what I should do."

Juliet's chest grew tighter than a wedding band one size too small. Not in a million years would she allow him to make a sacrifice that impacted an entire kingdom. He'd make an ideal ruler with his innate kindness, strength, and intelligence. "Absolutely not. Bascandy needs you, and you'll be a wonderful King."

"Thank you, and perhaps." He tucked a lock of her hair behind her ear. "Does that mean you have agreed to come with?"

Her heart thumped wildly. Was she truly considering traveling abroad with him? Was she a mad woman? "When would we leave?"

"After we round up a few of my men who still search for me. However, they shall return on another ship if we do not find them soon."

Juliet's thoughts continued to leap back and forth and sideways. Not for a second did she yearn to become a queen who resided in a palace while others scraped to exist. Also, being judged for the rest of her life soured her stomach.

But she had to push past her fears, take this next step, and finally let herself dream of having more in her life. Because the truth was, she didn't want to live without Gray for a fraction of a second if the possibility of a life together existed.

Maybe, and hopefully, she could help minister to the downtrodden in Bascandy one day. Less fortunate folks lived everywhere in the world, didn't they? She'd be a fool to turn down the opportunity, especially with Gray at her side.

And yes, she needed to start thinking of him as, and calling him, Henry. Because that's who he really was, and that's the life she would have to accept for him and for them.

He ran his finger over her wrist, stirring up an explosion of tingles inside her. "What are you thinking?"

To kiss him until their troubles faded was one idea. Instead, she drew a sharp intake of breath. "If I travel with you, I have three conditions. First, I'd like to seek guidance from my bride-ship friends."

"A perfectly reasonable request. What else?"

"While your engagement remains intact, you and I won't share intimacies."

"I agree." His brow rose. "And your third requirement?"

"It's more of a revelation than a stipulation." She had to tell him the truth, even though he still belonged to someone else. "I love you unconditionally and to a dizzying degree."

His lips trembled as sincerity filled his warm eyes, giving her hope they'd find a way to piece together their vastly different lives. "I am lightheaded with love myself."

"Then it's good we're sitting down."

"Indeed, and it is good we established firm rules for our relationship." His gaze flickered to her lips, then rapidly away. "For I am dying to kiss you."

Slowly, she nodded. As much as they loved one another, her future remained unresolved. Would she travel to Bascandy only to turn around and retrace the waves back to Everly because he couldn't break his engagement to Faith? If so, she'd return alone. Never would she permit Henry to forfeit his country on her behalf.

Twenty-eight

JULIET AND HER FRIENDS—SAGE, WILLOW, and Daisy—stood around a table in the elegant, sunlit breakfast room of Victoria's Royal Hotel. The room was empty, save for them and the anticipation that filled the air. A lovely Christmas and a busy two weeks had flitted past since she agreed to travel to Bascandy with Henry.

"You're giving me a wedding dress?" Juliet traced the beaded bodice with her fingertip, then the length of a silky white sleeve. The gown matched perfection, as did the thoughtfulness behind the gift.

They had gathered to ogle Daisy's creation, a wedding dress tucked inside a long, white carton now serving as the table's centerpiece. Henry, always eager to help make Juliet's life easier, had arranged for the private meeting space and refreshments.

Quite pregnant, Daisy rested her hands on her extended stomach. Darling dimples dented her cheeks, and freckles dotted her nose. She'd tamed her dark brown hair into a long braid as usual. "Though I sewed the gown, it's a wedding gift from us all. Believe it or not, you inspired the design before I knew you had even met someone special."

"That is me." Juliet chuckled. "Miss Inspirational."

Willow laughed as her blue eyes sparkled. She and her sister Sage had the same heart-shaped faces, dainty chins, and reddish-blond hair. Willow's teal blue hat sat at a jaunty tilt, adding to her charm. "Tell us more about your mystery man."

"And make it snappy." Clad in a smart burgundy dress trimmed with black bric-a-brac, Sage grinned. Twin tortoise shell combs locked her flowy red-blond hair from her lovely face. "Will your wedding take place soon? It was hard to tell from your letter."

"Not exactly." More than a little, she wanted her friends to approve of her decision, but a big fat knot sat in the middle of her stomach.

Juliet had mailed them invitations two weeks ago to meet her today. Now, with all eyes on her, she questioned how to explain her complicated situation. Maybe the same way she'd told Livy and Tabitha during their teary goodbye yesterday back in Everly. *I'd risk everything to spend the rest of my life with Henry.*

She gestured to a nearby table before a sunny floor-to-ceiling window trimmed with velvet gold drapes. Attractive ivory wallpaper with tiny pink roses on either side added to the room's appeal. "Does anyone care for coffee or tea?"

They all moved to a nearby table and sat on the well-cushioned chairs with Willow across from Juliet. A tray of pink-and-green petit fours perched between tea and coffee urns. Cream and sugar containers completed the spread.

"You've stalled long enough, Juliet." Daisy leaned back in her chair. "We want details about your fiancé."

He wasn't exactly her fiancé.

"Yes," Willow added. "You've only told us his name is Henry and he's handsome."

"Not a very vivid picture, Juliet." Sage poured coffee into her cup and her sister's, the rich scent circulating. "Give us the particulars."

Juliet squared her shoulders and one at a time locked eyes with her friends. "I may have neglected to mention one little detail—odds are, I'm about to marry a king. Well, in a few months."

"A king?" Willow lowered her cup, clattering it on the saucer. A few drops of coffee spilled onto the white linen tablecloth. "A flesh and blood king?"

"With a crown?" Daisy's big eyes doubled in size. Perhaps tripled.

"I assume." Juliet hadn't pondered such things and figured she'd have plenty of time on the ocean journey to think about palaces, kingdoms, and everything royal.

Sage finally closed the wide gap separating her rose-pink lips. "That'll make you a queen."

"But I fell in love with a carpenter."

"Back up." Willow raised her palm. "Give us the full story, then we'll badger you with questions."

After Juliet filled her cup and Daisy's with tea, she shared everything important since meeting Henry. Finding him in the woods, learning he suffered from amnesia, converting the carriage house into a tearoom, dancing together, and learning to become a lady. "Trust me. I was as equally astounded as all of you when I discovered his identity."

Daisy's animated face suddenly grew serious. "Wait a minute. I want my wedding dress back."

"No, ma'am." Juliet knew wholeheartedly that wearing Daisy's gown on her wedding day would be like having a friend by her side. She suspected she'd need the support if a ceremony ever occurred.

"You can't wear . . . a homespun dress." Daisy sputtered and stood. "You need something beautiful, fancy, and . . . expensive."

Juliet stretched and tugged on her friend's sleeve, guiding her back into a sitting position. Then she reached for a petit four and placed it on her plate. Even though it wasn't ladylike, Juliet couldn't resist saying, "I'd prefer to walk down the aisle naked than to give you back my gown."

Laughing, Sage shook her head.

"I've missed you all more than you know." Juliet meant every word as she sampled the dessert. Tasty but inferior to Icala's treats in the tearoom.

Willow wiped her mouth with her linen napkin. "Since you're in love, I'm curious why you seek our advice. Does his station in life unnerve you?"

"Yes, but something else disturbs me more." She explained the situation regarding his engagement to Faith. "Even so, I intend to leave for Bascandy with him tomorrow because Henry has no intention of wedding her. I apologize for bringing you here under pretenses."

Sage's eyebrow cocked. "What pretenses?"

"Initially, I wanted your advice but then realized I knew my mind and heart's desire. I'd never forgive myself if I didn't do everything possible to have a life with him."

Sage patted Juliet's hand in a rallying, supportive manner. "I'd do the same thing if I were you."

"And I'd never forgive myself if I left without telling you all goodbye." Her friendship with Willow and Daisy had only existed for one year, yet they'd shared dreams, fears, and hearts during their voyage. In a sense, they'd created a makeshift family. She'd known Sage for a shorter time, though they'd instantly formed a quick, solid fondness for each other.

A hefty lump wedged in Juliet's throat. Maybe she'd return to Victoria one day, or they'd pay her a visit in Bascandy. A person never knew what life had in store.

She smiled at her friends. "But enough about me. Tell me what's the latest with you. Willow, please go first."

"All right. Caleb adores farming in Salt Springs. We both do. However, with winter upon us, work has slowed. Yet we've stayed busy."

Sage laughed and swatted her sister's arm. "Tell them."

Either Willow blushed or the room's heat flushed her rosy cheeks. "My flowy dress hides the fact, but I'm with child."

A chorus of congratulations followed from Daisy and Juliet.

"Caleb is ready to bust his buttons and claims he wants a girl just like me," Willow said.

Of course he desired a wee one like his wife, lovely through and through. "How wonderful. What is the date?"

"Late spring."

Daisy applauded, and Juliet liked that the first person she'd met before boarding the bride ship hadn't lost her whimsy. "One day, perhaps we'll arrange for our children's future marriage."

Everyone chuckled but Juliet. "In my opinion and experience, arranged marriages are dreadful and should be avoided at all costs."

"A fine point." Daisy tapped her chin with her finger. "I'm happy to report our sewing shop thrives, and Mother arrived before Christmas. Fortunately, she and Seth get along like long-lost friends. Sometimes, I can't get a word in edgewise when they start chattering."

Willow cocked her brow. "I find that hard to believe."

Daisy sheepishly grinned. "You're right."

Sunshine streamed directly from the window onto Sage, brightening her happy face even more. "In my world, Jackson and I married while out of town."

All four women squealed.

"That's wonderful." Gratitude sank to Juliet's toes. Each woman had been transformed since leaving Manchester. Who would have guessed they'd find prosperous, precious futures in foreign lands? And husbands who adored them as they were—unique, brave women willing to cross the oceans for better lives.

"Juliet, I never heard why you left the Firth mansion." Sage poured more coffee into her cup and added cream. "When I returned to Victoria, I was surprised by your letter that you'd uprooted and moved to Everly. Once again, you were vague regarding the reason why."

Juliet summarized the situation that had led her across the strait and how Ruby had tried to blackmail her. "But she's in jail now and shouldn't bother anyone anytime soon."

"Huh." Slowly and perhaps absently, Sage stirred her coffee. "Shortly after my arrival in Victoria, I saw Ruby bury something behind the Firths' house, close to the fence line. Suspicious, I went over and investigated."

Juliet's muscles grew taut. Was Sage involved with the stolen jewel fiasco? "Don't tell me you dug up the missing jewels."

Sage nodded, lowering her spoon onto her saucer. "Before I rushed out of town, I tried to return the jewels to the Firths but couldn't gain an audience with either Mr. or Mrs. Firth. So I left the jewels in my drawer and forgot all about them."

It had never crossed Juliet's mind to associate Sage with Ruby's crime. What a strange turn of events. "I assume you'll return the jewelry to Mrs. Firth. At least one piece is a family heirloom."

"Of course. I'll do it later today. I'm sorry if my actions caused you distress."

If Juliet hadn't lost her position with the Firths, she wouldn't have met Livy, Tabitha, and, most importantly, Henry. Perhaps she should stop by the jail and thank her old roommate before leaving town. "Everything has worked out for the best."

Well, not for Ruby.

Someone cleared his throat, and they all turned toward Henry, tall and masculine in his dark blue tailored three-piece suit. He grinned, his eyes on Juliet as he strode forward. She deemed his smile the perfect combination of friendliness and breathtaking. Even before she'd learned of his lineage, she noted his impeccable manners, perfect diction, formal speech, and almost regal bearing.

She had grown more accustomed to his title, albeit slowly. Deep down, he hadn't changed. He was still as sweet and kind as ever.

Standing beside her chair, he gave a slight bow. "Hello, everyone. I am Henry."

The women stood, looking in awe. Daisy curtsied and whispered to Juliet, "He is ridiculously handsome, much like Seth, Caleb, and Jackson."

Juliet nodded, her heart adding an extra beat. "Oh, I am well aware."

After introductions and tight farewell hugs, the women departed. Not one tear fell from Juliet's eyes because her gratitude for their friendship outweighed her sadness.

"Did you enjoy visiting with your friends?" Henry stood across the table from her and popped a petit four into his mouth, his eyes grazing on her face.

"Immensely, and they were duly surprised when they heard our tale."

"I can only imagine." He swallowed, and she watched his Adam's apple rise and fall. "And did you seek their guidance on how to proceed with your future?"

"I did not—"

"Because you had already made up your mind?" He pinched the bridge of his nose, obviously distressed.

Dobbin entered the breakfast room, postponing her response. He approached their table. "I have fulfilled your request, Miss Dash."

"What is this secret you two share?" Henry slipped his hands into his pockets, worry filling his eyes. "I find this development utterly disturbing."

Laughing, she moved to the table holding her bridal gown and passed the large, cumbersome container to Dobbin. "Will you please deliver this to my room, as well?"

"To clarify, your room on the steamer?"

"Yes, please. Put it with the rest of my belongings aboard the royal ship."

Henry raised his face to the ceiling before directing his focus back to her. His eyes shimmered with emotion, and she wanted nothing more than to plant her lips against his. But no kissing was allowed for a dreadfully long time. "I love you."

Without a word, Dobbin turned to leave, but not before Juliet caught sight of his bright smile.

She drew her shawl tighter around her shoulders. "Are you ready to escort me to the dock?"

"Yes, but first, I have a surprise for you." He nodded toward the doorway. "What could it be?"

"I'm wondering the same thing." Side by side, they moved toward the room's exit, the noise in the lobby growing in volume. She raised her voice. "I require a hint."

"It is furry."

"A cozy blanket to keep me warm on the steamer?"

"Ideally, I would perform that task myself, but alas, I cannot."

Before becoming a lady, Juliet may have readily ignored the no-kissing rules. Not anymore. My, how her life had changed.

Henry reached for her hand and led her to the lobby. After rounding the corner, he pointed at a wicker basket alongside the wall, no bigger than her new side-laced brown boots. A white-and-blue checked cloth concealed what hid underneath until a furry gray head revealed itself—an adorable puppy.

"Since you left Bells behind in Everly, I thought you needed another female traveling companion besides your new maid."

Dobbin had hired Miss Walker to accompany her on the voyage. She'd protested having a maid of her own when she'd only just been one herself, but both Dobbin and Henry had insisted she have a woman companion for the long voyage.

"How thoughtful, and I love puppies." She placed her hand against her chest, her heart ticking excitedly. "You are the best man on earth."

"Am I?" His grin held a mischievous slant.

"Oh, yes." Juliet picked up the bundle of fur and hugged the squirmy pup to her chest. A cold, wet nose tickled her neck. "I'll name her Junior."

"Interesting choice."

"I always make interesting choices, and isn't it obvious? She has gray fur."

"Ah."

She glanced at the hotel guests rushing up the staircase or out the wide brass door. Everyone had somewhere to go, and so did they. With her arm joined with his, they strolled toward the exit and departed the hotel.

The bright sunshine drew a squint to her eyes as the brisk air kissed her cheeks. Across the street sat the brick Brown Jug Saloon and a lovely church. "Goodbye, Victoria," she whispered under her breath.

As they approached the harbor, she let her gaze linger over the breathtaking view of the Olympic Mountains beyond the ocean. Snowcapped and exquisite, the scene always stole her breath. She sighed and tried to capture the image to remember forever.

The large royal ship couldn't weigh anchor in Victoria. Therefore, they'd first board a smaller steamer to reach the harbor in Esquimalt, where she'd arrived on the bride ship. In many ways, it felt like yesterday, but almost a year had passed. "How long until we reach Bascandy?"

"Roughly four months."

Juliet glanced over her shoulder, expecting to find Dobbin shadowing their steps. Sure enough, two additional uniformed men and a middle-aged woman with an exceedingly large hat, presumably Miss Walker, accompanied the group. What a strange, royal world.

She moved her gaze to the man at her side. "Plenty of time to achieve my goal."

"Which goal is that?" He swung the empty basket's handle, his steps matching her stride.

"Since I learned to be a lady in less than two months, I assume learning to be a queen in four will be a luxury."

His cheerful laughter serenaded her heart as he guided her around a pile of melting snow and down the hill toward the waiting ship. "Dobbin and I shall happily teach you everything you want to know. But never forget, I adore you as you are."

"Likewise." She squeezed his arm. "How long until you speak with Faith?"

"Immediately upon our return. I do not care to waste two minutes."

"Then how long after that until we wed?"

"As soon as humanly possible. One of us can barely wait for the honeymoon."

A pleasing warmth settled inside Juliet's belly. She agreed with him, but mentioning the truth would be unladylike. "What an outrageous thing to say."

"My only excuse is that I am outrageously in love with you."

Little girl Juliet could have never imagined this moment. Even now, all grown up, she barely believed it was happening. "And I love you just as much."

Twenty-nine

The Bascandy Palace
June 1864

JULIET HAD NOBODY TO BLAME BUT HER-self.

Last night, she informed her attendants she would open her door in the morning when ready for assistance. But then she'd barely slept, too excited about her ceremony at the Royal Chapel, her upcoming romantic honeymoon at Henry's second home on a shell-covered beach on the coastline, and marrying someone as wonderful as her betrothed.

Thus far, the forenoon had flown past in a blur. People rushed in and out of her bedchamber to deliver a five-course breakfast, a romantic message from her groom, last-minute advice from her soon-to-be mother-in-law, and the announcement of a wedding gift arrival—a horse. A genuine horse in the courtyard.

What a day, and it had barely started.

Now, attired in a satiny robe, Juliet sat before a gilded dressing table and gazed into a diamond-shaped mirror. She stretched to trace her image with her fingertip. A lady stared back at her with pinned-up hair, a bridal wreath of orange blossoms and myrtle sprigs crowning her head. She blinked aside a joyous tear.

Who'd have predicted her path to happily ever after? Certainly not her.

Church bells chimed in the distance, and she closed her eyes, cherishing the sweetness. According to Henry, bells typically played an hour before a wedding ceremony, calling guests to the chapel. But he had arranged for the music to clang hourly because she adored the engaging sound, resurrecting precious memories of her grandfather and the nighttime bells in Everly.

Her soon-to-be husband was charming like that.

"Will there be anything else, Miss?"

Juliet's eyes popped open as she turned and smiled at a lovely lady-in-waiting named Adelia. She'd forgotten all about her presence. "Thank you, but no. Not until it's time to don my gown."

She could single-handedly toss on a dress, but that would be a royal mistake, particularly today.

After a curtsy, the woman left Juliet alone with the puppy curled in the sunshine near the window. Juliet rose and glided around the vast room, running her finger over a deep blue tassel tieback, the embossed floral wallpaper, a velvety petal in a vase of three dozen red roses, a quaint music box of gold, and a tiara she hesitated to touch. But she gently tapped the highest point.

It was all too much, yet part and parcel of marrying her future husband.

The voyage from Victoria had passed in a whirlwind. She'd

learned enough to write a book on Bascandy and the monarchy. Fine dining and moonlit strolls on the deck with Henry occupied her evenings, naturally with Miss Walker or Dobbin chaperoning. One night, she dropped her knife, the one generally strapped to her calf, over the ship's railing, causing barely a ripple in the water.

She didn't need it anymore.

Henry had forewarned his mother of Juliet's upcoming arrival and unprecedented plans via a letter. Although the Dowager Queen hadn't initially welcomed Juliet with open arms, she'd softened her stance after learning Juliet had little interest in her son's wealth. His lovely sisters had accepted her in a heartbeat and vice versa.

Juliet paused beside the bed, larger than her entire room at the Firths' mansion. Her gorgeous gown draped across the plush royal blue covering. If anyone had objected to her decision to wear Daisy's dress, the whispers hadn't reached her ears. She ran her finger across the high, satiny waistline.

According to her ladies-in-waiting, the square neckline matched the latest fashion, yet an inch too low for Juliet's taste. But she'd adapt. Maybe she'd start to feel like a bride after she slipped into the gown.

She still felt like ordinary old Juliet with orange blossoms in her hair.

True to his word, Henry had met Faith the same night they arrived in Bascandy. She had no desire to wed him or anyone else for an excellent reason—she still mourned Sutton. Soon, she'd leave the country for a worldwide tour of her own, perhaps the first step in mending her broken heart.

Official duties had filled much of Henry's agenda, and his easy-going manner had balanced Juliet's initial awkwardness at the palace. Fittings, introductions, and parties—where she met duchesses, viscounts, and marquesses—had busied her days.

She halfway knew what to expect regarding the upcoming

ceremony—a flock of bridesmaids, a fanfare of trumpets, a cake weighing more than two stones, and guests in made-to-measure court dresses and tails. A tad overwhelming. Yet she held tight to Livy and Tabitha's last-minute advice—when unsure how to respond, merely nod and possibly say, "Indeed."

Someone rapped on the closed door from the adjoining room. Juliet hurried forward in her slippers from Tabitha, stopping inches from the door. "Henry?"

"Were you expecting someone else?" Her future husband's voice rumbled.

"I wasn't expecting anyone. You've been sleeping in a different wing."

"Not anymore." They'd discussed countless topics on the ocean steamer, though never sleeping arrangements after the wedding. Surely, they'd share a bed, would they not? "Open the door. I have a gift."

Another one?

In the last week, he'd purchased her a music box, books of poetry, and a new wardrobe, complete with more riding habits than weekdays. "I appreciate you, but I don't need lavish presents. Besides, we're not to view one another until the ceremony." Even then, she'd don a veil.

"But it is cake."

Cake? Juliet opened the door a notch, and he handed her a plate containing an apple dessert with a heavenly cinnamon scent. Temporarily, she set it on a nearby ornate table with wooden legs and a granite top. "I am royally impressed you brought me food. It's perfect."

"You are perfect," he said through the narrowly opened door.

A lady never rolled her eyes, but nobody watched, so Juliet did. And yet his flattery worked its magic, and she smiled. "I'm anything but. Are you nervous?"

"I am beyond excited to wed you finally."

"Finally? We haven't even known each other for a year."

"But I have waited for you my entire life."

Her heart slammed against her chest as she laid her cheek against the thick wooden door. "Sometimes you say exactly what I'm feeling. It's uncanny."

"Did Livy also give you a marriage manual as a wedding gift? Mine is titled *The Proper Young Husband's Book*."

"Yes. She handed me *The Proper Young Wife's Book*, which has an entire chapter devoted to kissing rules."

He laughed. "I do not believe we need guidance on the subject."

Silence hung between them until she said, "Indeed."

"Are you garbed in your gown yet?"

"Why are you asking?"

"I am trying to recall if tradition dictates that I cannot gaze upon you fully attired before the ceremony or if I cannot see you at all beforehand."

She had no idea, but adored his eagerness and recalled the last time they'd spoken through a barely open door back in Everly. Back then, she feared she wasn't worthy of him and had been pushing him away. But Livy and Tabitha helped her understand she had to open her heart more and depend on God to help her.

Henry wrapped his big hand around the door's edge, inches from her lips. The temptation to kiss his fingers, one at a time, prodded her to act. Dare she? Soon, they'd wed. Juliet gently pressed her lips against his warm knuckle before straightening.

He drew a sharp breath, and the air they shared sizzled. Neither believed in superstitions, and one little peek should not cause a kingdom-shaking catastrophe. "Do you want to forego tradition?"

"You have no idea." His voice carried a huskiness she craved.

"Please enter if you wish." She backed up as the door slowly opened to reveal her future husband.

Impeccably dressed, he wore a royal uniform of gold trousers, a white cummerbund and same-colored shirt, and a blue jacket with brass buttons. His freshly shaven face carried the scent of sage on his skin, and she wouldn't mind messing up his neatly coiffed hair. But she'd wait until the honeymoon.

What a blessing to have such a charming and impossibly wonderful husband-to-be.

When Juliet opened her mouth to tell him not to mess up her hair, he dropped his finger to her lips, tracing the top, then the bottom. "Do not say anything. I want to stare at you for a minute or two silently."

His tawny eyes held a fire. It wasn't like they hadn't seen each other in days. They'd shared a candlelit meal last night. But standing in a bed chamber, with her wearing nothing but slippers and a silky robe, had a distinct intimacy. She tightened her belt.

Shivers danced over her skin as the desire for her future husband built. He cupped her neck, and her knees weakened. Thank goodness he embraced her, or she might have collapsed. Their lips met, as did their souls.

She didn't want to think about someone arriving to help her dress for the ceremony. Or that Henry should have left for the chapel by now. Or that they had a lifetime to share their affection. No, she only wanted to savor the here and now.

His feathery kiss teased and sped up her pulse. Her hands roamed, exploring his broad shoulders, thick neck, and lush hair. When his fingers made a trail up her cheek, warmth enveloped her, yet a shiver crept upward as well.

They had traveled on far different paths, but she knew all the way to her toes that God had brought them together. Ideally, she'd awaken in his arms every morning and they'd share the same pillow each night. And she believed he yearned for the same thing. But they had to stop sharing their affection now, or she'd mess up more than her hair.

Reluctantly, she placed both of her hands against his muscular chest and shoved enough to break their embrace. They stared at each other, breathless.

She softly smiled. "I'll see you at the chapel."

With love in his eyes, he rubbed his thumb over her chin and whispered, "Once upon a time, a scrappy orphan and a rebellious prince fell in love and lived happily ever after."

"And they grew fat but incredibly delighted, eating cake every day."

He laughed before sobering, his voice husky. "Thank you for rescuing me and agreeing to become my wife. You, my love, are truly unforgettable."

Brimming with joy, Juliet reached for his fingers and squeezed. "And thank you for being my fairy tale."

Bonus Epilogue

Thank you for reading *His Unforgettable Bride*. We hope you loved this story. Find out what happens next for Henry and Juliet with a Bonus Epilogue, a special gift, available only to our newsletter subscribers.

This Bonus Epilogue will not be released on any retailer platform, so get your free gift by scanning the QR code below. By scanning, you acknowledge you are becoming a subscriber to the newsletters of Patti, Jody, and Sunrise Publishing. Unsubscribe at any time.

Reader Questions

1. Would you have climbed onto a bride ship to improve your life if you were Juliet? Like her, would you have wanted to become a lady?

2. When Henry awakens after his attack, he's deeply grateful Juliet saved his life. Why and when do you think his gratitude changed to love?

3. What kind of pressures do you think Henry faced as a royal family member?

4. How would you describe Juliet's relationship with Tabitha and Livy?

5. How was Juliet a good influence on Henry/Gray and vice versa?

6. How is Juliet's rags-to-riches life a Cinderella story?

7. Do you feel sympathy for any of the characters?

8. Do you believe people can fully reinvent themselves or never entirely?

9. What do you think of Juliet's reaction to learning the man she loved was a prince? Do you think you'd have responded similarly?

10. Would you consider marrying a king? Why or why not?

11. What did you like the most about this story?

Thank you for reading His Unforgettable Bride!

Make sure you haven't missed any
of our romantic Bride Ships novels
by Jody Hedlund and Patti Stockdale.

AVAILABLE NOW!

More Sunrise Historical Romance

No one writes Western historical romance like Lacy Williams! Journey to Wyoming and discover five mail-order brides and the men who love them in our Wind River Mail-Order Brides series.

START YOUR COLLECTION TODAY!

Read on for a sneak peek at the first book in this wonderful new series!

A CONVENIENT Heart

LACY WILLIAMS

One

December 1892

MISS HARDING, PAUL COPIED FROM my slate!"

Merritt Harding stood beside a school desk with one finger pointing at a line from *McGuffey's Eclectic Reader* while little Clarissa Ewing struggled to sound out a difficult word.

The tiny town of Calvin, Wyoming, had seen growth over the past years, and her one-room school was bursting at the seams with students.

"Miss Harding, he's copying my mannerisms again!"

With a prayer for patience slipping silently from her lips, she patted Clarissa on the shoulder and left the girl to sound out the words on the page.

Ignoring whispers from the front of the classroom, Merritt turned toward the back of the room, where the older students were seated.

Thirteen-year-old Daniel Quinn had his arms crossed and was

glaring at twelve-year-old Paul Gowen, who was indeed sitting in an identical pose, down to the pinch in his lips.

"Boys, what are we supposed to be working on?" she asked.

Both boys swung identical mulish looks at her. She didn't know whether to laugh or cry.

"He's mocking me!" Daniel cried.

Indeed, Paul mouthed the very same words.

Daniel was new to her classroom this year, his parents having moved to town last summer. She'd taught Paul in this schoolroom since he was six years old.

The two boys were alike in nearly every way. She'd been stumped since the first week of school, unable to understand how they had ended up as rivals instead of friends.

The whispers from the front of the room had grown in volume. A glance in that direction revealed Clarissa with her head bent over her book, lips moving as she silently read. Her seatmate was distracted by whatever conversation was happening amongst the six students in the three desks in front of her.

Merritt tapped the desk in front of Paul. "Why don't you continue your arithmetic work from my desk? Take your slate and chalk with you."

For a moment, she thought he would argue, but he reluctantly stood up and tucked his slate beneath his arm to trudge to her wooden desk at the front of the classroom. There were thick books stacked on one corner of the desk and paintbrushes lined up along the opposite side, but the center surface was clear. He should be able to do his work there.

"Please keep working," she told Daniel before she walked to the front of the room. With every step, the whispers became more muted until she stood before the front two desks with her eyebrows raised.

"Would you like to share with the rest of the class?" she asked

Harriet Ferguson. The eight-year-old was small for her age and hadn't joined the schoolroom until last school year.

Harriet flushed and ducked her head, folding her hands in her lap as if Merritt had meted out a grand punishment, not asked a simple question.

"We was wonderin' if it's time to start practicin' for the pageant yet." Harriet's seatmate, five-year-old Samuel Ferguson, was practically bouncing on the wooden bench.

The slate-gray winter sky outside the window was no help determining the hour. It had been threatening snow all day, but only an occasional flake had danced past the window today.

Merritt consulted the watch pinned at her shoulder. "We've another half hour of work at least." She made her voice loud enough for the entire class to hear.

She felt the collective sigh of impatience and heard one audible groan. Though her glance encompassed the entire room, she couldn't tell where it had come from.

The Christmas pageant was scheduled to take place in this very classroom on Monday evening, a mere seven days from now.

Christmas was three days after that.

Between the two events, it was no wonder her students were restless and distracted. After nearly ten years in her position as Calvin's schoolteacher, Merritt expected it. Just like the tradition of holding the pageant in the schoolhouse had been upheld since she'd sat in one of the desks as a student, it was also tradition that the closer the performance loomed, the more distracted her students would be.

She had her own reasons for being distracted. This day had stretched interminably long already. *How* much longer until dismissal?

She'd be happy if she could wrangle fifteen more minutes of work out of her students. Then they could all practice reciting lines. A glance at the nearly completed canvas backdrop leaning against the wall at the back of the classroom made her shoulders droop slightly. She'd meant to make more progress on that project over the weekend but had spent her time planning meals for the next few days, shopping for each one as the special occasion it was, and scrubbing and dusting her entire house from floor to ceiling.

The work will get done, she told herself.

But not tonight. Tonight she had an engagement.

"Miss Harding, what's this?"

Paul held up a folded piece of paper. One crossed with cramped handwriting in even lines. One that she recognized.

Paul must've opened the drawer in her desk and found the letter.

"That's personal—"

"Are you getting married?"

Her words tumbled over his blurted question. It was too much to hope that no one else had heard.

She felt sixteen pairs of eyes swing in her direction as she hurried toward her desk.

"That's private," she snapped.

Paul's eyes widened as she came to stand beside where he sat in the hard-backed wooden chair.

She rarely used such a tone with the children.

But as she took the letter from his hand and slipped it into the pocket of her skirt, she felt blazing heat in her cheeks and realized she was breathing hard, as if she'd run up here instead of walked.

"You're gettin' married?" Harriet asked in the sudden empty silence.

"Course she ain't." Bobby Flannery piped up from across the room. "Miss Harding is a spinster and everyone knows it."

His seatmate must've elbowed his side, because Bobby yelped. "What? My ma even said so."

"That ain't nice," Clarissa said. "Miss Harding is pretty enough to get her a man if she wanted one."

"Children—"

Merritt's attempt at regaining control of the class went un-heeded. Two students began arguing about her looks while Paul said, "I thought you couldn't be our teacher anymore if you get married."

Little Samuel looked at her with sad eyes and a now-trembling lower lip. "You don't want to be our teacher no more?"

"Of course I do," she told him.

But it was more complicated than that.

"She's old!" A voice burst out from the middle of the room.

And Merritt felt her temper spark.

"Enough!" She rapped the edge of her desk with her ruler, and the children went silent.

Twenty-five might be a spinster here in the West—most girls married before they were eighteen—but Merritt wasn't *old*.

She bit back the words to defend herself, knowing that debating a ten-year-old would not be an effective use of her time. Though it was tempting.

"I was not planning to tell you this yet"—her heart pounded as she made her voice loud and clear—"but I am . . . possibly . . . considering getting married."

"To who?" demanded a single voice from the back before Merritt's raised eyebrow quelled any more noise.

"*If* you complete today's work diligently and make it through our rehearsal, I will tell you a bit more."

It had been years since she'd lost control of her classroom like this. Even longer since she'd had to resort to bribery. But these were desperate times.

Her plea worked, and the last hour of the day flew past—probably because she dreaded what the children would ask.

The inquisition was as terrible as she'd imagined, but she was able to shorten it a bit as she rushed the children into their coats and out the door.

"I have known him for months." Technically true, though she'd never met her intended groom in person.

"He is a businessman." John had told her about investing in the railroad, though she hadn't understood it all from his letters. There would be time to discuss it at length soon enough.

"No, he isn't from around here." They hadn't discussed where they would live, other than agreeing that she needed to stay and finish the school term as her contract stipulated.

"Where did we meet? I answered an ad in a newspaper."

These last words were said as she ushered the children out the door with her own woolen cape on and arms wide lest they dawdle any longer.

As she crossed out of the doorway, she caught sight of a familiar figure standing on the boardwalk just outside.

Drew McGraw. Her cousin and his three younger brothers owned a ranch well outside of town. She hadn't seen him in weeks, and he had a couple of days' worth of scruff on his jaw.

Her stomach was already twisty with anticipation and nerves as she crossed the boardwalk to him, watching the last of her students scurry toward their homes.

"What's this I just overheard?" He stretched out his arms as she walked toward him.

"What are you doing in town?" She asked the question as she joined in the affectionate hug. Maybe he'd be distracted . . .

But he was just as inquisitive as one of her students. He squeezed her shoulders, then stepped back to look into her face. "You met someone?"

She bit her lip and nodded. Icy wind bit at her cheeks but didn't cool the blush there.

"How come you haven't told the family?"

She saw the hint of hurt in his eyes and felt a pang of remorse. "I wanted to make certain that it . . . that he . . ."

She couldn't say the words aloud. There was still a part of her that worried that John would step off the train, take one look at her, and change his mind about the whole thing. Finding a husband to marry, bearing children of her own . . . her long-held dreams were coming true. Finally.

Drew didn't seem to know what to say to that, and that was all right too.

"Did you bring the children with you?" she asked.

Drew's thirteen-year-old son David, ten-year-old daughter Josephine, and five-year-old daughter Tillie were as close as if they were Merritt's own nieces and nephew, and Merritt missed them dearly.

"Not this time. Gotta grab a load of supplies and head back. Wanted to check if you're still coming for Christmas."

In the excitement of John's arrival, she'd forgotten about her promise to come and stay with the McGraw cousins for Christmas next week.

She'd be a married woman by then.

And John already knew how much her cousins meant to her. "I'll be there."

We'll be there.

The train whistle blew, the sound carried on a stiff wind, still far in the distance.

Her gaze flicked toward the end of town where the station was located. Her heart pounded.

"I've got to go," she said. "I'm meeting . . . him."

This was the moment her life would change forever.

"We're supposed to get married on Sunday. That's less than a week away. I mean, isn't it a lark? When I get off the train, she'll be looking for my hat and coat." He patted a red flower—a poppy?— in his lapel pocket.

Jack Easton didn't turn his head from where he sat in the railroad car. He didn't have to. Between the quiet, mostly empty compartment, a reflection in the glass window beside him, and the acoustics in the arch of the train car, the young man's conversation with an older gentleman who wore a neatly trimmed gray beard, in the seat across from him, carried perfectly to Jack's ear.

"She's a schoolteacher, been in the classroom for years," the young man went on.

"How many years?" Gray Beard asked.

Both men were dressed in suits—not the best quality, but a sign they were doing all right financially.

"Nine, I think." The younger man wore a bowler hat that made him look a mite foolish.

Jack favored a cowboy hat, but he'd lost his in a barroom scuffle a few days ago and hadn't replaced it yet. He riffled one hand through his hair at the empty feeling on his head.

"Nine years in the classroom?" Gray Beard sounded skeptical. Jack couldn't see his face in the reflection, but he had a clear view of the prospective groom's face. "Don't you think she's a little . . . long in the tooth?"

It was a rude thing to say, and Jack took offense on the unknown bride's behalf.

"She's twenty-five." But the groom suddenly looked uncertain.

"Or that's what she wants you to think. She could be lying. She might be forty."

It seemed to Jack that a schoolteacher would probably be someone upstanding in the community. Why would she lie? Especially when a lie about her age would be instantly revealed when the two met.

"What's wrong with her, anyway? Why'd she need to get a husband from a mail-order ad?"

The groom obviously hadn't considered anything like this, and Jack watched in the reflection as the man tugged at his shirt collar and then swallowed hard. "I've jumped into this, haven't I? Maybe I should've thought about it longer than I did."

Jack lost track of the conversation as he watched the landscape change outside the window. The woods and trees they'd been passing through opened up to a plain where everything was dusted with snow. The Laramie Mountains were visible in the far distance, purple shadows against the gray sky.

"Next stop, Calvin, Wyoming!" The conductor's voice called out, and then the man himself passed through the train car.

Jack had been all over the West in the past few years. Montana, Nevada, Colorado. He'd never stopped in Calvin. Passed through once and judged it too small.

But that'd been . . . three years ago? Maybe things had changed.

"Perhaps I should go home." The groom's voice sounded clear as a bell, and Jack saw that he'd loosened his tie now. He took off his bowler hat and ran his hand through his hair, clearly agitated.

He'd be an easy mark across the poker table. His tells were as big as a brand on a cow's hindquarters.

"You don't want to meet her? What if she's a great beauty?" Gray Beard said. Was the man toying with the groom? He seemed to be playing devil's advocate now.

"It's almost Christmas," the young groom said.

Christmas.

Jack should find a game. Put aside a few dollars and hole up in a hotel room. Shops would be closed during the holiday. Restaurants too.

Jack didn't have a home to go back to. No one to celebrate with.

And he liked it that way. The nomadic life he lived suited him just fine.

He decided to stretch his legs. Standing up, he slipped his leather satchel over his head and shoulder. He had to hold on to the seat in front of him with one hand as the train swayed and rocked.

Jack strode through the nearly empty train car, then moved through the door at the end and into the next car over.

This one had a small water closet, its door slightly ajar, and was more crowded, with people in almost every seat. Many had packages around their feet or on their laps. Another sign of Christmas.

The conductor was calling out, and several people stood up in this train car, moving toward the door.

The brakes weren't screeching yet, but Jack could feel the slowing motion.

Looking down the car, he recognized the head of dark hair beneath a ten-gallon hat, the matching dark-brown mustache. The man was a head taller than most other travelers in the train car, and his lined face showed hard living.

Morris.

Jack turned to go back the way he'd come. He didn't have any desire to bump into Morris.

But two passengers blocked his way back into the other train car, and the only exit was to slip into the water closet.

Jack latched the door behind him.

He had a revolver at his hip, though he'd only had occasion to use it shooting cans off a branch or fence post. It was mostly for show, to keep other poker players from trying to rob him.

But Morris was a hired gun for the owner of a silver mine back in Colorado. Jack had judged him as unpredictable the last time he'd seen him.

The conductor called out again, his voice sounding just outside the water closet door. He must be returning through the compartment and re-entering the car Jack had left.

"I'm looking for a man named Jack Easton."

That was Morris's voice. He must've followed the conductor. Sounded like he was standing right outside the water closet.

"He's got some aliases," Morris went on.

Whatever the conductor said in response, it was muffled.

"He's got light hair. Wears a beard sometimes. Ugly as sin."

There was a tiny spotted looking glass high on one wall, and Jack glanced in it now. His nose had been broken once, a long time ago. It had the slightest bend in it. His eyes had crow's feet from being in the sun.

He wasn't ugly.

At least, not judging by the looks he got from the women who kept company in the saloons. He never took them up on the offers their eyes made.

Jack appeared a little disreputable, maybe, with the scruff on his chin—hadn't seen a barber in weeks. Not ugly.

"He stole five hundred bucks from a friend of mine. I'd like to get it back."

Jack watched in the looking glass as his reflection scowled.

He hadn't stolen a thing from Clark Henshaw. Jack had won at the poker table fair and square—without even a card up his sleeve.

He'd learned early on how cards made more sense than people. How to predict what was coming up next—ace or deuce or anything in between.

Reading people had come later, out of necessity. He'd learned to predict when a fist might come his way and that an empty bottle meant trouble.

He was good at reading people now. And he didn't drink much. Saw it as a weakness after what he'd been through as a child. Which meant that the longer the night went on at a poker table and the more drunk the men around him got, the sharper Jack's senses became.

He didn't have to cheat to win.

And the men he played could afford to lose. He didn't play otherwise.

"I'd like to get the money back to my friend," Morris said.

Good luck.

Jack had fifty cents in his pocket. He'd passed the winnings from Henshaw's table to a group of widows whose husbands had died in a mine accident. Henshaw had sent men into an unsafe shaft, and they'd been lost to a cave-in. The unscrupulous owner had made no reparations to the widows left behind—women who had children to feed but no source of income. Likely those women had paid overdue bank notes or settled up accounts at the local general store.

Jack had righted that wrong.

There was no money for Morris to collect.

And Jack didn't want to think about how the man might try to enforce the debt. He winced.

The train braked with a hiss and screech. The voices outside the water closet rose and fell as passengers disembarked.

Jack edged open the door to find the small vestibule empty.

He cautiously moved out of the water closet and tried to guess where Morris had gone. Would he get off the train at this stop?

Jack crept through the doors and back onto his original train car.

It was empty.

As he tried to guess whether Morris had gone through here, Jack rushed forward to see that both the young groom and Gray Beard were gone.

But the groom's coat and hat were abandoned on the seat. The coat was crumpled, flower hanging precariously.

The door opened at the end of the train car, and Jack's pulse pounded as if he'd drawn a pair of aces.

It wasn't Morris but a grandmotherly-looking woman. Short.

Over her head, Jack had a clear view of Morris's back, his head and shoulders, in the train car beyond.

And then Morris started to turn.

Jack ducked, instinct pushing him to don the abandoned coat. He quickly shoved his arms into the sleeves, hastily pulling the coat over his own. His satchel hung awkwardly between the coats, but he ignored it for now. He reached for the hat, mashing it low on his head. It wasn't much of a disguise, but maybe if he moved quickly, Jack would be all right.

He kept his back to where Morris had been and walked calmly away.

"All aboard!" the conductor called from the platform outside.

He couldn't stay on this train with Morris on board.

He stepped off the train and onto the platform. Another train would pass by. Maybe this afternoon or maybe tomorrow. He'd get on it and find a place to hole up for Christmas.

"John?" A feminine voice called out.

He turned on instinct and came face-to-face with a woman who was pretty as a picture.

Snow dusted her dark hair, pulled behind her head in a low bun. Her dark eyes were intelligent, and he saw a moment of hesitation pass through them before she took one step closer, her pert chin rising just slightly.

"It's me." She sounded the way he felt—breathless. Anticipation shimmered between them.

"I'm . . . I'm your bride."

Note to Reader

Last year, I polled my newsletter readers, asking for their favorite tropes. The results stirred my decision to write a book with amnesia, royalty, and fairy-tale elements. Another contributing factor was an Oscar Wilde quote taped to my printer: "Memory is the diary we all carry around with us." The words touched my heart and inspired me as I created my story.

I loved researching etiquette rules from the 1800s. Two books helped shape my story: The Gentlemen's Book of Etiquette and Manual of Politeness by Cecil B. Hartley and The Ladies' Book of Etiquette and Manual of Politeness by Florence Hartley. The quotes on the first page of each chapter are from these books, which were first published in 1860. Although Livy consults a fictitious manual when instructing Juliet, much of her teachings echo these two volumes.

Bascandy is a fictitious country, but I patterned it after Guernsey, a place I adored visiting. If I had known I would one day set a story there, I'd have spent time researching. Instead, I slipped into old churches, strolled the hilly cobblestone streets, and roamed through quaint little shops.

Everly is loosely based on early New Westminster, British Columbia. Even though someone generously donated the bells to the community in 1865, two years after this book takes place, I couldn't resist adding the charming detail to Juliet and Henry's story.

Having Jody Hedlund as my mentor was a master class in writing. I owe her a kingdom of gratitude. Thanks to the Sunrise team for believing in and investing in me. It means the world, and I was blessed by the experience more than they probably know. Thanks to Heather Feeney from the Maritime Museum of British Columbia. I appreciated her steamship knowledge.

I also want to thank my talented daughter, Kelli. She served as my sounding board, offered terrific advice, and helped brainstorm the trickier parts. When it came time to pick a name for my make-believe country, she suggested using the first letter of my grandsons' names to create Bascandy: "B" for Boone, "A" for Archer, "S" for Sawyer, and "C" for Charlie. The "andy" part was all me.

Likewise, thanks to the rest of my family and friends for understanding when I need to prioritize my writing instead of doing something fun and fabulous with them. They're the best!

Thanks to God for His steadfast love.

Patti

Connect With Sunrise

Thank you again for reading *His Unforgettable Bride.* We hope you enjoyed the story. If you did, would you be willing to do us a favor and leave a review? It doesn't have to be long—just a few words to help other readers know what they're getting. (But no spoilers! We don't want to wreck the fun!) Thank you again for reading!

We'd love to hear from you—not only about this story, but about any characters or stories you'd like to read in the future. Contact us at www.sunrisepublishing.com/contact.

We also have regular updates that contains sneak peeks, reviews, upcoming releases, and fun stuff for our reader friends. Sign up at www.sunrisepublishing.com or scan our QR code.

About the Author

Patti Stockdale is a historical romance author and freelance writer who lives in Wisconsin and creates tangled-up characters full of heart and hope. Patti married her high school sweetheart and has two kids and four grandsons. She loves traveling somewhere new, planting flowers, drinking tea, reading fiction, and dancing with her family when she's not plotting stories.

Visit her at www.pattistockdale.com.

About the Author

Jody Hedlund is the best-selling author of over fifty sweet historical romances and is the winner of numerous awards. She lives in central Michigan with her husband and is the mother of five wonderful children and five spoiled cats. When she's not penning another of her page-turning stories, she loves to spend her time reading, especially when it also involves consuming coffee and chocolate.